Plagues and Princes

AND

Princes

THE GREAT MORTALITY

Thomas Schultz

Print ISBN: 978-1-54393-053-5
eBook ISBN: 978-1-54393-054-2

With appreciation to the Kansas City Writers Group for their well-thought commentary and guidance and to my parents who taught me to appreciate adventure.

This is a work of fiction. Names, characters, places, and incidents are either the product of the author's imagination or are used fictitiously. Any resemblance to actual events, people, or locations is purely coincidental and not intended by the author.

For additional information, contact:

Russell Street Publishing, LLC
9410 N. Tracy Ave.
Kansas City, MO 64155

Table of Contents

Prologue

Mindless in its pursuit and reckless in its own desire for life, the pestilence did not care if its host lived or died. Nor did it care if the pattern of stars in the night sky looked like animals or mythical beasts or if their alignment portended dreadful days ahead. The pestilence did not sin nor dream nor wonder what tomorrow might bring. The pestilence had only one goal: to exist. The death of one human could not stop the collective power of the plague; a power that gained force with every infection until that power became the embodiment of evil—the Great Mortality.

Kingdom of Naples, March 1348

The *Marie de la Rosa* entered Naples on a quiet breeze to take on fresh water and make repairs. In less than a fortnight, she'd be home. Almost two years had passed since the sea-toughened cocha and her crew left Genoa. The ship's hold now overflowed with fine silks and rare spices from Black Sea ports. To the crew, the end of the journey meant a brief respite before the next adventure. To Antonio, a young apprentice seaman on his first voyage, the end meant reunion with his wife, Angelina, and his son, Francisco, and the fulfillment of his promise to be faithful. Antonio loved the sea, but he loved his wife more. He vowed never again to leave home.

After the crew dropped anchor, Antonio helped secure the rigging and organize the deck. A commotion farther along the dock drew his gaze. When he completed his task, he jumped onto the pier and approached a fishmonger who stood next to a long wooden table covered with tuna, eel, scallops, and hake.

"Is there trouble?" he asked the fishmonger, whose once-white tunic reeked of fish guts.

Pointing, the man replied, "The crew of that ship was very ill. At least three had to be carried off. I think they were dead. The captain is looking for more men, but I doubt anyone will be interested. Everyone is afraid of the strange sickness."

"Strange sickness. What strange sickness?"

The fish seller leaned close. "Yesterday, a merchant from Salerno told me about a great pestilence ravaging the port towns of the eastern Mediterranean. Many thousands are dying, and no one is willing or able to attend to them. It is all very hard to believe."

"A great pestilence, you say?" Antonio stepped back.

"No one seems to know where it came from or what it is. I think God is punishing us for our sins." The fishmonger nodded as if looking for agreement.

That evening, Antonio remained with the ship. The fishmonger's ominous tone and visions of ill winds blowing in from the sea to lay waste to entire towns cycled through his mind. He had survived the journey without sickness or injury and maintained the purity of his soul with prayer and penance. The men scoffed at his concern. "Afraid you'll get drunk and bed a woman?" they taunted. Antonio ignored them as they left to seek the pleasures available at a nearby whorehouse.

When the order came to raise anchor, Antonio climbed down to release the lines. Moments later, a crowd approached from the center of town. The din of angry voices soon eclipsed the splash of waves against the wooden hull. The most boisterous echoed above the others.

"You killed our children."

"Send the ships away."

"Close the port."

With the help of the tidal current, the *Marie de la Rosa* pulled away from the pier. Antonio watched in horror as the townsfolk chased seamen to their ships and set warehouses on fire. As word spread among the crew about the violence in the harbor, the captain did his best to reassure the men that they would soon be home.

On the fourth day out of Naples, the captain decided to make for La Spezia to restock supplies and attend to a growing number of sick crewmen. At sunrise the next day, Antonio called down from the mast, terror clear in his voice, "Ships are blocking the port, Captain, sir."

Angry citizens manned every manner of boat in order to block the entrance to the harbor. The *Marie de la Rosa* had no choice but to turn away.

"What now?" the crew asked.

"We sail on," the captain said. "The wind is with us. We will make good time."

But time turned against them. One by one the crew met death at the hands of an unknown sickness. The men cursed the heavens, the saints, and each other. Tempers flared. Fights irrupted. Those still strong enough tossed the dead and near-dead overboard. Soon, the ship lacked sufficient crew to man the rigging. As the days passed, the ship's course became known only to God.

Below deck, in the shadowy reaches of the crew's quarters, Antonio lay in his cot. He struggled to find a comfortable position. Neither the gentle sway of the ship nor the muffled beat of waves eased the intense pain in his body. Large black buboes, one the size of a goose egg, marred the weathered skin of his neck, underarms, and groin. The stench of dead bodies and Antonio's own waste, vomit and rotting flesh, permeated the air. As the last member of the ship's crew, only he now knew their misery and suffering. He had no words to explain what had happened; why everyone died so quickly. He refused to believe that God's wrath caused their pain.

Consciousness came and went without regard for Antonio's desperate desire to live. A vision of Angelina appeared. He reached to caress her cheek, to feel the smooth, rose-pedal softness. Why had he left? He strained to remember. He pictured her standing on the pier, her long black hair, like wisps of silk, waving in the cool spring breeze. He wanted to hold her, to feel the tenderness of her breasts pressed against him.

As he lowered his arm, another shot of pain coursed through his body. His muscles tensed. He had to confess his sins, but there was no priest. "God forgive me," he shouted. His limbs now motionless at his side, he strained for vision but saw only blackness. He feared his soul would never find peace as the *Marie de la Rosa* would never find land. He gasped. The strength to breathe left him. A quiet peace washed over him as his pain retreated. The last sounds he perceived were the splash of waves and the creak of rigging in the salty breeze.

Chapter
ONE

Chepstow, Wales, April 1348

"I prayed at my mother's tomb and promised I'd become a monk," Thomas said.

"What does that have to do with calling your father a liar?" Andrew asked, as he sipped ale from a clay mug.

"The day I left home, my father stood next to me by her tomb. I was too small to see the face carved into her marble effigy. He told me she loved me, but I have no memory of her."

Andrew's brown eyes glinted in the mid-day light that shone through the front window of the Broken Oar. He shoved aside his empty bowl of leek and rabbit pottage.

Thomas wiped his mouth with his sleeve and piled his bowl on top of Andrew's. Without the sweet scent of leek under his nose, the stale, musty odor of spilled ale and vomit again ruled the air. He waited for Andrew to say something, but Andrew's silence goaded him. Another sip of ale loosened his restraint. "I left home eight years ago, and not once did my father visit me. He said he would, but he never did." Thomas drained his drink and slammed the mug on the table harder than necessary. "And now Abbot Michael wants me to wait until after Michaelmas before I take my vows."

"At least you know who your father is."

"I meant no—"

"I know." Andrew emptied into Thomas's mug the last of the ale from the pitcher left by Eva, the young barmaid.

"I want to believe my father cares. But all I heard on our trip to Tintern was 'Study your Latin' and 'Mind the abbot.' He was adamant I'd become an abbot one day and make the family proud. Is that all I am? A means to make my father proud? I'm sixteen now. What else can I do?"

"Is this all because William is coming to Bristow?"

Thomas looked out the window and watched a horse-drawn cart rumble down the street toward the wharf that edged the River Wye. Andrew was right; he missed his older brother more than he wanted to admit. "William never came to visit either. I'm sure my father drove him away. William wanted to be a knight—like every second son. What would my father say if I told him I no longer want to be a monk?"

"Abbot Michael said the abbey could make a lot of money if William's plan to sell wool in Calais goes well."

Loud voices from a table of freemen on the other side of the room stole Thomas's attention.

"The pestilence is already in Marseille," the loudest voice said.

"When did you hear that?" another man asked.

"I was in Bristow last week. A merchant from Navarre told me. He said death comes quickly once the bad humors drift in."

Disbelief thick on his tongue, a third man chimed in, "How can that be?"

"By Christ's blood, how should I know? The merchant said ghostly ships wander the sea, dead men covered in horrible sores, the reek of Satan every-where. God forgive us if this sickness comes to Wales."

A vision of William sailing home aboard a slow cog flashed in Thomas's mind: an evil-looking ship close behind, its torn sails and rugged wood shrouded in a haze of bad air.

Andrew jerked his head toward the men. "Do you think William is safe from that sickness those men are talking about?"

Thomas dismissed the frightening image and shrugged. "Calais is a long way away. Once I take my vows, we won't be able to go hunting anymore. The Broken Oar will have to buy its rabbits and squirrels elsewhere. And you'll need to find another excuse to come to Chepstow to see Eva."

Eva waved to Andrew. He smiled back and sipped his brew. "Do you think Eva is pretty?"

Thomas forced a look. Her long brown hair had the sheen of polished walnut and her cream-colored kirtle highlighted the budding figure of a girl of sixteen. He had to admit her full lips and her soft, round face were pleasing to the eye. "She's shorter than you. Do you enjoy her attention?"

"I never thought about that." Andrew looked into his mug and motioned to Eva for a refill. "Why do you ask?"

"All you have to do is walk down the street and the girls flock to you like ants to honey."

Andrew shrugged and emptied his mug in one long gulp. "You should try talking with girls. I hear them say they like your blue eyes."

"What good would it do? Monks are not allowed—"

"Now's your chance…before you take your vows."

"My chance? What about you? Lay brothers are celibate too."

"I haven't decided if I'll join the lay brothers. Quiet. Here comes Eva." Andrew's gaze followed Eva as she approached and filled his mug. "Thank you, Eva."

Her voice giddy, Eva tugged at her hair while she spoke. "My mum sends her blessings. She misses seeing you at the Three Monks Inn."

Thomas's stomach turned at Eva's tone. She never talked to him that way. He leaned back to finish his ale and gestured for more, but Eva ignored him.

"If Talfryn paid more for squirrels or blackbirds, I might stop by more often," Andrew said.

"Well, if you want to walk me home after I finish work, my mum would like that. Then you could tell her you are well. She worries about you."

"How long are you working?"

"I'm almost finished. My mum wants me home before the dockhands get too drunk. The men have a tendency to let their hands wander. I can take care of myself, but my mum worries. You know how she gets sometimes." Her brown eyes sparkled when she smiled.

Andrew winked. "Do I need to watch where my hands go?"

Thomas banged his mug on the table. Eva absently poured the remnants of her pitcher into the mug, spilling some on the table, and walked away. His speech slurred, Thomas said, "She hates me."

Andrew watched her walk away. "What gives you that idea? Maybe you should slow down on the ale. We have to get back to the abbey."

Thomas straightened his posture. "I'm fine." In his ale-induced confidence, it didn't matter that Andrew had the physical size to better handle his ale. Andrew's muscles came from turning piles of seasoned logs into firewood, whereas his skinny arms struggled to heft leather-bound manuscripts from shelf to lectern. He felt the room sway. "You go take care of Lena."

"Eva."

"That's what I said. Just leave me to sit here all by myself." Thomas chugged his ale, then leaned forward with his head on his arms. When the priory bells rang the mid-day call, the metallic song morphed into a muted twang that drifted to garbled noise.

Andrew checked to make sure Thomas slept soundly in the chair. He then joined Eva at the counter where Alfred, the owner of the Broken Oar, drew ale from a firkin.

"Would you watch Thomas for me, Alfred? Eva wants me to walk her home."

"Mind your manners," Alfred said. "I need her back here tomorrow morning."

Eva took Andrew's hand and led him out of the alehouse and up the hill from the riverfront toward High Street. Ruts carved into the dirt road during the morning rain had hardened and made Andrew divide his concentration between watching where he walked and gazing at Eva.

People and carts hustled along High Street. Shops and narrow, two-story cottages bordered the road. Horses and oxen clamored in a mixed tune of whinnies and bellows. Located near Chepstow's main gate, the Three Monks Inn usually filled its beds, which made for long hours of work for Eva's mum. The sound of laughter poured out the windows of the inn's main hall. As they turned down the alley beside the three story inn, Andrew asked, "Is your mum home?"

"My mum has to work late."

A shot of excitement sparked within Andrew's gut at the prospect of what 'work late' meant. Their past interludes had been quick and furtive; never a chance to truly enjoy the moment like he thought sex should be. Of all the days to come to Chepstow with Thomas, today had to be the one Eva's mum worked late. His sensibilities told him to turn around, but he followed her to her cottage in the corner of the fenced yard behind the inn. The clang of the iron latch on the simple wooden door sounded like a crack of thunder in the stillness. Adrenalin surged throughout his body washing away the effects of the alcohol.

"No one's about. You can come in."

Eva's voice hypnotized him into forgetting everything he should have known. Anticipation dried his mouth. He licked his lips. He knew exactly what was going to happen, yet he was powerless to stop it. Eva sat on the bed in the sparsely furnished, one-room cottage. She looked at him and motioned for him to join her. Unable to resist, he sat beside her.

She put her hand on his thigh and leaned close. His entire body tingled. Reason and hesitation disappeared. He embraced Eva and drew in the warmth of her slender body. Their lips met. He held his breath as a rush of pleasure filled him with lust. Lost in a frantic desire to feel his skin next to Eva's, he gave over control to the inevitable.

Time passed without meaning. When Andrew looked out the window, shadows stretched across the back of the inn. "How long have I been here?" He jumped up from the bed.

"Not long enough. My mum will be home after dark."

"I have to go. Thomas and I need to get back to the abbey."

Eva snatched his clothes. "Not until you give me another kiss."

As Andrew stood naked before Eva, guilt tore through him like a panicked bull. "Eva, please. I have to go."

"Just one little kiss." She closed her eyes and pouted her full, tantalizing lips.

Andrew looked at her slender body and voluptuous curves. He was trapped. Should he leave or stay? The choice was obvious, but his mind had not yet regained full control of his body; his youthful desires still ruled. He leaned over and kissed her long and tenderly, his hands wandered over her silky skin. "Sorry. I must leave."

Eva scowled, but gave him his clothes. "You have to come back soon."

He dressed quickly, dashed out the door, and ran back to the Broken Oar. He barged in and stood a moment while his eyes adjusted to the dim light. Every table was occupied. He looked at each in turn, but Thomas was nowhere to be seen. At the table where they sat, a group of three ill-mannered dockhands now drank away the remaining hours of light. He knew the men to be unfriendly on the best of days so he hurried to the counter. "Alfred, did you see where Thomas went?"

"He said he had to piss. That was some time ago."

Andrew searched behind the alehouse. The privy was empty. He searched the alley and the nearby hiding places he recalled from his days roaming the streets as an orphan. The sun continued its relentless descent. They would need to run the five miles back to the abbey to make it by vespers, and Thomas likely wouldn't be able to run five feet.

Desperation sapped his strength as he looked under porches, in barrels, behind piles of rubbish. He kept a constant watch on the sun and refused to give up hope. At the priory, the Benedictine monks said they hadn't seen Thomas. He circled around the walls to the south side of the priory where he felt the tug of his past. There was the hole in the wall that he once called home before Brother Gilbert brought him to Tintern Abbey. With no sign of Thomas, he fell to his knees. "How could I have been so selfish? God, please forgive me." What would he tell Abbot Michael if Thomas was abducted, or worse?

He heard a noise like wind howling through trees; except, there were no trees and no wind. The noise came again, like a moan. He followed the sound to his old hole in the wall. He bent down to see into the shadows.

"I feel sick," Thomas said. His eyes refused to focus on the shadow standing outside the tiny space. He brushed his brown hair out of his eyes and squinted.

Someone reached in and gently shook him. "Wake up. We have to go now."

His speech groggy, Thomas said, "Andrew? Is that you? Why did you leave me?"

"I took Eva home. But I'm here now. We must go."

"I wanted to see your home. I thought I might find you there. This place is small. I had a really hard time getting in. Now, I can't get out." He wiggled his foot, but it was stuck.

"Let me help you." Andrew took hold of Thomas's arm.

Thomas recoiled. "I'm ugly. Leave me be."

"Who told you that? Why would you say such a thing?"

"When we walk down the street, all the girls look at you. No one pays any attention to me."

"None of them know you like I do. You have eyes that see everyone as equal. Your soul never judges. Where else in this world could I find a friend like you?"

"You just say that." Even though he knew in his heart Andrew had never lied to him, the ale amplified his fear that he would be a monk soon and nothing would ever be the same.

"Come now, or I'll get angry."

Andrew's stern voice jolted him into submission.

Andrew again took hold of Thomas's arm. "Watch your head." Once freed, Andrew embraced him. "I'm sorry I left you. I shouldn't have done that."

With his arm over Andrew's shoulders, Thomas walked out the stiffness in his joints and staggered along Upper Church Street following Andrew's lead toward Striguil Castle. Perched on a high hill overlooking the River Wye, the castle dominated the town and gave it life. One of the guards recognized them and waved. "Greetings, boys. What seems to be the trouble?"

"Bran, I need help. Thomas got sick from too much drink. We need to get back to the abbey. May I borrow a horse?"

Moments later, Bran returned with a bay palfrey. "She can handle two riders, but don't push her too hard."

Thomas looked at the horse and vomited.

"Best you got that out now," Andrew said. "I'll bring her back tomorrow, Bran."

At a steady canter, they reached the abbey's stable as the moon's silvery rays overtook last light. While they missed supper and vespers, Thomas didn't feel hungry; his knotted stomach ached, and his throat hurt from having regurgitated a belly-full of ale. He leaned against a post while Andrew secured the horse in an empty stall.

"Is your stomach settled?" Andrew asked.

He felt his stomach and nodded.

Andrew picked him up in his strong arms and cradled him like a child. They sneaked through the lay brother's refectory with its long wooden tables and into the yard behind the kitchen. Brother Samuel stepped out the back door of the kitchen just as they passed by, his short, wide profile framed by the light within.

"Are you boys well?" Brother Samuel asked.

"Thomas got sick at the Broken Oar. He is fine now, but a little tired. I'll take him to his room and watch him for a while."

"Shall I call Brother Ignatius?"

"No, thank you. If we need to go to the infirmary, I'll take Thomas myself."

In the darkness, they climbed the rear stairs of the abbey's new great hall and crept along the passage to Thomas's room. The narrow bed was a squeeze for the two of them. While his body begged for sleep, Thomas's mind rejected rest. He couldn't stop thinking about his future, whether he could be like the other monks—obedient, reserved, humble. He would soon move to the monks' dormitory and become one of many who followed a routine of prayer and work. The youngest son of a nobleman could expect little more. But what of Andrew? Monks and lay brothers weren't supposed to be friends—and that sickness the men at the Broken Oar talked about. What if the evil humors come to Wales? Andrew's breathing slowed; he always fell asleep first.

London, England, April 1348

"Did you bring the money?" With bent fingers, the old scribe extended his hand.

"Forty shillings is a lot," Hastings said. He stroked his black beard and wondered if he should bargain for less. The number of bribes it had taken to bring him to this point drained his purse. Were it not for an opportune encounter with an overweight lord in a quiet alley earlier that evening, he might have missed this opportunity. But now, he had money and new clothes. He reached under his warm, woolen cloak for the bag of coins tied to his belt. If Jankin was right, this crumpled man held the key to a prosperous future.

"We agreed," the man said. "Forty shillings."

In the dark of the London alley, amid the slop and feces of a muddy path bordered by timber framed buildings, Hastings counted out twelve half-noble coins. Reduced to a washed-out shade of gray, the shiny bits of gold reflected moonlight as they fell into the informant's palm—never again to be held or touched or gloated over. "What is it you found that's worth the price of a fine riding horse?"

The man fingered the coins and slipped them into a leather pouch. "There is an abbey near Sempringham, in Lincolnshire. The Gilbertines they are called. You will find an interesting tale there if you care to follow the lead."

Hastings waited, but the man remained silent. "For this I paid forty shillings?" He reached for his dagger. "Jankin said you had information that would make me rich."

"Put away your weapon. Jankin did not exaggerate. I found a letter in a folio at Westminster Palace. The letter contained a request for support from the king for someone at the abbey. The handwriting was unclear and my Latin is only fair; I could not make out all of the words. However, from the words I could read, I discovered something."

"And?"

"It is unusual for the king to send money to an abbey."

"Must I cut the words from your tongue? What's my advantage?"

"Find out why the king sent the money and, by chance, you will find many who will pay."

Chapter
TWO

Thomas marveled at the serenity of the flowing green landscape, but the beauty turned to decay as tiny black dots danced across the field to his left. As the dots grew in number, the grass withered and turned brown. To his right, a lush field, dotted with sweet smelling lavender, offered a soothing respite from the dismal scene. A three-foot-high stone wall separated life from death. Along the top of the wall, water ran in a trench like an ancient aqueduct. The tiny dots ascended the wall and halted at the water's edge. Out of the corner of his vision, three children ran and played among the flowers. They approached the wall and looked over the diseased land as if its sickness lay unseen.

Unable to move or cry out, Thomas watched, transfixed by a feeling of impending doom. The children climbed over the wall and chased each other in a game of catch-me-not. The black dots swarmed and covered the frolicking younglings like an evil shroud, but they continued to jump, run, laugh, and sing.

When the children scrambled back over the wall, the dots clung to them like sap. As their feet touched the emerald green grass, the dots fell off and trailed behind as the children ran away. Grass shriveled, flowers wilted, and the sweet perfumed air turned rancid. At last, Thomas found the power to move. He stomped on the dots until the soles of his feet became numb.

An icy wind whipped across the decaying field. "Stop," a cruel voice shouted. In the distance, a dark form appeared, its edges, indistinct, its voice, as familiar as a remembered terror. "You are too late."

Thomas cowered before the evil presence. He turned and ran; his body floated over the landscape.

The voice followed him. "Run if you must, but I will find you."

"Are you awake?"

Pulled back to reality by a friendly voice, Thomas woke to rumpled blankets and his heart beating like a galloping horse.

Andrew nudged him. "You stink of ale. Best get up before Abbot Michael comes looking for you."

First light came too early for Thomas. "Were you here all night?"

"Most of it. I went back to the lay brother's dormitory after night prayers."

As best he could, Thomas ignored his dry mouth, upset stomach, and headache. The musty smell of fresh plaster and whitewash did little to clear his stuffy nose. Tucked away in a corner of Tintern Abbey's new great hall, his first floor room was meant for storage, but served as his accommodations until he took his vows. His furniture included a small bed with a straw-filled tick, a narrow oak chest, and an old table with a wobbly, wooden stool.

"Move over," Andrew said as he straightened the bed and folded the wool blanket. "I have to go. Hurry up and get dressed. And wash your face."

Alone again, he mustered the resolve to get up for his morning lesson with Abbot Michael. He opened his window to clear the hazy thoughts clouding his concentration and caught the sweet-sung refrain of a goldfinch. The cool, fresh air made him shiver but did its job of waking him. A quick trip down the back stairs to the latrine gave him a few more moments to think on his lesson for the day.

Abbot Michael's private chamber occupied the entire first floor of what used to be the guest lodge and was now connected to the recently completed great hall by a vestibule at the top of the main stairs. Archways, covered with elaborate arcading, framed the doors. The complex designs seemed out of place for the Cistercian simplicity emphasized by the Rules of St. Benedict he had spent long hours memorizing.

He stared a moment at the cross-shaped knocker on Abbot Michael's door, uncertain if he was ready to recite his assigned list of Bible verses. Words spun in his memory like wind-blown leaves. He raised the knocker half way and let it fall.

"Enter."

Thomas grabbed the cold iron ring and turned the latch. He walked into the spacious chamber with its plain plastered walls and minimal decoration. Seated behind a table strewn with documents and scrolls, Abbot Michael wore an unbleached woolen robe and black scapular tied at the waist with a cord of the same fabric as the robe. His gray beard neatly trimmed, he mouthed words as he read from a document tilted at an angle so the light from the trio of south-facing windows behind him lit the page.

"God's blessings, Father Abbot." Thomas's voice cracked.

Abbot Michael continued to read from the document in his hand. While Thomas waited, he gazed at the wide shelf that hung from the wall to the left of the door. The shelf held several of Abbot Michael's favorite books, a mix of pewter mugs and candle holders, and tokens from travels abroad. He wondered what it would be like to travel so far that you'd want a remembrance of the trip.

"God's blessings, Thomas." Abbot Michael motioned for Thomas to come closer. "I am pleased that you have mastered Gregory the Great's *Dialogues* and the *Lives of the Fathers*. Your novitiate will benefit from your hard work. You are now ready to take on more substance in your training and participate in some of the spiritual activities around the monastery. You must become acquainted with the sense of community we share. After all, you will be spending a great deal of time with your fellow monks as you proceed through your training. You must learn to accept the guidance of those who are more experienced."

"Yes, Father Abbot." Thomas grasped his hands together behind his back.

"Your day will start at prime with reading from the books in the armarium while the rest of us attend the Chapter meeting. At terce, you will attend morning mass in the nave with the lay brothers. Then, you will proceed to the cloister and join the monks for their daily reading, the *lectio divina*. In particular, I want you to read from the Psalms." Abbott Michael handed Thomas a list of Psalms to read. "Understand each word and, as you say it, make it a part of you. Reading is a time for concentration and communal solitude."

"Yes, Father Abbot." Thomas gripped the stiff sheet of parchment with both hands and scanned the list as Abbot Michael continued.

"Before the monks go about their daily work, you will join them in the refectory for dinner. Silence is an important part of the routine. The reading during the meal is food for the soul. You must seek to savor the words you hear rather than the food you eat. After dinner, check with Brother Samuel to see what work he may have for you. In work, you must seek to be humble before God; we toil for Christ. Your contribution aids the community and keeps you from sloth. Once Brother Samuel has seen fit to let you go, you may return to your studies."

"Yes, Father Abbot."

"I hope this will be instructional for you and help to ease your way into the routine of a novitiate. I am proud of you, Thomas. You have shown a great aptitude for learning."

Thomas made to leave.

Abbot Michael raised his hand and said, "One moment. Brother Samuel told me he saw Andrew carry you to your chamber last night. Is there anything I should know?"

It was too much to hope Abbot Michael would remain unaware of his indulgence with drink. The urge to vomit seized him, but he swallowed hard. His thoughts jumbled, he stood still, arms stiff at his side, his face frozen. Then, a plausible response flashed in his mind. He rubbed his stomach. "I'm fine now. I must have eaten or drank something that upset my stomach while Andrew and I were in Chepstow." Relieved by the choice of words, he felt certain a confession was unnecessary. The drink was to blame for his upset stomach; he spoke no lies.

Abbot Michael crossed his arms like he always did when he wanted to make a point. "I take it you learned something from this experience?"

"I did. Thank you, Father Abbot."

"Good. Let us say no more about it. However, I am concerned about your friendship with Andrew. When you take your vows, you will be expected to devote your time to prayer and the work of the abbey. Even if Andrew joins the lay brotherhood, which would be years away, he will be busy with his own work. You will not have time to associate with lay brothers beyond the need to coordinate tasks you are assigned. Brother Gilbert tells me Andrew's willingness to work is an example for all, but I am troubled by the influence he has over you. Shall I ask him to leave?"

Stunned, Thomas's mind went blank. If a chair had been placed behind him, he would have collapsed into it. He never imagined the conversation would take this turn. He found his voice and said, "Andrew is my friend. It was my fault. I was the one who drank too much and caused us to be late. You can punish me if you must."

"It is not what I must do, Thomas. It is what you must do. Andrew is an orphan who has no future beyond the fruits of the labor his hands can provide. You will be a monk. Nothing can change that."

Holding back tears challenged all his self-control. "Why does it matter where Andrew came from?"

"It is the way of things."

Thomas clenched his fist. An unexpected energy filled him. "Jesus didn't care who his disciples were. You are friends with my father, are you not?"

"That is different. In the service of the Order, I am obliged to build relationships with benefactors and men of authority—like your father. If you become abbot, then you also may find it beneficial to make friendships outside these walls. Until then, your goal is *opus Dei*, the work of God."

"But I'm not yet a monk."

Abbot Michael frowned. "It is best that you spend less time with Andrew and more time with your studies."

"I don't understand."

"Everyone has his place. You are the youngest son of a nobleman and therefore your destiny lies with the church just as your brother, Robert, is destined to inherit your father's lands and title. Andrew has no father whose trade or lands he might inherit. It is not possible for him to rise above his station in life."

Thomas thought of the two boys who helped Matilda in the kitchen back at Kendalwood Manor. His father never allowed him to play with them. From his window, he sometimes caught glimpse of them running and laughing outside the castle walls. It seemed wrong, unnatural even, that he be forbidden to join them. "I don't care where Andrew came from."

"When you learn to choose your friends wisely, you will come to understand."

He took a deep breath and tried to relax his fist. "Thank you, Father Abbot. I'll try to understand."

Back in the vestibule, Thomas stifled ill-favored thoughts of defiance. It was his duty to obey, but how could he ignore his friend? In a world of adults, Andrew, at two years older, was nearest to him in age, and when they were younger, they did everything together. Abbot Michael seemed no longer the kind, understanding, father figure who gave special favors to his favorite son. He had become the Abbot of Tintern Abbey and Thomas, the soon-to-be novitiate.

He disliked the unexpected change. Life as a monk would be serious, rigid, and repetitive. There would be no opportunity to follow simple pursuits with Andrew like running through the woods, pretending to fight dragons and evil knights or shooting rabbits and squirrels for sale to the Broken Oar. The church would be his only friend and God, the Blessed Virgin, the Lord Jesus Christ, the heavenly saints, and the other monks, his only companions. He was determined to keep Andrew a part of that mix.

To Thomas, it seemed more than a coincidence when the next day Andrew left with Brother Gilbert to meet with the lay brothers at Aluredeston Grange. Andrew had gone on other trips but never for more than a day or two. To be gone a fortnight struck him as unbearable—and untimely.

"They left early this morning," Brother Elias had said when Thomas asked where he might find Andrew. At least he now had more time to think. How would he tell Andrew that Abbot Michael wanted him to spend more time with his studies—and less time with him? He wandered toward the abbey's main gate and stood outside intent on wasting time. A raven pecked at something on the road. With keen interest focused on the raven's actions, he paid little attention to a merchant leading a horse-drawn cart until the man called out, "May I interest you in some skirrets?"

The raven ruffled its feathers at the approach of the cart, turned its beady eyes toward the horse, squawked, and flew away. Thomas bothered a glance at the merchant. Food wasn't on his mind. Instead, his thoughts jumped to the story of the strange sickness told by the freeman at the Broken Oar. Where was the pestilence now? Was William in danger? He eyed the man and asked, "Have you any word of the pestilence?"

The merchant snapped to attention as his black cape fluttered in the brisk breeze. He took a step back and looked around, eyes wide, and said, "Why do you ask?"

"I heard stories and wondered if they were true."

In a soft tone, the man said, "Talk of that evil menace is nothing for the faint-hearted, lad. It's dreadful what I've heard."

"Is it true ships drift on the sea with only ghosts to man the rigging?"

"I don't know about ghosts, but I've heard it said anyone who breathes the vile humors dies a horrible death. Bodies covered in blotches and sores give off an unbearable foul stench. Mind you, I haven't seen anything myself. Only God knows what the truth may be. Best to say your prayers, lad, and ask God for forgiveness."

Thomas shuddered at the description. It was bad enough listening to the men at the Broken Oar, but now another story to add to the mix. He quickly put out of his mind an image of William covered in blotches. Could the pestilence really be that bad?

The merchant reached into his wagon for a clump of the skinny white roots. "I can assure you these are the finest skirrets—sweet and crisp."

"You'll have to speak with our cellerar, Brother Samuel. I'll get him for you." Thomas ran off happy to get away from the uncomfortable talk.

For the next week, Thomas did his best to hide his frustration over Andrew's absence. The few minutes it took to walk from his room to the armarium became a walk of miles rather than yards. The windowless room amplified his sullen mood. He turned off his desire to learn and grabbed books at random. Some of the heavy volumes in the abbey's collection were scripted in letters so small it was nearly impossible to read in the dim light of a candle. Instead, he turned the smooth vellum pages of folios that contained colorful drawings.

When the bells sounded for mass, he trudged along the covered arcade to the abbey church and made his way to the nave. Rather than listening to the melodic chants of the monks and reciting the communal responses, he let his gaze wander over the decorative rood screen and upward along the massive stone pillars, bigger than the grandest oak trees. He tilted his head back and stared at the graceful curves of pointed arches and decorative ribbed vaulting.

Bells sounded and it was time for reading. He took his copy of the Old Testament from the nook in the wall of the cloister and found a spot near the passage to the lay brother's refectory. He wanted to be as far removed as possible from the gathered monks. With his list of verses from Abbot Michael in hand, he leafed through the pages to find the corresponding scripture. As the others read, he mumbled his words without regard for proper diction.

More bells signaled dinner. Did the monks ever get tired of bells? Rushes, laid on the refectory's slate floor, lessened the chill and filled the air with a musty dustiness reminiscent of a stable. Benches scraped and grinded as the monks took their places at trestle tables lined along the two longest walls. A voice from the balcony began the reading. Abbot Michael said he should savor the message rather than the soup in his bowl, but his thoughts got stuck wondering if the slice of carrot he poked at was one he had cut for Brother Samuel the day before.

A slight variation in his new routine came in the form of manual labor. Brother Samuel usually kept him busy in the kitchen, which Thomas didn't mind. Kitchen work kept him warm and dry during the unseasonably cold and wet spring. But on the rare occasion of a nice day, Brother Samuel sent him to help Brother Aldwin tend the vegetable garden.

Thomas thought of Brother Aldwin as a calm and gentle man, but he nearly broke his vow of silence when Thomas failed to properly follow instructions on the use of a hoe. Thomas often stepped on plants in one row while he worked on another. Brother Aldwin waved his arms and gestured frantically in an attempt to get Thomas to hoe correctly. When Thomas accidentally chopped off a new shoot, Brother Aldwin snatched the hoe and pointed toward the church.

"I thought that was a weed. You pointed at something that looked like that before."

Brother Aldwin shook his head and acted out the motion of hoeing around a similar plant. He pointed at a broad-leafed plant, yanked it from the ground, and held it close to Thomas's face.

"Is that the weed?"

Brother Aldwin nodded, his lips a thin, tight line. He again pointed at the church.

"Am I to do penance for killing the wrong plant?"

The question garnered a huge smile and exaggerated nods from Brother Aldwin.

Near Sempringham, England, April 1348

Jostled on horseback for five days, Hastings wished he'd been the one to steal the horses instead of Rowan. "This is the dumbest rouncy I have ever ridden." He shifted his ample weight to ease a sore spot.

Rowan chuckled. "Are you sure it's not the rider?"

"Your swordsmanship may be the best I've seen, but your lack of foresight astounds me." He glanced at the three-inch scar under Rowan's right eye, a risky move if detected, but hard to resist. More than a few men regretted the explosion of hate triggered by an intrusive gaze.

"Don't forget, I'm also the best thief you've ever known."

Hastings sighed. He didn't want to encourage Rowan's arrogance more than necessary. "I'll admit you're no longer the ill-mannered, arrant wretch I met a year ago, but when I asked you to find a good riding horse, I was expecting a palfrey—even an old one."

"It's not like we had much choice. You spent all our money on bribes to those fools at court."

Hastings thought of the grand halls and plentiful platters of hot food and warm bread dished out by lords and ladies eager to show off their wealth and connections to the king. At times, he considered the price he paid for a slice of information insignificant compared to the sumptuous feasts given by those willing to sell their souls. His stomach growled as he recalled the pleasure of chewing a slice of mutton, the firm flesh oozing sweet juices. He was unsure which he hated more: lack of money or lack of food.

As he assessed what he now knew of the benefactor of the king's generosity, he expected there could be more to the story—much more. The seemingly unrelated facts surrounding Edmund of Sleaford held an intrigue that percolated in his mind. Sleaford had a son and grandson, both now deceased, and his castle was near the priory. There must be a connection to the Gilbertines.

The spires of Sempringham Priory rose above the Lincolnshire fens like needles jabbing at God; at least, Hastings found it amusing to think so. He had no time for God, or the supplicants who groveled at the feet of the church—unless there was profit to be made. "Merchants travel these roads. Perhaps you can make yourself useful and replenish our stock of coins while I meet with these Gilbertines."

"What if the monks don't tell us what we need to know?"

"Leave that to me. Your blade is better served elsewhere."

Rowan kicked his heels into his horse's sides to discourage it from stopping to munch on a bed of newly sprouted grass. "Then why did I come along? I was happy at that whorehouse in London."

"I may soon have a task better to your liking."

"Traveling the robber infested roads eating whatever tasty animal comes my way?"

"Nothing so exciting." Hastings stared down the long road ahead plotting his contingencies for whatever bits of information he could glean from the poor sots waiting to be played like a well-tuned psaltery.

Chapter
THREE

Tintern Abbey, Wales, April 1348

The rare opportunity to sleep late felt like an indulgent gift. With Abbot Michael away tending to affairs of the abbey, Thomas pulled his warm, but scratchy, wool blanket over his head to block out the light. As his thoughts drifted between the coo of a morning dove and the comfort of his bed, a *whack* jarred him out of his half-sleep. Another *whack* followed, and then another. By the third *whack*, he knew the source of the intrusive noise. Andrew split wood with a rhythm unmatched in speed and consistency. Happy that Andrew had returned from Aluredeston Grange, his momentary excitement collapsed with a pang of dread; he had to tell Andrew what Abbot Michael said about ending their friendship. As he lay in bed, he wished everything could stay the same, but each swing of Andrew's maul brought a cringe. Avoidance seemed pointless. He got dressed and ran down the stairs. In the yard, Andrew stood shirtless, his blonde hair bright in the early morning sun.

"You never get tired of work, do you?"

With his ever-cheerful expression, Andrew turned and said, "Someone has to do the work around here. And we all know that excludes you."

"Are you cold?"

Andrew glanced at his well-muscled arms. "Working keeps me warm. You must have some books to read."

"After more than a week away, all you can do is ask me about books?"

"What's wrong now?"

"Did I say anything was wrong?"

Andrew shrugged. "I can tell. Your head must be spinning with thoughts."

Thomas opened his mouth, but nothing came out as if all the words in his head vanished. He sat on the ground cross-legged and tugged on tall blades of grass. Andrew sat beside him and waited. After an agonizing moment of listening to the high-pitched chirps of a dozen sparrows flitting about the yard, Thomas said, "Can we go hunting for squirrels?"

Andrew motioned to a large pile of wood amounting to about a full cartload already cut to length. "I have to split this wood. Then we can go. Why today?"

"Did Brother Gilbert say anything to you about coming back from Chepstow late and missing vespers?"

Andrew's face scrunched into a puzzled look. "No."

Thomas stared at the ground and tugged faster at the blades of grass.

Andrew grabbed his hand. "One word at a time."

His throat tightened. Andrew's hand was warm and sweaty; rough from years of work. The hand of a commoner with no future—or so Abbot Michael would have him believe. He rejected the thought. This was the hand of his friend. Even if he wanted to pull away, Andrew was too strong. The grip was firm but not painful. He had to speak. As if ripped from his soul, he repeated the words that had rattled around in his mind for days, "Abbot Michael said I have to spend less time with you. I can't be your friend anymore."

Andrew maintained his grip. "Look at me. Since when did we listen to Abbot Michael's commands about what we should and shouldn't do?"

Thomas shrugged. He studied the face he knew better than his own; brown eyes, pointed nose, narrow jaw, and a mouth that spoke the truth without hesitation. The soul within could no more be separated from his own than heat could be taken from fire.

"You can help me split this wood and then we can go hunt squirrels, take them to Chepstow, and sell them for a mug of ale—only one mug this time. And no Eva."

Thomas did his best to make a meaningful contribution. He fetched—more precisely rolled—logs from the pile and stacked the split logs into smaller carts. They finished as the church bells rang sext.

"This is hard work," Thomas said.

"As soon as you take your vows, you'll be too busy reading from those books in the armarium and praying all night in the church to worry about splitting wood or shooting squirrels."

"I know. I think I'd rather go hunting with you. But, Abbot Michael wouldn't approve, would he? And my father expects me to become the abbot some day and no amount of wishing is going to change that. I need to have faith and accept it, right?"

"You think too much. Seems like everyone else has decided your future for you. At least no one expects anything from me."

Thomas helped Andrew deliver the wood to the infirmary and then the warming house where a small pile sufficed to keep the fires stoked until Good Friday. They took the rest to the bin by the rear door of the kitchen.

Brother Samuel came out to greet them; the distinctive, heavy flop of his sandals announced his approach. Sunlight brightened the grayish-white of his woolen habit and highlighted his brown hair cut in the style of a monk's tonsure.

"Thank you for the wood," Brother Samuel said. His fat cheeks bulged with a grateful smile that matched his jolly disposition. "Andrew, I have a task for you. I would appreciate it if you would go to Trelleck Grange and remind Brother Gilbert that we will need a fine, plump pig for the Easter feast. The Countess of Norfolk will be attending so we will need to serve meat at the abbot's table."

"I was going to clean the lay brother's dormitory."

Brother Samuel pointed at the newly filled bin. "Please bring an armload inside."

Thomas struggled with half as much split wood as Andrew as they carried their loads into the kitchen, a generous room with a high ceiling. A wild mixture of smells filled the air from the pleasant aroma of fresh bread, to the sharp sting of diced onion and the complicated bouquet of a simmering pot of soup. They piled the wood in a chest beside the massive fireplace that took up most of the east wall. A large, black cauldron hung from a heavy iron arm that swung over the fire.

"Your other tasks can wait," Brother Samuel said, as he stirred the contents of his cauldron. He waved the vapors toward his nose, took a deep breath, and let out a sigh.

Thomas cocked his head toward a basket of fresh biscuits. The inviting feast sat at one end of the long, rectangular oak table that stood in the center of the room. The soft, gray patina of the wood and numerous cut marks bore witness to its many years of use. A collection of different sized bowls, pots, and baskets vied for space on the table.

Brother Samuel reached for the bowls filled with chopped leeks and carrots and added the vegetables to his pot. "Brother Gilbert has a way of forgetting things so a little reminder would be in order." Brother Samuel's attention seemed focused on the contents of his cauldron.

"Anything else?" Andrew asked. He winked at Thomas. "Maybe Thomas can come with me in case Brother Gilbert has anything to send back."

Before Brother Samuel turned to respond, Andrew dashed out the door with a large biscuit in each hand and Thomas close behind.

The errand meant Thomas now had a legitimate excuse to spend the day with Andrew. They gathered their bows and arrows from the stable and headed out on the four-mile walk. The constant spring rains caused deep ruts and wide puddles in the road.

As they approached Trelleck Grange, they heard shouting. Andrew motioned to Thomas to stay close.

Not more than ten paces farther down the road, the sound of a branch cracking echoed through the trees, and a grubby little man with stringy black hair moved through the undergrowth. The man knelt beside a bush, laid down his bow, and broke several long branches in front of him.

Andrew nodded and drew his hunting knife. He crept toward the vagrant. "What are you doing here?"

In a squeaky voice, the man said, "We're jus' 'ungry. Didn't mean no 'arm."

"How many are you?"

"Jus' me and Owen. I swear."

Andrew motioned to Thomas to come closer.

Across an open field, freshly plowed for spring oats, Brother Gilbert argued with another man in front of Trelleck Grange's manor house—the distance too far to make out the words clearly. Even in his brown habit and black scapular, Brother Gilbert looked more like a soldier than a lay brother, hands on hips and feet firmly planted, his stature reminiscent of his past military service at Striguil Castle. The other man looked to be about the same size as Brother Gilbert but wore rust-colored breeches, an over-sized tunic, and a cap that appeared too large for his head.

Andrew glanced around. "Others are about, I'm sure of it."

Without warning, the grubby little man turned and jumped at Andrew like a cornered rat. They tumbled down a slope about ten to fifteen feet. Thomas watched, helpless to aid Andrew. The man kicked and squirmed free of Andrew's hold. Andrew grabbed the man by the legs and yanked him to the ground. As they wrestled, they crushed shrubs and snapped fallen branches. Thomas cringed at the noise. When Andrew regained the advantage, he swung his fist and struck the man's left cheekbone knocking him unconscious. Andrew then quickly gathered his weapons and hurried up the slope. Panting, he asked, "What betides?"

"Over there. Near the wood shed." Thomas pointed at a man coming out from behind a border of tall shrubs.

"Do you think you can hit that shed from here?"

"I think so," Thomas tried to act brave as events swirled around him.

"I know you can. As soon as I step out, you land an arrow just in front of him as he comes around. Ready…now!" Andrew dashed out from the bushes and into the open.

Thomas shot his arrow with perfect timing.

As the third man rounded the corner of the shed, Thomas's arrow landed two feet in front of him. The thud of the arrow stopped the man in his tracks. He looked around and called out, "Adwar. What are you doing?" He drew a knife and yelled, "Owen!"

Andrew jumped over ridges and furrows in perfect step as he ran across the field. With an arrow in one hand and his bow in the other, he shouted, "Brother Gilbert! Another man comes. By the wood shed." In the middle of the field, he took a stance, set his arrow, and targeted Owen.

Thomas drew another arrow and quickly gauged the correct angle. This time, he aimed for the man, not the shed.

Brother Gilbert threw a punch, knocking the wind out of Owen. He grabbed the sword he kept by the front door of the manor house. "I think our discussion over your lost pig is finished."

After he recovered his breath, Owen managed to say, "Give it up, Fane."

Brother Gilbert called to Andrew, "A pleasure to see you, Andrew. You can relax. Is that Thomas over there?"

"Yes." Andrew lowered his bow and approached, but kept the arrow set on the string.

"Who's Adwar?"

"He must be the man we found in the bushes. It looked like he was going to shoot somebody. We made sure he didn't."

"Thank you, Andrew. I imagine I was his target. Is that correct?"

Owen remained silent.

"What did you do to him?" Brother Gilbert asked Andrew.

"I punched him in the face. Just like you taught me. Knocked him out, I think."

"Good job, son. You best help Thomas carry the poor sot. That other fellow by the shed is going to walk over here real slow and not cause any more trouble, right?"

Once all three of the misfits stood together, Brother Gilbert asked, "Which of you is going to tell me the real story here?"

Owen fidgeted and said, "It's this damn weather. Made a mess of our crops and most of our stores have gone moldy with all this rain. We just thought that since you had all these pigs and sheep you might be able to spare one or two. We would've paid you back when we could. God's truth. Isn't it so, Fane?"

"Just as he said," Fane replied. His shaggy, dark brown hair hung over his eyes like a mangy sheepdog.

Adwar didn't say a word. The bruise on his cheek and the beginnings of a black eye merged with the rest of his ugly face.

Brother Gilbert stroked his beard. "We've all suffered from this weather. Let me make you an offer. If you'll work here until Easter, you can have a dry place to stay and something to eat. Then, I'll send you on your way with some victuals. Or, I can send Andrew with a message to my friend, Eudo, Captain of the Guard at Striguil Castle. I'm sure he can find a pleasant place for you to stay. What's it going to be?"

Owen quickly responded, "We'll do as you say. We don't want any trouble. I speak for all of us, right boys?"

Fane grunted a barely intelligible "Yes." Adwar flashed a toothless grin.

Brother Gilbert called to the other lay brothers gathered around the manor house and asked them to help escort the three misfits away. When they were alone, he turned to Thomas and Andrew and said, "Thank God you boys came along when you did."

Andrew said, "I almost forgot. Brother Samuel asked us to remind you that he needs a fine, plump pig for the Easter feast."

"I'm sure Brother Samuel was losing sleep wondering if I would remember. You can assure him that I'll have his fine, plump pig delivered in plenty of time. And by the way, best not tell Abbot Michael about all the trouble today. I'll get around to it in due time. I think they learned their lesson. Or, at least I hope so."

Thomas and Andrew returned to the monastery with enough time to gobble down a bowl of Brother Samuel's thick soup before running off to vespers. They made their way into the church through the heavy oak doors leading from the cloister.

Thomas found it hard to concentrate on the service. He kept thinking back to Adwar's attack on Andrew and all the "what-ifs." What if he had missed the shed—or worse, killed Fane. He never before faced the prospect of killing a man. The idea that he might have caused a death distressed him.

When the service ended, he continued to stand in the nave as the monks and lay brothers filed out. With his head bowed, his thoughts raced in every direction except the one that told him to move his feet.

Andrew returned a few moments later. "Are you coming?"

Thomas remained silent, his gaze fixed on the patterns in the tile floor.

Andrew put his arm around Thomas's shoulders. "Are you worried about what Abbot Michael said?"

Straining for volume, Thomas said, "I could have killed that man today. Is that what a monk is supposed to do? Monks are supposed to lead peaceful lives and pray and work for humility and God's blessing." Tears welled up.

"What happened at Trelleck Grange was beyond our control. We did the right thing."

"Did we?" Thomas's voice cracked.

"You have nothing to be ashamed of. I was scared too. But no one died. You saw how forgiving Brother Gilbert was. He had no anger toward those men. In the end, he only wanted to help them. What is it Abbot Michael says? 'We can try to help the less fortunate, but they have to become responsible for their own actions.' That's what we did today."

"Is it?" Thomas sniffled and wiped his nose with his sleeve.

"You think too much. And that's never a good sign."

After a moment of silence, Thomas said, "I love being here at the monastery, Andrew. This has been my life since I was eight years old. You were only ten when Brother Gilbert brought you here. Everything will change once I become a monk. We won't be able to go to Chepstow or have fun or go hunting. Life will be serious."

"And you'll have to learn how to tend the vegetable garden with Brother Aldwin."

The birth of a smile formed at the corners of Thomas's lips.

"See. You can still smile. The world won't end because we have difficult choices to make. I believe God gives us only what we can handle. I never thought I could defend myself in a fight. Yet today, God put me in a situation to show me I could. I can still remember that beggar clubbing me on the head and then everything going black. Had Brother Gilbert not found me and brought me here, I may have died then and there. For the longest time, I had so much anger toward that beggar. But Brother Gilbert taught me to turn that anger into something useful. All I want is to be able to protect myself and my friends." Andrew looked into Thomas's innocent blue eyes. "You are my friend and no one, not even Abbot Michael, is going to change that. All that time shooting at rabbits and squirrels prepared you for what you had to do. Your shot was perfect. God certainly had something to do with that, did He not?"

Thomas shrugged. All he could think about was Abbot Michael telling him that he and Andrew could no longer be friends and how lonely life would become.

"I like it here too. There's work to do, food to eat, and Brother Gilbert will need someone to take over one day at Trelleck Grange. If that's what I'm to do, then God will direct me down that path. If not, well, I can't force it now, can I? Tomorrow will come when it comes. Agreed?"

Thomas nodded and straightened his posture. As they left the church, he tried to keep his thoughts in the moment. Letting go like that frightened him.

Snug in his bed, Thomas drifted off to sleep and fell into a happy dream. He stood alone on the deck of a pristine cog drifting on a warm sea. A gentle breeze stirred the rigging. Waves splashed against the hull with a hypnotic beat. The bright sun shined in a perfect sky. He gazed out to the horizon enjoying the fresh, salty air.

A change in the wind brought a putrid odor drifting up from below the forecastle—the scent of Satan. Curiosity got the best of him, and he descended a narrow ladder into a small dark room.

He paused as his eyes adjusted to the dim light. The foul stench, like decomposing fish covered with honey, assailed his sense of smell. He shivered and held back an urge to vomit. Looking around the eerie confines, he saw what appeared to be bodies lying on cots. An overpowering urge drove him to look at the motionless forms. With a clap of thunder, light flashed and revealed the space. The sunken shape of old death stared at him from faces frozen in looks of impossible anguish. The eyes reflected the blackness of rot and decay. Ugly black growths grew from pale skin at the base of necks and from under arms.

He jumped back and fell against a cot, disturbing the occupant who fell on him in a horrifying embrace. Terror engulfed his senses. He threw off the emaciated carcass and scurried up the ladder. A sinister laugh trailed off behind him as he dove over the side of the ship into cold water.

Swimming in sweat under a draft from the open window in his room, he woke to the darkness of a moonless night. A strange foreboding unsettled him. He felt his neck and underarms and relaxed when he found nothing growing. Comforted that the experience was only a dream, he drew up his blankets and went back to sleep.

Chapter
FOUR

Calais, English Possession, April 1348

Sir William de Parr reveled in the tension of the conquered city, but making good on his plan to sell wool at a huge profit, turned out to entail logistics he never thought about. The rumored naming of Calais as the staple port for wool fueled his plan, yet confirmation of that proclamation proved elusive. He walked the muddy streets from his room in the fortified section of the city to an alehouse near Calais's wharf and merchant quarter. The Rusty Anchor seemed the best place to talk business with his new-found acquaintance, Edward Crawford. William hated the ale they served; it tasted like piss, but at least his bowels didn't object.

The setting sun glinted off his new suit of mail purchased with his share of the spoils of war. The smithy said the color of the leather straps went well with his auburn hair. Noticeably absent from the smithy's flattery was a comment about William's struggling attempt at a beard. At twenty years of age, William hated the comments he received about looking too young to be a real knight. If only others could recognize his abilities as a commander—his company of Welsh archers seemed to appreciate his efforts.

He spotted Crawford under an overhang outside the run-down alehouse. The long shadows of evening shrouded Crawford's wrinkled features and worn, rumpled clothes made from tattered, out-of-style cloth. If someone wanted to hire a successful merchant by appearance alone, Crawford exhibited nothing to desire, but William needed specialized talents—someone who knew his way around the edges of legality. Crawford waved at his approach.

Once inside, Crawford asked, "What's this idea you had?"

"Have you heard the rumors about the staple port for the wool trade moving to Calais?"

Crawford shook his head. "What have you heard?"

"Shall we find a spot in the corner?" The dilapidated appearance of the Rusty Anchor's exterior perfectly matched the ramshackle décor of its interior. The wattle and daub walls offered little protection from the elements. Rats ran free through holes in the wood plank floor. The lingering smell of stale ale, burnt fat, and vomit saturated the air. Tables and rough-hewn benches made for primitive seating in the large, square room. William pointed to a table by the far wall. "That hole will give us some fresh air."

"Good idea. I'll get us mugs."

When Crawford returned, William leaned close and said, "I figured it out several months ago. Once the king got control of a port on the continent, he'd be certain to move the wool staple there. Wool is England's most valuable export. And the king needs better control over tax collections. What better place than here where the army is in control."

"What's your point?" Crawford wrinkled his nose as he took a sip of ale.

"I know a good source of wool available for export from England. If I can arrange for that wool to be among the first delivered to Calais, when prices are at a premium, I'll make a fortune. The only thing I need is a ship to carry the load. What do you think?"

"Who's got the wool?"

William sat back and crossed his arms. "That information is not part of the conversation."

Leaning forward with a pointed finger, Crawford said, "If you want a ship, I need to know where it has to go and how much it needs to carry."

William considered his alternatives; he had none. He needed this plan to work if he was to prove to his father that he was worthy of respect. "This is just between you and me. Yes?"

"You have my word." Crawford smiled, but only with his lips.

William took a long swig from his mug and looked around the room. "My father, Lord Geoffrey de Parr, has land up river from Chepstow east of the River Wye. He has good relations with the Countess of Norfolk who has extensive pastures around Chepstow. Tintern Abbey is also nearby and high quality wool is one of the things they are known for. My brother, Thomas, is a ward of the abbot there. Between my father, the countess, and the abbey, I'm sure they have close to a hundred sacks of wool to export, maybe more. They can store the wool in cellars at Bristow until a ship arrives. The sheep are sheered in June so there is plenty of time to make arrangements."

"Bristow is a busy port. Are you sure you want to load the wool there?"

"As I said, my father has good relations with the Countess of Norfolk. No one is going to trouble the king's aunt."

"Clever. You've thought about this for a long time, I can tell. You'd make a good merchant."

William smiled and finished his ale. "I want to show my father that I can succeed. I had to learn everything on my own. This is my chance to make a lot of money."

"Let me think on who best can manage that kind of bulk. I'm sure I can find someone. Give me a few days."

The crescent moon provided scant light for Crawford as he sloshed through the muck. He sidestepped the biggest puddles in the narrow streets leading to the wharf. In an alley, the dark outline of a tall, broad figure came into focus against the lighter gray of the building.

"You best have a good reason for this meeting," the man said.

"I've a good reason, Rufus."

"Speak quickly. I don't want to get caught by the night ward."

"I hired a ship coming from Marseilles to ferry a shipment of wine from Bordeaux to Bristow, but it went missing after leaving Barcelona and never reached Bordeaux. I'm sure the pestilence is to blame. Finding transport is getting difficult. I made contact with another ship on its way to Navarre, but after Bordeaux, its return route took it to Jersey and then Bruges. My wine now sits in a warehouse in St. Helier."

"Why do I care?"

"A fellow by the name of William de Parr is looking for a ship to ferry wool from Bristow to Calais."

"And?"

"If you take Parr to Bristow to pick up his wool, I'll make it worth your while to stop in Jersey. I need to move the wine before it spoils. Parr doesn't care when he gets to Bristow as long as it's by the end of July."

Rufus cleared his throat and spat at a large puddle. "What if Parr objects to the course?"

"Tell him whatever you have to once you're under sail. Just don't throw him overboard. Once we have the wool, we can get rid of him."

"You best be in Bristow by the end of July." Rufus shook his fist. "I'll not be minding this owler while you're enjoying yourself at some whorehouse in London."

Crawford scoffed. "I'll be there. And don't worry about Parr. He's too worried about what his father thinks to cause any trouble."

Near Sempringham, England, April 1348

Situated in a gully, the wooden hut leaned against a tree just as the man at the alehouse described. Hastings looked over his shoulder toward Rowan and the setting sun. "Wait here." He glanced at the angled path that meandered up the brush-covered slope and back toward the main road to Sempringham.

Rowan nodded and rested his back against a large oak, its breadth wide enough to hide his profile.

Hastings knocked on the loose-fitted door and, without waiting for a reply, entered the hut.

A frail voice asked, "Is that you Father John?"

"I brought food," Hastings said, as he set the sack of bread and cheese on a table next to an old man seated in a three-legged chair.

The old man's unsteady hands groped for the canvas sack. He untied the knot with crooked fingers and felt the contents. His expression as blank as his stare, he asked, "Who are you?"

As much as Hastings hated to act kind, he switched to his pleasant voice. "A friend."

The old man sniffed the loaf of bread and set it on his lap. "I sense you have a question."

Hastings stooped for a better look at the old man's eyes. Odd that this blind, white-haired sot could perceive such a thing. "I understand you once worked at the priory. I'd like to ask you some questions."

"Who sent you?"

"I came to offer you food and drink in exchange for information."

"Give me your hand."

Hastings resisted the urge to ask the purpose and presented his hand as any trusting soul might oblige.

The old man placed his hands over Hastings's and massaged Hastings's palm and fingers in an intrusive sort of way. "You are selfish and greedy, but I'm hungry and thirsty. What is it you wish to know?"

Hastings pulled back his hand and looked at it. "What kind of enchantment is this?"

"No enchantment. The blind can see what most men are too busy to notice."

He shook off an odd feeling that this man already knew the questions he intended to ask. "Yes, well, I can see you know more than most folk around here give you credit."

The old man broke off a piece of cheese, sniffed it, and put it in his mouth. "Enough with the flattery. Ask your questions."

Hastings looked around for another chair, but there was nowhere to sit except a mat of straw covered with torn strips of canvas. He opted to stand. "What do you know of the person who was held at the priory at the king's command?"

"If you mean by the first King Edward, that King Edward ordered many to be tucked away to die. The lucky ones lost their heads. Others, spent their lives in lonely silence."

"This woman received support from the king. That's odd is it not?"

"Not if that woman was a princess."

"A princess." Hastings stroked his black beard. "How do you know she was a princess?"

"Not many alive today were there when she arrived."

"You saw her?"

"I was a lad then, but yes. I saw her. The child was taken to the nun's side of the priory. Men are not allowed there. I never saw her again, but I overheard talk that her father was a prince."

"How did they keep such a thing a secret? Having a child at the priory, I mean."

"Babies are not uncommon. When men and women are confined, even within a house of God, Satan easily finds willing souls to corrupt."

Hastings looked to the ceiling. With the speed of a practiced conniver, his mind played out multiple avenues of deceit. He explored the risks and opportunities in a flash of insight. "What do you know of Lord Sleaford?"

The old man tore off a fist-sized piece of bread and handed it to Hastings. "Where's the wine? This may take a while."

Sleaford, England

Hungry for something more than bread and cheese, Hastings leaned back in his chair while the innkeeper laid out the evening meal: platters of pork, long beans, carrots, and a basket of fresh, dark bread. "By the blood of the saints. It's about time you served the food."

"Sorry, m'lord. I'll get more wine."

Hastings caught a glimpse of the innkeeper looking at the scar under Rowan's right eye. He sighed when Rowan didn't take notice. It had taken long hours of explaining for Rowan to acknowledge the advantage gained when an opponent paused, even for an instant, to gawk at his deformed cheek. But whether logic prevailed when no threat was imminent, Hastings was never sure.

Rowan stabbed a chunk of pork with his knife and shoved it into his mouth.

"Careful, you might choke," Hastings said.

Rowan chewed and swallowed hard. "I'm still here."

"You might try to taste your food once. When we move into Sleaford Castle, you'll need to control that anger of yours." Hastings took a sip of wine.

"Are you sure we'll be invited to stay?"

"Before I finish with him, that old sot Sleaford will beg us to stay as long as we wish."

His mouth full of bread, Rowan mumbled, "What of the daughter that blind hermit talked about?"

"Yes. Curious, that. If the parish priest is to be believed, Sleaford's wife was unable to bear children after their son was born. And now, the wife, son, and grandson are dead. With all that death, grief is easy to exploit. We need only find a credible enemy and the right tale to secure our future."

"Did the priest give you an introduction?"

"Tomorrow morning."

Sleaford Castle, Lincolnshire, England

While Rowan sought to fill their purses with coin, Hastings approached Sleaford Castle from an elevated causeway that rose above the fens. A broad moat covered with a thin layer of wispy fog surrounded the castle. In the early morning light, Hastings urged his horse across the drawbridge. The chatter of a flock of blackbirds faded under the heavy clomp of hooves on the wooden planks. Another finger of land, long enough to accommodate a horse drawn cart, separated the bridge from the twin towered gatehouse.

A guard raised his hand and called out, "What's your business?"

"My name is Hastings. Your master, Lord Sleaford, is expecting me."

The guard called to someone within the castle yard and motioned for Hastings to proceed.

In the courtyard, an ugly man who walked with a limp ambled over and grabbed the bridle of Hastings's horse. The horse jerked its head with a defiant bob, but the man held fast with unkind hands.

"Steady, there," Hastings said. "I treat my whores better than that."

The man ignored the comment and, in words almost indecipherable, said, "Lord Sleaford's in the great hall."

Hastings dismounted. "What did you say?"

The stable boy ran over and repeated, "Lord Sleaford is in the great hall. Up those stairs." He pointed in the direction of the stone keep. His mop of tawny hair framed a youthful face smudged with dirt, his breeches decorated with bits of hay and manure.

The ugly man scowled. "Tend to the man's horse." He thrust the reigns into the boy's hands and walked away.

Hastings recalled hearing an old sot in a London prison talk the same way. The reason for the awkward speech came to him: half the man's tongue had been cut out. It seemed funny to remember such a thing. He wondered what lie this man told to lose his tongue. Whatever it was, the ugly bastard must not have been very convincing. A smile pulled at Hastings's cheeks. He stroked his beard to cover his delight. None were better at lies than he. Before the stable boy led his horse away, he tossed a coin to him. "Rub her down well, lad."

Another guard at the entrance to the keep escorted Hastings into the great hall where an old man sat in a high-backed arm chair next to a grand stone fireplace. Draped in a red and gold wool cloak, the man rose to greet his guest.

"Hastings?"

"I'm pleased to meet you, my lord. Father John has said many a kind thing about you."

Lord Sleaford gestured to a chair. "Please, have a seat. I am anxious to hear the information you have about my grandson."

Hastings paused to look into the old man's tired eyes. The mention of his grandson brought a reflective glare from the light of the fire; a tear perhaps? "Before I relay my story, I want to be sure it's truly your grandson of whom I speak."

"I understand. What is it you wish to know?"

Hastings pulled the chair close. It was time to pick this old man for every detail that could be used to advantage. "I understand you have a daughter."

"Had a daughter. Katherine. She married a man by the name of Geoffrey de Parr. She is dead now."

"There was no mention of other relatives in your grandson's records. His name was Edmund, is that correct?"

"Named after me. His mother died in childbirth. His father died in London some years later. I raised him as my own son. There are no other relatives."

"Yet you say you had a daughter named Katherine. I fail to understand."

"She was not my natural daughter. She was five years younger than my son. He adored her. They were supposed to marry, but she refused. The church sided with her so I relented and let her go. Why do you ask about her? What does she have to do with my grandson?"

"Forgive me, but I needed to clarify the relationship. The information I have is delicate and I wish to reveal it to the right family. You can understand?"

"Yes, of course."

"My messenger should return within a fortnight. I'm confident yours is the family I seek, but I want to be sure. May I beg your kindness and wait for him?"

"My servants will show you to the guest chamber. When you are settled, you may join me for dinner."

The thought of fine platters of food made Hastings salivate. He nodded. "Thank you, my lord." His calculations for the success of his plan improved beyond his best guess only an hour ago. The wheels of deceit turned quickly and evolved into a masterful idea. In his mind's eye, he pictured his hands thrust into a chest of coins. The image brought a smile upon his face.

Sleaford, England

Hastings entered the cramped alehouse after dark. Four men lined a counter where one woman served mugs of ale and sweet-smelling wine while another flirted with the men, her compliments as crude as the company. Another group of men carried on an argument about something. The word "pestilence" twice rose above the rambles and drew his attention. He pursed his lips and frowned at the men for the unwanted reminder of that evil sickness.

"Where is Rowan?" he mumbled to himself as he glanced around the room. A door at the back led to a series of smaller rooms on either side of a passageway. The place reeked of musky sex. He drew back the curtains of each room until he found Rowan, naked and groaning like a dog on a bitch in heat.

"God's bones, do you ever think of anything besides bedding a woman?"

"What now?" Rowan said, without slowing the pace of his thrusts.

"When you finish, meet me in the other room."

Rowan soon appeared, his clothes disheveled and his face greasy with sweat. He grabbed a stool and pulled it next to the table where Hastings sat. "What brings you out of that fancy castle at this hour?"

"I certainly had no desire to endure the stench of this rat infested piss pot. I need you to take a message to Herefordshire. This is complicated, so pay attention."

Rowan glared. "When did I ever mix up your instructions?"

"There's not enough time to answer that. Listen carefully. Clean yourself up and trim your beard. Get a change of clothes, something a servant from a noble family might wear. Deliver this message into the hands of Lord Geoffrey de Parr at Kendalwood Manor near Ross-on-Wye. Ask for a reply; I expect you may not get one—it'll surprise me if you do. Take note of who else you see and find out if there are children. And this is most important, take note of Parr's reaction. If all goes as expected, we'll have found the person who'll get old Sleaford's rancor sufficiently provoked."

Chapter
FIVE

Calais, English Possession, May 1348

William arrived early at the Rusty Anchor. Crawford arranged for him to meet a man after the mid-day wards. Except for two men asleep at a table, the alehouse was empty of customers. He ordered a mug and found a bench in a corner opposite the front door. Streaks of light shone through holes in the walls and a shuttered window near the counter. He sat in the shadowy darkness waiting; his gaze fixed on the door.

Two mugs later, the door opened and light invaded the room. The sudden glare hurt William's eyes. He squinted. A dark shape filled the doorway for a moment and then approached. "Parr?" the man asked.

"Yes," William replied.

"I've got a ship and crew and the means to deliver of your goods."

"Are you Rufus?"

"I go by many names."

As his eyes readjusted to the dim light, William studied the man. Rufus stood about six feet tall. His greasy, black hair merged into a greasy, black beard. A dark brown overcoat hung down to the floor tattered and dragging with it smells—the origin of which better went unsaid.

"Did Crawford tell you my plan?"

"Sixty marks. In advance."

"That's outrageous." William's hand settled on the hilt of his sword. "That's four or five times what delivery contracts cost."

"Those are my terms. If the king's agents intercept my ship, you lose your goods. I lose my ship—and maybe my head. If you don't like the terms, seek another to do your business."

William raised his hand. "I'll pay your price, but I need to accompany you on the voyage. Not because I distrust you; the wool will only be released to me. Once I send word, we can prepare to leave. I need to be in Bristow by the end of July."

"We leave when I'm ready. If you get in the way of my crew, you'll sit out the voyage in the hold."

William nodded.

"Wait for word from Crawford. Then look for a cog called *Lady of the Seas*. Be sure you're ready. And bring the gold." Rufus cleared his throat and spat on the floor. As he left the alehouse, his overcoat dragged through a patch of dried vomit.

Sleaford Castle, Lincolnshire, England

"God's teeth," Hastings said, as he opened the letter sealed with the mark of Lord Geoffrey de Parr. "He sent a response."

Rowan gave an exaggerated bow. "At your service, my lord."

"For once you outdid yourself." Hastings grinned as he read the letter. "How do you feel about delivering another message?"

"I found a lively stew in Leicester. One of the whores begged me to return."

"I have no doubt of that. Did you find out if there're any children from the marriage of Sleaford's daughter to Lord Parr?"

"Two. William, the oldest, serves in the king's army in France. The younger son is called Thomas."

"William in France? How fortunate. Sleaford's grandson died there." Hastings stroked his beard as his thoughts quickly coalesced. "While you were away, Sleaford kept asking me about the information I had on his grandson. He's ready to believe anything. And now, I have an idea that should serve as excellent fodder for a profitable tale of revenge. This story is indeed getting interesting. I think it's time we tested the interest of the chancellor."

Tintern Abbey, Wales, June 1348

The first weeks of Thomas's introduction to spiritual activities soon turned into a month and then two. Now seventeen, doubts over his future as a monk remained. He refused to give up the idea that he and Andrew could remain friends. But if he didn't become a monk, what then? The question had no answer.

While efforts to gather wool from the abbey's Welsh granges got underway, Andrew spent more time at Trelleck Grange. Thomas was sure Abbot Michael had a hand in Andrew's move, but Andrew didn't put up a fuss. "Brother Gilbert is going to teach me how to sword fight," Andrew had said with a glee that made Thomas angry. How could Andrew enjoy doing something that didn't include him?

After mass on a particularly nice day at the end of June, Thomas overheard one of the lay brothers tell Abbot Michael that a messenger sent by the countess had arrived. *Word from William perhaps?* He took his seat for the daily reading and pretended to read from his Old Testament book. He fidgeted with the pages and glanced around at the deep concentration etched on monk's faces as they perfected their communal solitude. Instead of focusing on the ancient lands of the prophets, his mind flitted from Bristow to Calais.

Abbot Michael soon returned and motioned for Thomas to join him in the outer parlor. "I did not want to disturb the others. This will only take a moment. The countess sent word that your brother will depart Calais mid-July on a ship called *Lady of the Seas*. He plans to arrive in Bristow by the end of the month. It is unclear if your brother will return with the ship. As I must be present to negotiate the price of the abbey's wool, I thought you may appreciate the opportunity to join me in case William is unable to stay for very long. The experience may also be helpful should you someday be elected abbot."

"But what of my vows?"

"We will be back well before Michaelmas. There is no reason to change the date."

Sparked into a happy mood by the prospect of seeing William, Thomas returned to the cloister. Instead of his usual spot by the passage to the lay brothers' refectory, he sat next to Brother Aldwin, who flashed him an annoyed look. Thomas's gaze soon wandered from the vellum pages of his book to the tiled roof of the arcade. He tried to imagine how William might look after eight years. As his thoughts drifted his feet tapped the beat of a lively tune he had heard at the market in Chepstow.

When communal reading ended, Brother Aldwin motioned to Thomas to follow him to the parlor. A visit to the parlor meant only one thing: Brother Aldwin intended to say something. Monks who had pledged a vow of silence could only speak in the parlor and then, only if speaking was deemed urgent. What could be so urgent?

Once the door was closed, Thomas asked in a cheerful voice, "Are there lots of weeds to hoe today?"

Brother Aldwin scowled. "It appears you do not have the calm to properly tend the garden. I will not sacrifice any more plants to your inattention. Your help is not needed. You may tell Brother Samuel that you are free to do any other chores he may have in mind."

Thomas put on his best sad face. "Tomorrow then?"

"We shall see."

Since Brother Aldwin didn't say that he "must" tell Brother Samuel, he took the chance freedom as an invitation to tell Andrew the word about William. Careful to not draw attention to his amblings, he disregarded the time and set out for Trelleck Grange, making sure no one saw him leave. The delight at sneaking away brought back memories of when he slipped out of the monastery with Andrew when they were younger. They ran through the woods and attacked sinister looking stumps with sturdy branches that doubled as swords. Andrew loved to act out the brave knight who rescued his master from evil monsters.

About half way along the road to Trelleck Grange, a moan from behind a thicket stopped him mid-step. He listened, his head cocked toward the noise. The moans sounded odd—a woman for sure, but unlike someone in distress. He crept closer and hid among the shrubs. The moans grew louder, with a repetitive rustling of leaves. Deep grunts joined the chorus and then, a long sigh. A man's voice said, "Here's your coin." Footsteps trailed off into the woods.

Thomas waited a moment before going to investigate. On the other side of the shrubbery, he almost stepped on a woman lying on the ground, naked.

She rose on her elbows and laughed. "Come for a little fun boy?" she asked.

Thomas stared with his mouth agape; drool dripped from his chin.

"Never seen a naked woman before?"

Thomas shook his head.

"You one of them monks?"

Thomas again shook his head. His voice didn't work. His eyes stole every bit of brain power he had, with the exception of the bit driving the growing response in his groin.

The woman's breasts jiggled to the beat of her rapturous laughter. "Come here boy. Let me show you how to be a man."

He wanted to go to her. Desire trumped thought as his gaze remained transfixed on the curves of her body and her smooth skin. Her long, dark brown hair had pieces of dried leaves stuck here and there. She spread her legs and motioned for him to come closer.

He stared at her, unsure what to do. Her eyes seemed to call to him. She formed her lips into the shape of a kiss and winked.

What would God say? What would Abbot Michael say? He froze. His heartbeat raced like a wild drummer. Fear of not knowing what to do destroyed his animal lust. He turned and bolted. Gut-wrenching laughter faded behind him.

He couldn't tell Andrew he missed a chance with a woman, so he ran back to the monastery. He cursed himself for not following his desire. Soon, he would be a monk and the pleasures of a woman would be unknowable. Would he ever experience love? He wandered toward the river. At low tide, the bank smelled of rotten reeds. Over the past few months he felt out of place, more alone than ever before. The communal solitude the monks desired mystified him. At the river's edge, he picked up a stone and threw it toward the opposite bank. To be a monk involved more effort than he thought possible.

He looked downriver. Abbot Michael expected him to be delighted at the opportunity to go to Bristow, and he was excited by a chance to see William, but, the farthest he had ventured from the abbey over the last nine years was Chepstow. Perhaps he should stay and forget the prospect of becoming the abbot. At least, as a monk, he wouldn't have to make decisions. But then, he would miss the chance to see William.

Stay or go. His mind spun with possibilities and consequences until his head hurt. He grabbed another stone and threw it as hard as he could.

Sleaford Castle, Lincolnshire, England

"I apologize for the time it's taken, my lord," Hastings said, as he played the part of a supplicant. "But I'm certain of the details now. There's no doubt."

Lord Sleaford leaned back in his chair, his face red and his fists clenched.

"It is true. That arrogant bastard, William de Parr, ordered your grandson, and the rest of your grandson's company, to advance on the French lines. No purpose came from the attack and all the men were slaughtered. A waste of England's finest."

Lord Sleaford pounded the arm of his chair. "As you so eloquently put it, first the father steals the woman my son was to marry. Then, the son of that spiteful union became the instrument of my grandson's death."

Hastings hid his inner smile. He had mastered the ability to conjure any expression or voice at will. But there were times when his talents amazed even himself. After an hour of cajoling, Sleaford succumbed to Hastings's recounting of events. "I understand your anger, my lord."

"Anger? I am not angry, I am furious." Lord Sleaford again pounded the arm of his chair. The loud bang reverberated through the castle's great hall.

"It's at times like these when a man must stand up, at whatever the cost, and take revenge."

"Yes. You are correct. I need revenge. Before I die, the Parr family will suffer for my pain and grief."

"You shall have it, my lord."

"I want Geoffrey de Parr's life turned to despair and I want to look into the eyes of that young pup, William, before I commit him to the dungeon for all eternity—to suffer as my progeny have certainly suffered. Make that happen, Hastings, and you shall be well rewarded."

"It shall be done. I've a plan to bleed Lord Parr of his wealth. He'll be ruined for all time. And then, I'll present to you the son. You may do with him as you wish. It may take some time to set things in motion, but I'm sure you'll be well satisfied."

"Stay as long as you need. Do what you must. My servants are at your disposal. I have suffered for too many years. And now, at last, to find solace. I am old, Hastings. But you have fed me a meal to revive my strength. If I had known the prospect of revenge tasted so good, I would have called on you years ago."

"It's not too late, my lord. You have my word. Your satisfaction will be complete before winter's end. Revenge is best savored when dealt slowly, would you agree?"

Lord Sleaford nodded.

Hastings bit his tongue to curtail his exuberance. He wanted to shout for joy and hug this old sot. A rumble in his stomach gave him an idea. "Shall we celebrate your rebirth with a grand feast?"

Lord Sleaford clapped his hands, his wrinkled face suddenly beaming. "Call my servants. Empty the larder."

The future looked bright indeed. The means to buy his way to lands and a title never seemed as close as this moment. With the reward for proof offered by the chancellor and Lord Parr's desire to pay for silence, nothing could stop him from achieving his goal.

Chapter
SIX

Near Bordeaux, Duchy of Aquitaine, July 1348

Captain Larkin Montgomery of the *Margaret* paced the deck of his ship. Forty years at sea weathered his dark complexion with deep lines and thinned his white hair and beard. Not many captains lived so long to gain his level of experience. Yet this trip to Bordeaux tested his stamina more than he thought possible. A squall made havoc with the rigging and forced an unplanned stop in Brest, but it was not the sea or the damage to the ship that troubled him the most.

It was in Brest he first heard about the pestilence. While waiting on repairs, he frequented an alehouse near the wharf. The mere mention of this strange sickness sent shivers down the spines of hardened seamen. He overheard a spirited exchange between the local dockhands and a group of men who served on a ship that sailed out of Barcelona. The dark-skinned foreigners boasted about seeing ships drifting at sea, no captain or crew in sight.

Unable to quell his curiosity, he had asked the first of many questions. Later, he would wish he had never heard the answers. "Where did you see these ships?"

In broken English, one of the seamen replied, "Off the coast of Morocco at the western end of the Mediterranean. They looked like Genoese ships."

"And you saw no one on deck?"

"The sea was too rough to board her, but we were certain the ship was unmanned. Her sails were tattered and the rigging loose. Later, we passed an

Aragonese cocha. The captain said he saw a ship drifting in calm seas farther to the east. He claimed the crew was killed by the pestilence. And he warned of ports stricken by a deadly plague."

"Ports? Which ports?" Captain Montgomery asked, his gray eyes wide despite the glare of a nearby torch.

"Half of Marseilles is dead. The vile humors then spread to Avignon where the Pope surrounded himself with braziers. The people were left to die in the streets by the hundreds."

"Half of Marseilles dead?" He shook his head. "That cannot be."

In an angry tone, the seaman said, "It is the truth. I did not believe it myself. Then we heard the stories again in Lisbon. They say the bodies of the dead reek with an odor no man can stand. Horrible black growths ooze foul puss. They say it is God's punishment. For what, I know not."

"I think it is the Jews," one of the other seamen said. "They are poisoning the wells. What else can it be?"

In the days since leaving Breast, nothing in his experience prepared him for the visions of devastation that haunted his waking hours. *An evil plague?* It was too fantastic to believe. He wondered how such a thing came to be if God did not ordain it. *Half of Marseilles dead?*

"Rocks!" shouted one of his crew.

Bolted from his thoughts, he went below deck to check for damage. Water leaked through a five-inch crack that spanned three planks. "Get timbers to support this breach," he ordered. "Cursed voyage. What else can go wrong? By Christ's blood that mercer better be in Bordeaux to meet us."

Clouds blocked the mid-morning sun, laying a gray veil over an uneasy approach to Bordeaux. The *Margaret* traveled alone on its slow passage up the Garonne River. Flat fields stretched to the horizon.

A quiet wharf greeted Captain Montgomery. He puzzled over the odd lack of activity and felt a rising foreboding. What was wrong with these people? The other cogs that lined the wharf melted into a background of unnatural stillness. Men hurriedly unloaded the contents of their holds; speaking little as they maneuvered windlasses and ropes.

He called out, "Where is everyone?" There was no response, only blank stares.

With no one coming to greet the ship, he set out for the customs office. Shoving to the back of his mind the apprehension tickling his nerves, he strutted along with purpose. As he approached the main road, he realized the quiet of the wharf extended deeper into the city. The clamor of carts, the pounding of horse hooves, and the shouts of men going about their business sounded subdued. The usual assault of dust and foul odors retreated to minor annoyances.

The customs office occupied a single-story building set between a rigging shop and a shop selling fishing supplies. The door was locked, but through an open window he heard a man say, "What is your business?"

Peering through the window, he said, "I have a shipment of cloth to unload for Godfrey de Namur. I am Captain Larkin Montgomery of the *Margaret.* De Namur is a mercer from Flanders. Has he left a message?"

"Stay back! I do not know anyone by that name. People are dying around here. If this Namur arrived within the past few weeks, he may be among the dead. You would be wise to leave."

"Among the dead? What are you talking about?"

"The pestilence. We heard it came to Marseilles and Avignon, then Paris. Thousands die every day, they said. Now it is here. How it got here, no one knows. Some people go to sleep looking fine and then they are found dead the next morning. Others linger for days, praying that death will take them. I am not going to be found dead with unconfessed sins."

"What am I to do with the cloth?"

"You can dump it in the sea for all I care. Until the taxes are paid, your cargo can go no farther than the warehouses. Leave it there if you must. If Namur does not claim it, the cloth will be forfeited to the crown. Are you going to pay the tax or not?"

He shouted back, "I will not pay the tax, you bastard. You can rot in that hole for all I care. By the blood of the saints, is there no end to the misery of this voyage?"

His heartbeat quickened. He looked around. Worried thoughts of impending danger crept into his mind. Not sure of where to go or what to do, he folded his arms across his chest, pursed his lips, and stared off toward the wharf.

A well-dressed man with a balding head came up to him and said, "Excuse me, Captain Montgomery. I could not help but hear your conversation with the customs officer."

"Get away from me," Captain Montgomery said. "Are you afflicted with this pestilence? Stay away." He took several steps back and reached for his sword.

"Please, Captain. I am not afflicted."

"Who are you?"

"My name is James Stafford. I am from Bramshall in Staffordshire. I have been careful to stay away from the sick. I have not looked them in the eye. And I am an honest man. I have no quarrel with God."

"What do you want?"

"I am in great need of a ship to deliver a load of grain. I tried to hire a ship, but no one was going my direction. Maybe we can help each other. Tell me, what port did you come from?"

"I was in Brest about a week ago. I heard about the dreadful pestilence there. If it truly is here, by Christ's blood, I need to leave. But, my hold is full of cloth and I need to make repairs."

"I can help rid you of the cloth. The grain I have was supposed to be delivered to Jersey, but the captain of the ship I hired decided there was more money to be had if he sold it in Bordeaux. There was little I could do so I traveled along hoping to recover something out of his treachery. We arrived here just as the first deaths from the pestilence were reported. That was more than a week ago. The captain dumped my grain on the wharf and fled. I managed to move the grain into a warehouse. I will pay handsomely if you can oblige. I need to get to Jersey."

"It will cost you twenty-five pounds to cover my losses. You can do as you please with the cloth."

"I accept your price. What of your ship's hold? Can you carry two hundred sacks?"

"My ship can carry thirty tons. And Jersey is in the right direction. For all the saints, I am not going any farther south."

"God bless you, Captain. How long do you need for your repairs?"

"At least a day or two."

"The sooner we get under way the better. If that grain sits in the warehouse much longer, the rats will be sure to find it."

Near Kendalwood Manor, Herefordshire, England

The walls of Kendalwood Manor encircled a four-story stone keep. Hastings rode past the fortified gate and wondered if his own castle might look grander or more imposing than a simple knight's fee. How much would it take to buy such a place? He mused on the design as he neared the location for his secret meeting with Lord Geoffrey de Parr. Letters and messengers sufficed for the preliminary negotiations, but now he required a face-to-face assessment of his opponent. While he assumed Lord Parr would honor their terms and meet without escort, he came prepared— Rowan trailed at a cautious two hundred yards. It would take more men than a lowly lord could muster to defeat his one-man army.

At the marked spot on the road to Ross, he directed his horse down a lightly used path and into a stand of oak and ash trees. Out of sight of the road, the trail opened to a clearing of about twenty yards in diameter. At the far side, a man, at least ten years Hastings's senior and dressed in finery befitting a lord, sat astride a black stallion; his sword hilt glinted in the afternoon light. Hastings gave a slight bow. "Lord Parr?"

The man nodded.

"I assume we are alone."

"I am a man of my word," Lord Parr said. He nudged his destrier forward. "Are you a man of yours?"

Hastings dismounted. "You disparage me, my lord." He raised his arms to show that he carried no weapon.

Lord Parr scowled. "I am in no mood to treat with you. Get to your point."

He studied his adversary for a moment—the clenched jaw unmistakable behind the cover of a distinguished-looking beard, clean white surcoat fitted over a hauberk of fine metal rings, and boots that revealed only minor wear. A man of wealth indeed. But how much would it take? He stroked his beard. "A thousand marks and I'll forget everything I know."

Silence.

Hastings waited for any sign of distress—a twitch, a blink, or a jerk of the reins. Perhaps he underestimated the wealth and resolve of this lord.

"What are my assurances?" Lord Parr asked.

At last. He took a deep breath and smiled. A thousand marks would not buy an earldom, but it would grant him status as a baron. "You have none but my word, my lord. However, as I wish to enjoy my later years in comfort, I've no further plans for mischief."

"The amount you seek will ruin me."

"I'm truly sorry to hear that. But, you have your choices. I assume you wish not to offend the king."

"Very well. Meet me in Bristow at the end of the month. You shall have your money."

Hastings bit his tongue to quell his excitement. The fish took the bait.

Chapter
SEVEN

Tintern Abbey, Wales, July 1348

Thomas took a moment to rest in the abbey's main cloister before his afternoon work assignment began. An early morning shower had made the garden too muddy for inexperienced feet, as Brother Aldwin put it. The alternative, shoveling ashes from the kitchen fireplace and scrubbing the slate floor, would bring him indoors but at the expense of sore knees. As he stared at the gray sky, another rain cloud drifted overhead. He closed his eyes and listened to the gentle patter on the tile roof above him. How long would it be before he saw his work as toiling for Christ? Would he ever gain an appreciation for the communal solitude the monks desired? The heavy flop of loose fitted sandals cut short the search for answers he didn't want to find.

Brother Samuel approached with a big grin and outstretched arms. "God's blessings, Thomas. I bear good tidings. Abbot Michael says your father will meet you in Bristow."

A ping resonated in his gut. How could Brother Samuel say such a thing with a happy voice? "My father is coming too?"

"Yes, it appears so. Is that not wonderful to hear?" Brother Samuel sat beside Thomas.

"Why now? After all this time? When I finally have a chance to see William, he comes too?"

"Think kindly of your father, Thomas. He has many obligations and, as you well know, it is not encouraged for brothers of the Order to receive visits from family. That is a distraction from our spiritual endeavors."

"I know, Brother Samuel. But I'm not yet a monk. How am I supposed to feel? I hardly remember my father. Most of my life has been behind these walls. The chance to see William again is exciting. We were close growing up. I wish he had come to visit. Father too. But they never did. If I'm unable to see William now, I never will."

"We all have our crosses to bear."

"It's not a cross that I bear, Brother Samuel. I have no family. I suppose I do, in a way. You and the other brothers, and Andrew of course. But outside these walls, I have nothing."

"This is where we belong, Thomas. Our purpose is the salvation of mankind. If not for our devotion to Christ, the world will fall into anarchy. Satan will take the souls of countless innocents."

"Are you sure I'm ready for such a responsibility?"

"It is because you question that we know you are ready. You will make a wonderful brother, and, in time, you may become the abbot of this glorious monastery. But for now, I need for you to go to Trelleck Grange and let Brother Gilbert know we are ready for him to send the wool to Bristow. The countess offered to store our wool at her warehouse until your brother arrives." Brother Samuel patted Thomas's knee and in a soft voice said, "I am sure Andrew is there. You will have a chance to see him before you and Abbot Michael leave. Be sure to be back by vespers."

As Brother Samuel hurried back to the kitchen, Thomas remained fixed to the stone bench. *Why the sudden acknowledgement of Andrew?* Brother Samuel certainly knew of Abbot Michael's desire that his friendship with Andrew must end, didn't he? Whatever the reason, he didn't want to spoil the pleasant thought of going to see Andrew. He pulled the hood of his tunic over his head and set out for Trelleck Grange.

Four miles was a long time to consider the ways to greet his father and brother—glad, excited, formal. He pondered each and tested his voice. None sounded better than the other. A break in the clouds brightened his mood and he picked up his pace. Near Trelleck Grange, the distinctive sound of someone splitting wood pierced the quiet. He stopped and listened. Only one person could maintain that rhythmic pace. He ran the rest of the way.

In sight of the wood shed, he shouted, "Andrew!"

"Greetings, Thomas. What betides?"

"I missed you. While you were away having fun shearing sheep, I was learning how to be a monk before I actually become one."

"Shearing sheep is not something I'd call fun, but I missed you too." Andrew wiped his brow; tiny rivers of sweat ran down his shirtless torso in the sticky heat of a rare blast of sunshine.

"Is Brother Gilbert around? I need to tell him Abbot Michael is ready for the wool to be shipped to Bristow."

Andrew looked toward the pastures to the north. "I thought Brother Gilbert was working in the pasture over there. I'll let him know when he gets back."

"Do you have another axe?" Thomas asked, as he took off his tunic.

"I can only swing one at a time."

"You know what I mean."

"To split wood, you need a maul not an axe."

"I can help."

"If you wish to help, you could pick up these split logs and stack them over there."

When all the dry wood was split, they sat under the wood shed's overhang to rest. In the shade, cooler air blew across his bare chest and gave him a chill. He wanted to tell Andrew how scared he was to leave for so long, but he didn't know how to start. Andrew's voice stopped his spinning thoughts.

"Are you going to tell me what troubles you?"

Andrew always knew when something troubled him. It was best to simply say it. "I'm scared."

"About what?"

"Abbot Michael and I will be gone for at least a fortnight."

"What else?"

He plucked a handful of grass and tossed it. "My father is coming to Bristow."

"And?"

His gaze locked on Andrew's brown eyes. If anyone could calm his uncertainty and unfettered thoughts, it was Andrew. The heaviness on his shoulders vanished as the words spilled out. "How do I ask my father why he never came to visit? He is sure to have some excuse and say how wonderful it is I'm to be a monk. I know becoming a monk is what I'm supposed to do. But I still have doubts. And the pestilence. The villagers who come to the abbey talk about it. From what they say, whole towns perish once the plague sets in. What if the humors come to Bristow?"

"There's nothing we can do about the pestilence. As Abbot Michael says, all we can do is live right by God. Try not to think so much. You only get yourself upset."

Thomas nodded.

"Think about the time you'll have with William. There's no need to think about any more than that. You'll be fine. You best get back before vespers. I have to stay here tonight."

"Will I see you again before I leave?"

"Brother Gilbert wants me to go to Moor Grange. If I'm gone when you leave, have a safe journey." Andrew embraced him and kissed him on the forehead. "God be with you."

The walk back to the monastery dragged on like a sermon from a visiting bishop. Thomas had that ominous feeling again. Only this time, the feeling gave him the shivers.

That night, his unsettled feelings made for unsettled sleep. A dark dream took control. He found himself walking along the empty streets of a large town. Dilapidated houses and vacant shops leaned over the road at a dangerous slant; a thin line of light shone from above. An icy breeze blew on his neck, and shutters swung in the gloom with a ghostly silence, as if sound itself fled. Curiosity of what lay ahead drove him onward. He came upon the town square where he faced a grand church flanked by two great towers, each a hundred feet high. As he approached, he saw that the church and the towers were not made of stone, but rather of bodies—thousands and thousands of bodies stacked on top of each other like dead wood. The reek of rot and decay poured over him as a waterfall of misery and stench. A shrouded figure rose with evil menace from a waterless fountain at the center of the square and pointed toward the doors of the church beckoning Thomas to enter.

Thomas glared at the entity and refused to move.

"You cannot deny me. See my power. I take the souls I need to build a monument to my god, the destroyer of humanity."

The boom of the malicious voice broke Thomas's resolve and drove him back.

"There is no escape. You must give me your soul."

He hesitated. Doubt pricked at his will. He wanted to stand against the evil power, but fear overcame him. He trembled and looked for Andrew, but no aid was in sight. He turned and ran.

The creature bellowed, "I will not give up until I have you."

Chapter
EIGHT

Calais, English Possession, July 1348

William got up early. He had to gather his things and make his way to the wharf. Crawford had left him to greet Rufus alone and today was to be the day. He didn't trust Rufus. Why should he? Rufus was nothing more than a pirate, a rogue of the sea. And he was a knight, one of the king's men.

For as much as he wanted to get underway, Calais had yet to be proclaimed the staple port for wool. There was still time, or so he told himself. The thought of turning back rankled his soul; he had no other choice. He was committed.

A heavy mist clouded his view of ships moored at the dock. Closer, he passed the hazy outlines of masts and hulls and paused when he heard a gruff voice shouting orders. The weathered wood of a cog slowly materialized as an unwelcome carrier of men that had journeyed across an unforgiving sea. Atop the forecastle, he made out Rufus's tall silhouette. As soon as the anchor splashed into the gray water, William joined the men securing the lines.

Rufus cleared his throat and spat. "Get on board and stay out of the way. We leave as soon as the cargo is unloaded."

It seemed to take forever to get to open water. William hated the sea. His feet preferred solid ground, a firm base to fight like a proper knight. The ship tossed and swayed as waves crashed against the hull. After two years of trudging through the French countryside and living in war-ravaged Calais, he was headed home—a worthy knight with a fine new sword and a well-made suit of mail. And, he did it all without help from his father.

He took off his armor and stored it in a small room off the crew's quarters to keep it safe from the gritty salt of the sea spray. He kept his sword at his side, secure in its scabbard, as he learned the feel of the hilt.

Each morning, William rose to the same routine: he relieved himself in a disgusting bucket, collected a ration of food and water, and paced the deck for exercise. The crew paid him no heed. He spent most of his time standing near the bow, gazing to the horizon, and hoping for a strong breeze to blow away the bitter odor of a cadre of men who considered sea spray a bath.

Several days into the voyage, William realized the ship had yet to turn toward England. "When are we crossing the channel?" he asked Rufus.

A sinister smile peered through Rufus's greasy, black beard. "I need to stop at another port first."

"Another port? You said nothing about another port."

Rufus laughed, cleared his throat, and spat over the side of the ship.

Footsteps approached from behind. He felt a sharp pain at the back of his head. Everything went dark.

The Norman Coast of France

William's head throbbed. He rubbed the spot that hurt and cringed. His fingers found a bump and a crusty patch of hair—dried blood.

The planks of wood beneath him were hard and full of splinters. The dank smell of rotten grain filled the air. The stench brought tears to his eyes. He held back the urge to vomit.

Not a speck of light shined from any direction. He reached out to the darkness with his invisible hand and listened. Only the creak of wood and the beat of waves against the hull penetrated the unseen walls. *I must be in the hold.* "Let me out of here!"

Footsteps trailed across the deck above. Someone fiddled with a bolt and latch. The hinges rasped as the hatch opened, letting in a faint shaft of moonlight.

"So, the little master is awake," a surly voice said. "The captain is not to be disturbed. He'll talk to you in the morning, if you behave." Other voices joined in a chorus of laughter. The hatch slammed shut. Silence and darkness returned.

William now regretted taking off his suit of mail. He massaged his shoulder. With a slight hesitation, he reached for his sword—nothing. There must be a way out of his predicament, but the pounding in his head nagged too deep. Sleep became his best option, at least for now.

The hatch opened hitting the deck with a *bang*, waking William from his half-sleep. Stiffness limited movement in his neck and pain gripped his head like a vise. He squinted as he looked around his floating prison now lit by harsh sunshine. No means of escape presented itself.

"Did we sleep well?" Rufus sneered. "I'm letting you out for some fresh air. You best mind your step and heed the orders of my first officer. Understand?" He cleared his throat and spat.

"Understood. Where are we headed?"

"That's none of your business, boy," Rufus said. "We'll be in Bristow by the end of the month, as we agreed." A ladder appeared. It hit the floor of the hold with a loud thud. "Now get up here and do as you're told."

William slowly climbed the ladder and took a deep breath of fresh, salty air. On deck, ten burly seamen glowered at him; each carried a knife, a short sword, or both. The past few days on the ship now blurred in his memory.

William hated answering to Rufus's authority, and he hated being called a boy. He was no boy; he was a knight and one of the king's men.

The first officer stepped forward, a hairy-chested man called Grimsby. At his side, he carried a whip, and he seemed the type who enjoyed using it.

"Do as you're told, boy, and we'll get along just fine. We've got about two days before we reach port. The Captain likes his ship spotless." Grimsby jabbed his finger at William's chest. "That's your job. No more standing around like some important lordship. There's a bucket and a brush tied to the side rail. Start at the bow. Get busy. Ten lashes if I catch you slacking off."

William puffed his chest. The orders of a filthy seaman meant nothing to one of the king's men. He stared back at Grimsby with a coldness that revealed no emotion. "Anything else?"

Grimsby scowled and threw a well-aimed punch at William's stomach. William fell to his knees. "That's a warning, boy. Next time it'll be twenty lashes for insubordination. All I want to hear from you is 'Yes, sir.' Got it?"

"Yes, sir." William held his stomach as he got to his feet. Anger welled up. He gritted his teeth to keep from striking back.

St. Helier, Island of Jersey, Possession of the English Crown

A steady breeze pushed the *Margaret* along her course. Captain Montgomery stood on the deck and surveyed the Jersey coast as the morning sun broke free of the horizon. Stafford joined him.

"I do believe my luck has changed," Captain Montgomery said. "The tide has not gone out completely. Our timing is perfect."

"Why is that?" Stafford asked.

"The higher the tide, the closer we can get to the warehouses. We sail toward the parish church and then beach the ship on the sands. Then, at low tide, it is not so far to haul your grain. For the novice captain, it is quite daunting to beach your ship. But, that is the only way to do it here."

"As long as you know what you are doing, Captain. I appreciate your efforts to get us here with all speed."

"And none too soon by the looks of all those dead rats down in the hold. I cannot tell if they ate themselves to death or if they got seasick." Captain Montgomery chuckled.

"I suppose it was unavoidable that a few rats would find their way on board. With low tide, maybe you can get rid of them."

"Usually, I see far fewer dead rats. That grain sure kept them busy. They stayed out of sight nearly the whole distance from Bordeaux. It is the only good thing about hauling grain—the rats are too busy eating to venture out."

"I am just glad we got out of Bordeaux when we did. The city was rank with fear over the deaths from the pestilence. As soon as we get ashore, I will meet my contact and then I can pay you."

"Thank you, Stafford. I am anxious to get underway again. I wonder if there is anywhere safe from this evil pestilence. From what we heard in Brest last week, no act of penitence or intervention by the church seems to slow its spread."

As the crew unloaded the grain, rats scrambled out of the sacks and darted across the open dunes into warehouses and other buildings along the shore. Some stayed in the ship's hold to feast on the kernels of grain left behind.

Lighter by two hundred sacks of grain and half as many rats, the *Margaret* broke free from the clutches of the sand bar. With the rising tide, the ship picked up speed on its way to England.

When they entered open water, Captain Montgomery looked back toward the east. In the distance, he saw a cog with full sail coming around the southern tip of the island.

Rufus brought the *Lady of the Seas* into St. Helier with the rising tide. With no pier to aim for, he steered the ship as best he could so the laddeborde side faced inland at a good angle. Forward motion drove the ship deep into the sand. "Drop anchor here," Rufus ordered. "Grimsby!"

"Yes, Captain."

"Mid-day is upon us. Lower the nacelle. I want to meet with the customs official today. We need to load the wine at the next low tide." Rufus cleared his throat and spat.

When they reached the shore, Rufus said to Grimsby, "While I deliver this release, find us food and fresh water."

"Captain, the crew might like some time on shore."

"That's fine with me. It'll be early afternoon tomorrow before there's a low tide with daylight. But, somebody needs to stay with Parr. He's confined to the ship."

"Thank you, sir. I'll leave Jamison on board. He's more than a match for that young pup."

"Don't underestimate Parr. He's been too cooperative these past few days. I don't trust him. My gut tells me he's planning something. If we want any part of that wool, we need some leverage."

"What did you have in mind, Captain?" Grimsby asked.

"Crawford said something about Parr having a brother. If we can find out who this brother is and take him hostage, then we can force Parr to do as we say. Once the wool is on board, we'll dump the brother and sail away with a full load."

William scrubbed the deck until his hands turned as red as raw meat and his knees ached. He refused to let Rufus or Grimsby have an excuse to exercise the lash.

At sunset, only Jamison remained on board. The rest of the crew, including Rufus, went ashore to drink their fill and relieve the pressure in their loins.

Before Grimsby left, he ordered Jamison to tie William to the mast; it was more painful than the hard floor of the hold. William tested the rope and felt no give.

As the full moon ascended, William watched Jamison pace the deck. From time to time, Jamison stood by the laddeborde rail staring toward shore and grumbling under his breath.

William called out, "Jamison."

"What do you want, boy?"

"I have to piss."

"Is that so?"

"If the deck is covered in piss, you'll have to clean it up. Grab that bucket over there."

"I'm not holding a bucket for you."

"Then untie my hands so I can hold the bucket myself."

Jamison was large, but he wasn't quick. He uttered something unintelligible as he untied William's hands. When he turned to retrieve the bucket, William seized the opportunity and snatched Jamison's knife. With lightning speed, William stabbed Jamison in the back three times.

Jamison crumpled to the deck.

Blood still dripping from the knife, William cut his bonds. He took hold of Jamison's head and gave it a quick twist. An audible *crack* echoed off the deck. He dragged the body to the starboard side of the ship, heaved it overboard, and then searched for his sword and suit of mail.

The sword hung on a wall in Rufus's quarters like a trophy. The suit of mail he found stowed in a chest next to Grimsby's cot. "That bastard, Grimsby." He retrieved his armor, slammed the chest shut, and, mocking Rufus, spat on Grimsby's cot.

Low tide came after midnight. He climbed down the rope ladder hanging from the side of the ship and stepped onto the soggy sand. The full moon made it easy to navigate his way to the edge of town.

Light flickered through large windows at the front of a building that looked like an alehouse. William crept closer. Laughter and loud voices resonated from within.

The alehouse sat on a square not far from a row of single-story warehouses. William crouched among a line of low shrubs cursing Grimsby as he rubbed the soreness in his knees.

A group of men staggered out of the alehouse and zigzagged their way toward a two story building on the opposite side of the square. Three women stood by the front door holding lamps. Moments later, more men stumbled out of the alehouse and scattered in every direction like rats looking for a home.

William sized up the shapes. He spotted Grimsby's jabbing finger directed at a man who looked too drunk to feel anything. He waited while Grimsby started down the road toward the warehouse.

"Grimsby," William called out. "You should have left a few more men on the ship to guard me." Grimsby's eyes opened wide. William swung his sword at Grimsby's stomach spilling guts onto the road. "You should take care who you jab with that finger," William said as the man fell to the ground.

Adrenalin surged through his veins. An insatiable urge to find Rufus filled him. Rufus had to pay for the ill treatment suffered by one of the king's men, a Knight of the Realm.

William wiped his sword on Grimsby's back and sheathed it in its scabbard. He headed toward the whorehouse, the logical place to start looking for Rufus. As he approached, a woman in a snug-fitting kirtle that exposed an enticing portion of her rounded breasts, came out to greet him.

"What do you want?" she asked.

"I need to see Rufus. His first officer sent me."

"He doesn't want to be disturbed."

"This is important." William drew his knife and grabbed the woman by the arm. He held the knife to her neck. "Where is he?"

The woman didn't appear concerned by his threats. "Top of the stairs. First door on the right."

William pushed her aside and ran up the stairs to the first door he saw. He barged in. No one was there.

"I'll kill that witch."

As he turned to leave, he heard someone spit and then a fist found purchase on his face.

William spent an uncomfortable night tied to a sturdy support post in the St. Helier warehouse that held Crawford's wine. The rope around his hands cut into his skin. He cursed the woman who foiled his chance to dispatch Rufus. Once again, Rufus had stripped him of his sword and suit of mail.

At the sound of Rufus's voice, William perked up. The door to the warehouse creaked as it opened, letting in a shower of light.

Rufus walked straight to William, looked him in the eyes, cleared his throat, and spat at William's feet.

"I should kill you right here, boy," Rufus shouted. He struck William with a gloved backhand. "My first officer's guts lay dried in the road and Jamison is missing." Spittle flew from Rufus's mouth. "I know you killed them. Now, I have to deal with loading this damn wine myself. If not for Crawford, I'd feed you to the sharks. But he wants you delivered to Bristow—alive."

William glared. He didn't say a word. The metallic taste of blood filled his mouth.

"With two less crew, I don't have the men to keep watch over you. After we load this wine, you're spending the rest of the voyage in the hold. You can eat rats."

Locals helped to load the half ton pipes of wine. William lost count of the number of times Rufus spat while directing the men to tighten a rope or mind their step.

When the wine was cleared out, one of the men pointed to a dozen grain sacks piled in a corner. "Captain, whose grain is that?"

"It must belong to Crawford. Bring it along." Rufus looked at William still tied to the post. "When you untie him, have him carry the last sack. May as well get some use out of him."

Chapter
NINE

Tintern Abbey, Wales, Wednesday, July 23, 1348

Inevitably, the day came when Thomas had to leave for Bristow. He stood at his window overlooking the River Wye and tried to convince himself that Abbot Michael was right in saying he'd learn much on this journey. Truth be told, he only wanted to see William again. He wanted to tell William about hunting squirrels with Andrew, hoeing a garden, and seeing a naked woman. He wanted to hear about the fighting in France and ask William if he liked being a knight. But, why should it feel so strange to leave? He thought about his father; a tinge of anger brought back the doubts about his future. If he rejected the life of a monk, could he live among the dangers outside the walls of Tintern Abbey—dangers that included the pestilence? The odd dreams that troubled his sleep made him wish he never heard of the sickness. *What if the evil humors come to Bristow?* He had prayed for forgiveness, confessed his sins, and did his penance. And Andrew had wished him God's blessings. Was that enough to keep him safe?

His stomach tightened in knots thinking on his choices. He stuffed an extra tunic and breeches into his satchel; it seemed a good idea. After nine years living under the predicable rules of the Cistercians, the chance for something new broke through the mess of contradictions clogging his mind. He took one last gaze out his window and felt the warm, dry breeze.

The bells tolled terce. Abbot Michael disliked waiting when traveling to Chepstow by boat. By sunset, Tintern Abbey would be far behind. He looked around his room. His empty desk reminded him of the frustrations of memorizing the Rule of St. Benedict and learning to chant the Psalms. Memories of laughing and telling stories with Andrew lifted his spirits. He took a deep breath capturing the familiar smells of plaster, dust, and wood. For a moment, he closed his eyes, not wanting to forget. With thoughts of wonder for the unknown ahead, he turned and left his room behind.

Abbot Michael waited in the long boat moored at the abbot's pier. Four lay brothers, two in front and two at the rear, paddled the boat. The current drew them along at a swift pace. Thomas didn't know what to talk about, so he remained quiet and watched the river bank, content to listen to the birds and the pulse of the oars.

In Chepstow, Thomas and Abbot Michael boarded a larger long boat with four other passengers. Thomas's feelings of insecurity and dread, brought on by his impending reunion with his father, turned to marvel as he and Abbot Michael crossed the open expanse of the River Severn.

To reach their destination, they traveled along the Gloucestershire coast to the River Avon and then inland following the river's winding course. They traveled with the rising tide past open meadows, rugged hills, and sheer rock cliffs.

As the boat neared its destination, St. Augustine's Abbey loomed above the river on a high hill; the warm tan of the buildings and stone walls shined in the late afternoon sun in contrast with the green marsh below. The walls enclosed a grand church, remodeled in the gothic style. Delicate tracery sub-divided the pointed arches of its stained-glass windows.

"That is where we will find lodging," Abbot Michael said. "The abbey is away from the turbulent activity of the town center."

Passing the confluence of the River Frome, Bristow's wharf along the Avon came into view. At least a dozen ships from bulky cogs to slender long boats lined a wide span along the Welsh Back. Beyond the wharf, a row of rugged, wooden buildings faced the river. Thomas counted five church towers that pierced the sky above the town walls. Another magnificent spire rose above red cliffs to the south. A bridge crossed the Avon a short distance up river.

"Look, Father," Thomas said pointing to a large cart filled with barrels. "There are four horses pulling that cart. And the bridge has houses and a church on it."

"You will find many wonders here, Thomas. Bristow is a big city. You must also mind your step. Not everyone is as friendly as the simple folk of Chepstow."

"Yes, Father," Thomas said, as he concentrated on the commotion. Like a child, he didn't want to miss anything. Men loaded sacks of wool onto one ship and unloaded sacks of grain from another. Barrels swung precariously from windlasses. The street next to the wharf was filled with activity. Men in sweat-soaked tunics and dark-colored breeches went in and out of shops and warehouses carrying sacks of varied sizes.

As they approached an empty pier, the oarsmen braked the long boat's forward motion. Thomas jumped up rocking the boat.

"Sit down, boy," one of the passengers said.

"Throw that line," a man on the pier said.

Thomas threw the line and leaped from the boat. He was too busy watching the men on the wharf to offer any assistance to Abbot Michael.

"Thomas!" Abbot Michael said. "I nearly fell into the river."

"I'm sorry, Father. Look at all the horses with packs. And the buildings are all so close together. Some of them are two stories above the ground floor."

"Thomas, mind where you are going. Stay close now. We need to go through the center of Bristow to get to the abbey."

"Yes, Father."

The neighs of horses and the lumbering of carts soon obscured the sounds of the river. People hurried in every direction like ants at a feast. Thomas heard several languages that he didn't know; maybe Spanish or Italian. The air was filled with dust and smelled of manure.

As he and Abbot Michael passed into the old town through St. Nicholas's Gate and onto High Street, people pressed in around them. Thomas's smiles were repaid with looks as stern as stone.

A trench ran down the center of High Street. It served as nothing more than an open cesspool of filth and feces. The powerful odor assaulted his sense of smell and made him cough.

The shops along High Street displayed their wares through wide, open windows and on shutters that folded out to form tables and awnings: bread, leather goods, spices, silver, iron goods, and weapons. Signs above the doors of some shops were shaped like the goods inside. Other signs were painted with images and included the name of the shop like a goat's head and a bed for an inn called The Goat's Head Inn, and a well-dressed man next to a giant pair of scissors for a tailor shop called Timothy the Tailor.

Thomas stopped to admire the sign of the well-dressed man. The shopkeeper ran out and grabbed Thomas's hand, greeting him with an air of urgency.

"I am Timothy, the tailor. Are you looking for some fine garments, my boy? I have all the best fabrics from Flanders. Excellent weaves. Come inside. Let me measure you for a soft linen tunic or maybe hose. Those simple, wool breeches are much too common for someone of your looks."

"My ward is not interested in your wares," Abbot Michael said in a stern voice.

"Yes. Yes. I am sorry, Father," Timothy said, bowing in apology. "I did not know he was with you. Forgive me, Father."

"Come along, Thomas. If we dally, we will never get to the abbey."

They continued up High Street past the town center where High Street intersected with Corn Street, Wynch Street, and Broad Street. Proceeding north along Broad Street, they reached St. John's Gate—named after the church built above the gate. Outside the wall, they crossed a bridge over the River Frome. From there, the road wound on toward the abbey passing more piers along the Frome.

Thomas and Abbot Michael reached the east gate of the abbey before the supper hour. A stableman led them across the outer courtyard to an inner gatehouse. Brother Ezekiel, one of the Augustinian canons dressed in his white robe and mantle, greeted them.

"Good day to you, Father Abbot. It is good to see you again." He embraced Abbot Michael and gave him a kiss on each cheek. "I pray you had a safe journey. Please. Take a moment to wash your hands and feet."

"Thank you, Brother Ezekiel. I see your talents as the hosteller of the abbey have not diminished. This is my ward, Thomas de Parr."

"God's blessings to you, Master Thomas."

With their travel dust removed, Brother Ezekiel ushered them to a small public room in the abbot's lodge. "There is clean water in the pitcher." Brother Ezekiel motioned to an ornately carved wooden table. A silver tray, almost the same size as the table top held a silver pitcher and two silver cups. With a slight bow, he said, "Abbot Ralph will be along shortly. I bid you peace."

"Thank you, Brother Ezekiel. You are most kind."

After Brother Ezekiel left, Thomas rubbed his noisy stomach. "Do you think they will invite us for supper?"

"Patience, Thomas. As soon as Abbot Ralph arrives we will learn what lodgings they have for us and then we will see about supper."

Before Thomas's stomach growled again, Abbot Ralph appeared at the door. He also wore the white robes of an Augustinian canon. At fifty years of age, he walked with a youthful vitality. Of average stature and a little on the thin side, his face radiated a contemplative spirit. His long, narrow fingers clutched a gold cross that hung around his neck.

"My dear Abbot Michael, I bid you welcome." He greeted Abbot Michael with an embrace and a kiss on the mouth, the kiss of peace. "What brings you to Bristow?

"It has been too long since I was last to this splendid abbey, my friend. I praise the Lord that you are well and I pray that God's blessings protect you and your brothers. I would like to introduce my ward, Thomas de Parr. He is the youngest son of Lord Geoffrey de Parr of Kendalwood. Thomas is soon to be a novitiate of our Order."

Abbot Ralph held out his hand, bearing a heavy gold ring that seemed out of proportion to his slender fingers. Thomas knelt on one knee and kissed the ring.

"We are in Bristow to meet Lord Parr's second son, Sir William, who is traveling from Calais," Abbot Michael continued. "He should arrive sometime before the end of the month. I pray you may accommodate us while we wait."

"As always, Abbot Michael, you are welcome to stay as long as you wish. Brother Ezekiel will show you to the guest chamber here in the lodge. When you have settled, join us in the refectory for supper."

Thomas soon learned that the Augustinians did not practice the austerity of the Cistercians. The simple guest room he expected to be led to turned out to be a luxuriously appointed chamber with fine stonework, smooth plaster walls, and dark wood furniture. He looked under the bed cover and poked at a thin feather mattress that laid over a straw-filled tick. A small oak table under an arched window held a wide, wooden basin and a pewter pitcher filled with water; towels draped the sides.

Abbot Michael placed his extra robe in a chest next to one of the beds. "We will need to meet with Searle, the countess's steward, tomorrow. And, as I expect William will report to the customs office when he arrives, we will need to find out how best to keep watch for him."

"Do you know when my father will arrive?" Thomas asked, as he sniffed the freshly scented towels and admired the variety of religious ornaments and mementos that filled the shelves of an open cupboard.

"No, Thomas. We will ask if Searle can find out, as I am sure you are looking forward to seeing him again."

Thomas remained silent. As Andrew said, this was a trip to reunite with William, nothing more. He put his satchel in the chest and followed Abbot Michael to the refectory.

Chapter
TEN

Bristow, England, Thursday, July 24, 1348

Thomas met Abbot Michael at the inner gatehouse of St. Augustine's Abbey after morning mass. Departing from the church among a sea of white Augustinian robes, Thomas's tan tunic and brown breeches stood out like a dirty cygnet amid graceful swans. His youthful step and darting glances further contrasted him from the peaceful procession of solemn canons going forth to start another day of evangelism. For Thomas, the excitement of the unknown overshadowed every other thought and overtook his moody forebodings.

He and Abbot Michael walked along the River Frome where flat bottom cogs lined one side or the other of the mucky channel. The sharp odor of exposed mud drifted on the breeze. Men stood around on the piers or on the ships tending to repairs.

"At low tide, the river is not navigable for large ships," Abbot Michael said. "Captains must arrive or depart at the correct time or they become stuck along the way and have to wait until the next high tide to move on."

They passed through St. John's Gate and entered the bustling city of Bristow. Thomas held his nose, the gesture accomplished nothing. Tasting the dust and foul stink of the street was worse than letting his sense of smell become numb to the offense. Every now and then, someone yelled "Gardyloo!" Moments later, the contents of a chamber pot came splashing down from a first or second story window.

"There are many cellars below the streets of Bristow," Abbot Michael said as they turned off Corn Street onto St. Nicholas Street. "The countess's cellars should be beneath the warehouse just there."

Thomas followed Abbot Michael into a neatly maintained warehouse. A middle-aged man wearing rich tailored clothes stood by a lectern. He reviewed a piece of parchment making marks as he surveyed the goods scattered about the room. To the right, wide steps descended into the cellars.

"God's blessings, Searle," Abbot Michael said.

"Father Abbot, God be praised. I trust your journey was without incident." The men embraced.

"We arrived yesterday. I believe you know my ward, Thomas de Parr."

"Welcome to Bristow, Master Thomas," Searle said. "Your father's wool arrived several days ago. We have your wool as well, Father Abbot. Now we wait on Sir William and his ship. The countess has received no word that Calais has been made the staple port. The rumors persist, but the king has not acted. Without the king's proclamation, we may have to find other merchants and sell the wool in Bruges. The countess does not want to anger the king, especially during this time of war with France."

"I had hoped confirmation of the change of ports would be made soon" Abbot Michael said.

"That is not the worst, Father Abbot. There are numerous accounts of a savage pestilence moving northward along the coast of Guyenne and Poitou and through France from Marseille to Paris. Genoa and Sicily are in turmoil. Many captains refuse to take goods south for fear of contracting the sickness and not one desires to sail into the Mediterranean."

"I have heard mention of this pestilence. Is it truly as bad as they say?"

"I fear it is worse than we can possibly know. The madness of fear turns people against family and neighbor."

"We must pray for protection and ask God for forgiveness of our sins. God's grace is given to those who believe in Him and praise His word." Abbot Michael crossed himself with the signum crucis.

Talk of the pestilence rekindled Thomas's fears of leaving the safety of Tintern Abbey. He tried to recall the places that he had heard suffered from the sickness. "Has the pestilence reached Calais?"

"I am sorry, Master Thomas. I have heard no word regarding the fate of Calais." He patted Thomas on the shoulder. "As long as your brother avoids the French coast, he should be fine."

"Do you know when my father plans to come to Bristow?"

"Your father will be here Monday next. He takes lodgings at the Golden Fleece Inn on Corn Street. When I see him, I will let him know you and Abbot Michael have arrived."

Thomas's stomach fluttered. *I hope William arrives before then.*

"Thank you, Searle," Abbot Michael said. "Now, we must make our way to the customs office. Maybe they will be able to keep us informed when the *Lady of the Seas* arrives. And, if we are lucky, the rain will hold off until after sunset."

Thomas and Abbot Michael returned to Corn Street and then, passing out of the old town through St. Leonard's Gate, headed for the Key, the section of the wharf on the east side of the Frome.

The customs office fronted a wide, triangularly-shaped, open space that faced the river. It was a simple three-story wooden edifice with white-washed plaster covering the walls between dark stained beams. Large, square windows flanked either side of the broad door, which was open.

Inside, a single room stretched the width and half the depth of the building. Two notaries stood looking over scrolls and sheets of parchment piled on long oak tables. Open shelves, heaped with more stacks of parchment, lined the walls. As many as six cabinets with V-shaped shelves held scores of scrolls.

A counter separated the jumble of official documents from the public space where a man in a salt-stained tunic waited.

Thomas lingered inside the doorway while Abbot Michael went to speak with the notary who appeared to be the least busy. Just outside the door, two merchants, by the look of their brightly colored cloaks and hose, spoke in raised voices. Thomas tilted his head to listen.

"I must get my goods to Venice," the one wearing a red hat said.

"I cannot help you." The other man crossed his arms. "Sicily has been attacked by the pestilence. Naples. Genoa. Even Marseilles. I doubt Venice is safe. Death follows in the wake of this accursed sickness. Men are frightened and no one knows how to stop the advance of what must certainly be Satan's doing."

"Death does not frighten me. Not paying taxes to the king—that frightens me."

"I have heard it said that the ill humors are carried by the fish in the sea or by ships that sail on a foul wind. My priest says penance is our only hope."

"Priests say many things. I have no time for their calls of penance."

"Then suffer the fate of this evil menace. Pilgrims flock to the shrine of Our Lady of Walsingham seeking the protection and healing powers of the Blessed Mary's milk. You would do well to heed the advice of the church."

The man in the red hat waved his hand. "Enough of the church. If you cannot help me, I will seek aid elsewhere." He stormed off with a scowl on his face.

A few moments later, Abbot Michael returned and said, "That was rude. We will have to come back each day to check whether the *Lady of the Seas* has arrived. Let us take that walk around town."

For the rest of the day, Thomas and Abbot Michael wandered the busy streets. Abbot Michael filled in the place names as soon as Thomas pointed. Thomas's curiosity was insatiable. His fears vanished amid the intrigue of discovery. The Bristow Bridge fascinated him. Shop after shop, with homes above, lined the sides of the bridge. At the center, the Chapel of the Assumption straddled its width. The narrow road passed under the nave. Merchants, most of them jewelers, hawked their wares. People and horses crisscrossed paths in an orchestrated dance set to the melody of loud voices and the beat of hooves. The upper stories of buildings hung over the sides of the bridge and were supported by piles driven into the riverbed.

From the other side of the bridge, Thomas spied the incredible spire he admired when they first arrived.

"Look at the tower, Father."

"Yes. That is St. Mary Redcliffe. Sailors pray there before they leave on a voyage. When they return, they come back to give thanks."

"Then we must go there to give thanks for our journey and ask God to protect William on his." He tugged on Abbot Michael's arm, urging him on.

Rain gullies carved into the dirt of St. Thomas Street made it difficult to maneuver up the steep parts of the road. The warm, sand-colored stone of the church looked inviting. Fanciful spires decorated the exposed flying buttresses. In front of the north porch, Thomas leaned his head back to take in the full view of the tower.

"How did they build that?" Thomas asked, his eyes wide.

Inside the church, the vertical lines of the many columns drew Thomas's gaze to a ceiling that seemed to touch the sky. The decorated vaulting glistened in the light of the upper windows.

Thomas knelt at the front of the nave near the crossing and prayed for William. He insisted that Abbot Michael join in prayer. "It is a dangerous journey, Father. William will need all the help he can get."

After praying, they returned over the bridge and ambled toward Bristow Castle east of the city wall. Passing under New Gate at the end of Wynch Street, Thomas and Abbot Michael strode along The Weir, the section of road that ran between the River Frome and the Castle moat. In the shade of the castle walls, they enjoyed relief from the heat of the late afternoon sun. The breeze helped dry their perspiration.

When they reached the far eastern end of the castle wall, Thomas gazed in awe at the busy market. People of all classes paraded up and down Market Street between the castle gate and Lawford's Gate farther to the east.

"People come here from the surrounding villages and hamlets to sell their wares," Abbot Michael said. "On Saturday, there are many more merchants and it is much more crowded with activity."

A small stand with fresh vegetables and herbs caught his eye. "What is this, Father?"

"That is sage," a young woman said.

The young woman startled him. With his attention focused on examining the sprig of dried sage, he failed to see her. "What is it for?" he asked, as he looked to see who answered.

Time seemed to stop when he looked into her eyes—a deep, mysterious green like an ethereal forest of ancient pines. Her fair skin accentuated a kind face and a small nose. Her slender lips formed an inviting smile. Thomas's toes tingled.

"Sage is very good at removing bad humors," she said. "Cooked in wine, strained through cloth, and then drunk often, it helps to diminish phlegm. The same potion will help stiffening humors to pass."

Thomas didn't pay attention to what she said. His gaze remained transfixed by the glimmer in her eyes and the gentile movement of her lips. Realizing that she had stopped talking, he stuttered for something to say. "You eat it?" he asked at last.

"Yes," she replied. "It also adds flavor to pottage and soup. That sprig is one penny."

"I'm sorry. I have no money."

"Come, Thomas," Abbot Michael said. "We must be going now."

"But—"

"Maybe you can come back Saturday with a few coins." She reached out to take the sprig of sage.

Thomas froze. He concentrated on the sensation of her fingers touching his; they were rough, but pleasing. He let go. All he could do was smile in return. He wanted to say something, but nothing came to mind.

"Thomas," Abbot Michael called.

"Yes, Father." After Thomas left the stand, he thought of all the things he wanted to say. Most of all, he wanted to ask for her name. He turned to look back. She wore a white cap set back on her head, revealing chestnut brown hair and a white napron tied around her waist. A soft, green gown clothed her slender figure. She watched him and smiled.

Chapter
ELEVEN

Bristow, England, Saturday, July 26, 1348

While waiting for Saturday to arrive, a different kind of flutter gripped Thomas's stomach. He had nothing in his experience to make sense of it—other than the naked woman in the woods. Whatever it was that caused the giddy excitement that muddled his concentration, he enjoyed the feeling. To expend his energy, he earned two pence helping Searle at the warehouse. As soon as morning mass ended, he ran through light rain to the customs office undeterred by the damp. No word on the *Lady of the Seas*. Then, off to the market.

His feet splashed mud as he dodged his way through the soggy streets. By the time he arrived, a break in the clouds brought a respite from the gloom. Merchants and freemen selling everything from cackling chickens to expensive silk already filled many of the spaces. Crowds of people ambled about looking over the wares, haggling over prices.

Thomas searched the lanes of carts and wagons looking for the young woman with the sprig of sage. He thought he knew the place where she had been. He stood a moment next to a shoemaker's stall.

"Have you seen a young woman selling sage?" he asked. "She was here on Thursday."

"Sorry, lad. Can't say that I have. I'm usually at this spot every Saturday."

Thomas went to the fringes of the market hoping that she arrived late and had to settle for an out-of-the-way location. A noisy and cheerful crowd gathered to watch a group of minstrels. The music bounced and flowed with such abandon that no one within thirty feet stood still. All the dancing and frolicking made it difficult to see if anyone looked like her.

A frown forced its way onto his face. He wound his way back toward the center of the market. Suddenly, he glimpsed a young woman wearing a white cap. As he got closer, he realized it was her. He swallowed hard. His heartbeat quickened. He wanted to run away, but his feet kept going forward. Then, she turned and looked at him. Her gaze pierced him like an arrow.

"God's blessings, Thomas," she called out, waving.

He hurried to her cart. "How did you know my name?"

"That's what the priest called you, is it not?"

"Oh. That was Abbot Michael. He's the abbot of Tintern Abbey. I'm studying to be a monk there. I haven't taken my vows yet. I'm in Bristow waiting to meet my brother. He's coming from Calais. My father will be here too. He's coming on Monday. I looked for you at the spot I saw you on Thursday. I brought a few pence in case I saw something nice to buy. Yes. My name is Thomas…. What's your name?"

"My name is Isabel. You sure are talkative all of a sudden."

Thomas blushed. The memory of his awkward meeting with the naked woman in the woods flashed in his mind. He wanted to run away and hide from these strange yet exciting feelings.

"I'm sorry. That wasn't polite. You have such lovely blue eyes. I hoped you would come back today."

"Did you?" Thomas felt like he stood next to a forge. He was certain his face glowed like red hot coals.

"My father is in town getting some things for our farm. Would you like to keep me company until he comes back?"

"Yes, please. I mean, yes I would." A beautiful young woman, Isabel, wanted to talk to *him*. His cheeks hurt from smiling. He let Isabel talk on about the herbs and vegetables in her cart while he tried to pace the beat of his heart. But every time his mouth opened to say something, he stuttered. It didn't help that Isabel waited without a suggestion of ridicule. Her empathy made the stuttering worse. After one long, excruciating moment of silence, she took hold of his hands.

"Close your eyes and stand still." She rested his hands on the cart.

A rush of excitement filled him as he let go of the visible world.

"Breathe in deep through your nose. Hold it. Now, slowly breathe out through your mouth. Again. Once more. What do you smell?"

He breathed in and out several times as he pondered the sweet odor. "Lavender?"

"Yes. And what is lavender good for?

"It takes away the bad humors and eases the mind." To his great surprise, he didn't stutter. He opened his eyes. The gentle curves of Isabel's lips melted his fear. He wished the day would last forever.

"Here comes my father," Isabel said. She waved to her father as he worked his way through the crowded market. His long, white hair and matching beard stood out against the many younger faces. His drab attire was clean, but worn. He embraced his daughter and kissed her cheek.

"Father, this is Thomas. He's been helping me with the cart."

"It is a pleasure to meet you, Thomas. I am Hugh Fiske of Filton."

Hugh looked old for a man with such a beautiful, young daughter. His caring face put Thomas at ease.

"God's blessings, sir. Isabel has been teaching me about all these vegetables and herbs. I wasn't aware there were so many different kinds. She says you grow them on your own plot of land."

"It is a small plot, less than a quarter of a hide. It is part of the manor of Lord FitzNicholas. The land is not the best, but some of the herbs grow well on the rocky parts near the trees, the sage in particular. There is only myself and Isabel to care for the land so it is quite enough. Our rents are small. Maybe when Isabel is married, I will have more help." Hugh smiled at Thomas.

"Father, please. Thomas is studying to become a monk."

"Is that so? How wonderful. Just the same, you are welcome to come visit. Isabel gets lonely with only her aged father to keep her company."

"You're not that old, Father."

"None of us live forever, my dear. You will soon enough need help tending the land."

"Pay no attention to my father, Thomas. He thinks I should have been married as soon as I turned fourteen. He's been trying to convince every young man he meets that I'll make the perfect wife. I want to choose my own husband."

"Such foolish talk," Hugh said. He waved his hand in a dismissive gesture, but his eyes belied his displeasure.

Thomas blushed at the emotional twist of the conversation. Marriage was the last thing he wanted to think about. He was supposed to love the church, not a woman.

Hugh put his hand on Thomas's shoulder and gave him a fatherly squeeze. "If you are so inclined, just follow the Gloucester Road and you will come to the village of Filton. Anyone there will be happy to show you the way to our cottage."

"Thank you, sir. I must be going now. Abbot Michael will be looking for me at vespers."

"Come, my dear. We must be on our way also. The others from Filton will be leaving soon. We must keep together."

Isabel hugged Thomas. "I have a feeling we'll see you again. God be with you."

"God be with you, Isabel." Thomas tingled all over. After a few paces, he looked back to see if Isabel watched. To his delight, she waved.

On the way back to the abbey, Thomas shivered with newfound energy. The aroused feelings for Isabel excited him. Monks weren't supposed to be interested in women—at least not in the way his body told him.

"What am I to tell Abbot Michael?" he mumbled. He thought of different ways to tell Abbot Michael about Isabel, but none sounded innocent like a chance encounter, and saying nothing amounted to telling a lie.

Trelleck Grange, Wales

"The thatch is fine in this section, Brother Gilbert," Andrew yelled. "Let me climb a bit higher." Andrew took his time as he eased himself along the damp and slippery slope of the manor house roof. He threw his arm over the top and pulled himself up to straddle the peak.

"You seem to be over the spot where it leaks," Brother Gilbert shouted.

Andrew poked at the thatch with the handle of a small spade. "Here it is. The thatch is rotten here. We'll need to replace this section."

"You best come down, son, before you fall. We'll tend to the thatch come Monday. Hopefully, it'll be drier then."

Back on solid ground, Andrew brushed the dust and debris from his wool breeches. "Looks like a large section near the peak is bad. It'll take a half day at least to repair it. Not that I have anything better to do."

"You've been moody this past week," Brother Gilbert said. "If I had to guess, I would say you're wishing to be in Bristow about now."

"I've never been to Bristow."

"It's not that interesting, son. Lots of people, horrible smells, a bit rough in places, and women."

"I can't imagine Thomas handling any one of those."

"You sound like an older brother talking."

"I wish I was there with him," Andrew said, as his gaze wandered off toward the far field.

"I know. He'll be back soon enough. I think we need a distraction. How about we do some more sword training? You're making good progress."

"I need to be a lot better."

"Don't rush it, son. You'll get there."

"I want to be good enough to handle the likes of those men we ran into this spring."

"Perhaps you need some time with Eudo. I'm sure he'd be happy to teach you. He's one of the best sword masters I know. He handles a blade with style. Let me see if I can arrange an errand for you to go to Chepstow for a few days. I know that's not nearly enough time, but maybe you can work something out with Eudo for a day here and there when you have the chance. I'd welcome the extra sword arm around here."

Andrew beamed at the prospect to train with Eudo. Perhaps, he might even have a chance to see Eva again. A smile crossed his face as he recalled the feel of her smooth skin next to his.

At sea between Jersey and Bristow

Pipes of wine and sacks of grain filled the hold of the *Lady of the Seas*. William made a make-shift bed out of several grain sacks piled on top of the more secure barrels wedged in a corner. He propped more sacks against the wall to keep from falling between the barrels in rough seas.

Rats scampered about, sometimes nibbling at his hands and face when he slept. After four days, his senses no longer registered the repulsive odors of the hold. And, with each passing day, his strength diminished as his stomach gave up its desire for food.

The highlight of each day was when the hatch opened. He cherished the momentary vision offered to his sight-starved eyes. At the appointed time, the hinges creaked. Dusty shafts of light stabbed the darkness. A voice called down, "You still alive?"

"Yes," William said.

A bucket tied to a rope descended. William grabbed the bucket and poured the contents into the container he kept by his bed. The rope tightened pulling the bucket out of his hands. As quick as it opened, the hatch slammed shut extinguishing the light.

In the rush to replenish his water supply, William didn't have the chance to look at the itchy spots that developed on his legs. It was hard to resist the urge to scratch.

He cupped his hand to take a drink. As soon as the water reached his stomach, he vomited. The faint throbbing of a headache nagged for attention.

Chapter
TWELVE

Bristow, England, Sunday, July 27, 1348

As soon as Abbot Michael left to use the latrine, Thomas jumped from his bed. A night of anxious sleep did little to quell his guilt for seeking out Isabel. It was an innocent encounter, wasn't it? The six paces it took to walk from the table by the window to the door was all the space he had to ponder the words to describe his meeting. The moments ticked by and nothing but the truth sounded reasonable. As he turned toward the door, the sudden appearance of Abbot Michael startled him.

"What is the matter, Thomas?" Abbot Michael asked.

His pent-up energy had nowhere to go but to blurt a response. "I'm sorry Father Abbot. I've been afraid to tell you."

"Slow down. Tell me what?"

Thomas took a deep breath. "I met a young woman in the market yesterday. The one who ran the vegetable cart where we stopped on Thursday. She's very friendly. I met her father too. I hope you're not angry that I went to see her." He felt relief at saying the words, but immediately questioned the wisdom of confessing.

"I am not angry, Thomas. You are young. As a novice, you will learn to channel these desires for women into a desire to be of service to God. Earthly pleasures are distractions from the great work we do in God's name."

"Yes, Father Abbot." He stared at his feet. Being with Isabel made him feel unlike anything he felt before—excitement, yearning, acceptance—all rolled into an amazing experience. How could serving God replace those feelings?

"Come now. Do not be sad. We learn best when we fall short of God's will. Only then do we see His divine inspiration with clarity."

"I understand, Father. It's hard to remember all that I'm to do."

"After the morning mass today, I want you to stay here at the abbey. Abbot Ralph has agreed to hold a special mass and pray for protection from this pestilence. We must seek forgiveness for our sinful ways. Only with God's intervention will we be safe from the evil that ever seeks to destroy us."

The cool interior of the Augustinian church smelled old and musty. Thomas's attention to the mass faltered as his thoughts returned to Isabel. To keep from thinking about her, he studied the decorative, starburst carvings that surrounded the tomb recesses in the north and south aisles. Painted in rich reds, greens, and golds, the highlights created a festive display for the souls of the departed. He imagined grand processions down the center of the church as the bodies of those buried within the tombs were brought to their final resting places. He listened to the sublime chants of the Augustinian brothers as the sound echoed past the rounded arches of the pulpitum. The melodic tones melded with his mood. He sighed and tried to convince himself that if he was meant to meet Isabel again, God would create the means for him to do so.

The special mass for protection from the pestilence immediately followed the regular mass. The fervor of Abbot Ralph's words and the pleading tone of his voice made Thomas cower as if God's righteous anger had been unleashed against all who committed any sin, even the slightest infraction. He never before witnessed a mass so desperate for God's mercy and forgiveness.

He bowed and whispered: "Lord, hear my prayer. Please watch over Andrew and the brothers at Tintern Abbey. And watch over William as he travels to Bristow. It has been a long time since I last saw him and I pray you'll protect him on his journey. I have tried to do right as Abbot Michael taught me. But I'm sure I made mistakes and I thought of earthly pleasures. I pray you'll forgive me and let this pestilence pass."

Tintern Abbey, Wales

The delightful odor of a simmering soup drifted out of Tintern Abbey's kitchen. Andrew poked his head around the door. "Greetings, Brother Samuel. You wanted to see me?"

Brother Samuel stood over the cauldron with his usual cook's intensity. He gave the pot a quick stir with a giant wooden spoon and turned, sweat trickled down his temples and plump cheeks. "Brother Gilbert is pleased with your hard work."

"Thank you. I try my best."

"In recognition of his trust, I would like for you to deliver three sacks of coarse wool to Chepstow. A merchant will arrive from Cardiff between Wednesday and Saturday to take delivery. This is a new contract, so I would like someone to greet him. All you need do is make sure he is satisfied. Do you think you can do that for me?"

"I'd be glad to go." Andrew bit his lip to hide his excitement. "How long may I stay?"

"That is up to Brother Gilbert. I expect the merchant will be on time, but use your judgment."

Bristow, England

The second high tide on Sunday reached its peak as the sun set. The *Lady of the Seas* maneuvered into an empty pier along the Key. Crawford had an uncanny instinct for knowing when ships bringing his merchandise arrived in port. He walked along the wharf, watching the approach of the ship. Rufus appeared on the forecastle. Crawford waved.

"Where's Parr?" Crawford asked, as he looked past Rufus.

"That arrogant dog had the nerve to kill two of my men. He's in the hold. I kept him alive just for you. At least, he was alive the last I looked. He coughs like thunder."

"What?" Crawford scowled.

Rufus cleared his throat and spat. "I don't trust the little bastard. I'd rather have the devil as a passenger."

Crawford climbed on board the ship and spoke quietly. "There's a lot of money to be had here. We're too close to sailing away with a hold worth probably £600, or more."

Rufus shook his fist. "Don't talk to me about money. I sent a man down to see about Parr's coughing and now that man and another are coughing too. If it's that pestilence, by Christ's blood, I'll have your—"

"You can hire a hundred men for the money we'll make. But if Parr is dead we'll never get the wool."

"What about that brother?"

"Odd you should mention him. A lad named Thomas has been asking about your ship at the customs office. I'm sure he's the brother Parr spoke of."

"I say we seize the wretch and ransom him for the wool." Rufus cleared his throat and spat.

Crawford grinned. "Let me take care of that. You register with the customs office. Be sure to talk to the notary with the hunched back; he knows to expect you. Then, get the wine unloaded. Hire more men if you need them. The quicker we unload, the quicker we get that wool."

"Where do you want the grain?"

"What grain?" Crawford asked, his brow creased.

"We brought the sacks of grain from your warehouse in St. Helier."

"That's not my grain. No matter. Put it in the warehouse."

Chapter
THIRTEEN

Bristow, England, Monday, July 28, 1348

Monday morning found Thomas on his usual path to the customs office. People and horses packed the streets. After passing through the cool shadow of St. John's Gate, he had an odd feeling that someone followed him. When he turned onto Corn Street, he paused and turned around. Not sure what to look for, he continued on. Farther down Corn Street, he saw the sign for the Golden Fleece Inn and hurried past. According to Searle, today was the day his father planned to arrive.

At the customs office, ship captains lined up to register their goods. He waited his turn in the queue. "Good day," he said to the notary when he reached the front.

The hunchbacked notary rolled his eyes and said, "No one from the *Lady of the Seas* has been in today. Next."

His hopes dashed for seeing William first, he headed back into the old town. He turned onto St. Nicholas Street and stopped at the countess's warehouse. Boxes and barrels filled the main storage room. Two men sat at the top of the stairs to the cellars. "Is Searle here?" he asked.

"Greetings, Master Thomas," Searle called out from the cellar. "I will be up shortly."

Searle carried a lantern in one hand and a scroll in the other. He blew out the flame when he reached the top step. A puff of black smoke drifted upward filling the air with the smell of burnt fat. "How are you today, Master Thomas?"

"I'm well, thank you. Have you seen my father?"

"Yes. He arrived with the morning tide and stopped here on his way to the Golden Fleece Inn. I told him you and Abbot Michael are lodging at St. Augustine's Abbey. He said he had to meet someone this morning. After bells toll sext, he will be back at the inn. He seemed happy at the chance to see you."

Thomas smiled politely. After he left the warehouse, he proceeded down St. Nicholas Street in the direction of High Street. He sauntered along, wasting time. He looked for any excuse to not arrive early at the Golden Fleece Inn. Activity along the Welsh Back provided a welcome distraction. Sitting under a tree along the bank of the River Avon, he watched the tide go out. Cogs beached in the muddy river bed.

He wandered the alleys off Worship Street. Dodging manure and people in a hurry came as second nature. Passing narrow houses and shops, he wondered how people endured living so close together. He stepped into a shoemaker's shop. Shelves full of shoe forms lined the walls. The rich smell of leather masked the stink of the street. A slight breeze came from an open door at the rear. The shopkeeper looked up from his work and frowned. Thomas turned and left.

He stopped in front of St. Mary le Port church on Maryport Street. A fanciful mixture of colored stone from many shades of reddish brown to more plentiful gray infused the walls with a busy display that matched the chaos of people and animals going about their business. He watched the whirl of activity as he willed time to pass.

Back on High Street, the pleasant scent of fresh bread awakened his hunger. He remembered the few pence secreted away in his shoe and looked over the selection of breads, each looking tastier than the next.

"Greetings, young man," a woman with flour dust on her kirtle said. "Would you like to buy some bread? I can assure you everything is fresh."

He reached into his shoe and pulled out one of the coins. "How much can I get for a penny?"

"This loaf is too small to sell. You take it, my dear."

Thomas tried to give her the penny, but she refused. He nodded his thanks and tore off a piece. The firm crust made a loud crunchy sound. His cheeks hurt as his mouth salivated in anticipation of the feast. The bittersweet taste delighted his tongue and triggered a craving for something to drink.

He spotted The Goat's Head Inn across the street. As he approached the entrance, two men came up beside him.

"Greetings, lad." the larger man said. "You look like you could use a drink with that bread."

"Do they sell ale here?" Thomas asked.

"The Goat's Head Inn serves the best wine and ale in Bristow."

The men ushered Thomas into a paneled room off the receiving hall. The room was empty but for three square tables and a half dozen stools. Light filtered in through two small windows high on the wall toward the street.

"Send word to Crawford. We have his prize," the larger man said to the other. "And bring some wine when you come back. Let's have some fun while we wait."

"Who's Crawford?" Thomas asked.

"Don't worry about that, lad. My friend has gone to get something for us to drink. He'll be right back. So, what's your name?"

"Thomas."

"A pleasure, Thomas. I'm Alan. My friend there, he goes by Ifan."

Thomas broke off another piece of bread and munched on it while he waited. Ifan soon returned with another man called Nudd. They brought a pitcher and four mugs. Alan appeared to be the leader of the group, if size meant anything. His bulk equaled the other two combined. Ifan and Nudd looked like brothers; the same large nose protruded from their blank faces.

"Pour our friend Thomas a drink, Nudd," Alan said.

Thomas coughed as he took a swallow. "This is wine—and full strength. I just wanted ale."

"Wine is good for you." Alan smiled and motioned for Thomas to drink up.

Thomas took a larger swallow. The sweet wine soothed his throat. The tingle of the alcohol made him blink. After a few more healthy swallows, he felt warm inside.

"Here, have some more," Alan said.

Thomas didn't think to say no. Nudd refilled his mug as soon as it touched the table. The men encouraged him to drink up. Another mug followed. His senses didn't fully register the passage of time or the laughter of the men around him. He thought he heard church bells, but the sound faded to muddled noise. His eyelids got heavy, and the room appeared to spin. The mug took a roundabout and wobbly route to his mouth. He drained it, leaning his head back to get every drop. Some of the drink spilled down his cheeks and onto his tunic and breeches. The men laughed.

"Thomas, you spilled your drink," Ifan said. "You're not supposed to spill your drink."

Thomas slurred, "I'm sorry." He set the mug down. His eyes lost focus. Someone's hand rubbed his back pulling on his tunic. Then another touched his chest. The men laughed. He didn't understand the laughter.

His tunic pulled on his ears as it vanished above his head. He felt cold. He wanted to run, but like a bad dream, he couldn't move. His senses blurred. Rough hands gripped each arm forcing him to stand. Someone tugged on his breeches and they fell to his ankles.

"Now it's time to pay for the wine," a man's voice said.

Cruel hands force him to lean forward on the table. He wanted to say no, but nothing came out. Tears fell as he tried to rise up. The strength of the hands held him down. *Stop.* The thought screamed in his mind as he rejected reality. He closed his eyes tight to hide from the pain.

A loud commotion echoed in his ears. It sounded like men yelling, stools breaking, mugs crashing, metal clanging, men gasping. Then silence.

A gentle touch caressed his shoulders and encouraged him to stand. Someone helped pull up his breeches and helped him into his tunic. The touch seemed familiar, a remembrance from the distant past. Then, powerful arms hugged him.

"I am here, Thomas. You are safe now."

The low pitched voice of a man conjured up memories of comfort. He felt protected. He took a deep breath. The scent of the man broke through the fog of the wine and touched his soul. He opened his eyes to the blurry image of a strong man with dark brown hair and beard and warm, brown eyes—eyes that expressed the love of a father for his youngest son.

"Father?"

"Yes. I am here, Thomas. It is over. The men are dead." Lord Geoffrey de Parr stood among the shambles of broken stools, upturned tables, and dead bodies, his bloody sword still embedded in the chest of the largest man. He held his son tight and rocked him.

"I was afraid to come see you." Thomas shivered. Tears streamed down his face. "How did you find me?"

"The woman at the bakery remembered your blue eyes. She saw you go with those men."

"But how did you know?"

"When you did not come to the inn, I went looking. You are safe now. That is all that matters."

Chapter
FOURTEEN

Bristow, England, Tuesday, July 29, 1348

Thomas's head pounded and his stomach felt upside down and inside out. He blinked his eyes to focus. Light flooded through a large glazed window bordered by dark blue drapes. Sitting up on his elbows, the smooth, white sheets felt cool on his bare skin. The soft feather mattress enveloped him in comfort like a silk cocoon.

"Father." A smile came to Thomas's careworn face. "Where are we?"

"We are at the Golden Fleece Inn. How are you feeling, son?" Lord Parr leaned over and straighten his son's ruffled hair.

"Like I was dragged through the streets by a mad horse. Father, those men, why did they do that?" Thomas's eyes watered as he recalled the ordeal. He sat up in the bed.

"They were evil men, son. They paid the price for their cruelty."

"They're dead?"

"Yes."

Thomas felt shamefully satisfied. He wiped his eyes with a brisk swipe of his hand. His father had saved him. Maybe his anger had been misplaced; his father did care. The terror subsided, but a vision of the men's faces remained. He shoved the images and the feelings out of his mind, glad for the numbing effect of the wine. He studied his father's face; it was creased with more lines and his hair was streaked with more white than he last remembered.

An unexpected confidence invaded his soul. He no longer feared his father's reaction to the question he longed to ask.

"Father, why did you never visit me?"

Tired eyes that hinted at an all-night vigil looked back at Thomas. "I wanted to come, but it would not have been proper. My presence would only divert your attention from Abbot Michael's excellent teaching. I prayed that God would guide your thoughts and actions so you would find contentment in the service of the abbey. I could not deprive you of the opportunity to learn all that you have."

"But what if I'm not meant to be a monk?"

"I am surprised you would even think of anything other than joining the Cistercians. You have the potential for doing magnificent things within the Order. It is what you are meant to do. You may even become the abbot someday."

"But Father, if there was something else for me, would that be fine with you?"

Lord Parr sat back in his chair and stroked his beard. "Abbot Michael tells me you have learned much and despite the delay in beginning your novitiate, he may consider allowing you to become a monk by Easter. That would be a great honor."

"I know, Father. But I want to do other things too." He thought of Isabel. Would his father approve if he wanted to marry a peasant girl?

"We cannot always do everything we want, son. You have to think of your future. Tintern Abbey is a wonderful place to do God's work. I am sure you will come to see the truth in that. In time, you will be given more responsibilities. And as the abbot, you will have the opportunity to travel to many interesting places."

"Yes, Father. I pray that God will guide me in what I do." Thomas held on to the thought that God might see it fit to direct him down another path. He decided it best to change the subject.

"Has William's ship arrived?"

"I do not know, son. I will meet with Searle shortly. He has been trying to find out about a man by the name of Crawford."

"The man at the inn mentioned that name. Someone was supposed to tell Crawford they had his prize. Apparently, I was the prize."

"It appears so. But for what reason, I can only guess."

"Can I come with you?" Thomas looked around the room for his clothes.

"No, Thomas. I think it best if you stayed here. I will be back by supper." Lord Parr stood and kissed Thomas on the top of his head. "God be with you, son."

"God be with you too, Father." Thomas curled up under the sheets. As he drifted off to sleep he prayed, "Almighty and Merciful God, please watch over William and keep him safe. And thank you for sending Father to save me from those evil men."

Lord Geoffrey de Parr made his way to the countess's now well-guarded warehouse. The assault and attempted kidnapping of Thomas made him rethink his efforts to protect his sons. After all these years, why did Lord Sleaford contact him? Katherine's heritage should have been long forgotten. But this man Hastings. How did he become Sleaford's spokesman? And the outrageous amount demanded—a thousand marks. At least the wool would be loaded soon and William would be safely on his way. Then, he could take Thomas back to Tintern Abbey. If all went well, profits from the sale of the wool would cover most of the payment demanded. The rest he could borrow from the countess.

He greeted Searle and asked, "Have you discovered anything about the *Lady of the Seas*?"

"I was at the customs office this morning, my lord, and overheard one of the notaries mention the name. I saw a small purse change hands between a poorly dressed man and the notary. It all looked suspicious to me. I waited for the man and followed him to a ship on the Key. It turned out to be the *Lady of the Seas*. One of the crewmen greeted the man as Crawford."

"So, Crawford is connected with William and the wool shipment. Did you see William?"

"No, my lord. I watched Crawford from a distance. There was another man on the forecastle who appeared to be the captain. He was a large man with black hair and beard, the kind of man who could easily handle a crew of brigands. After they carted away the goods, I saw two men being helped off the ship. They were coughing hard. Another man was carried off, but I was not able to see if he was Sir William."

"My God! Do you think it is the pestilence?"

"I am uncertain, my lord. From what I have heard, the evil humors of the pestilence have not reached Calais. It seems unlikely that those men are afflicted with it, but I cannot be sure. The route the ship took is unknown. The men were taken to a warehouse facing the Key. It was only a short distance from the customs office. I discovered that the warehouse is leased to Crawford."

"Crawford must have bribed the notary to keep quiet about the ship's arrival. If William is still on board, we must hurry. The next falling tide is after sunset. This might be our last chance to find him. Maybe the High Sheriff can spare some men. I will go see him and meet you at the warehouse."

"As you please, my lord."

Crawford stood on the forecastle of the *Lady of the Seas* and glared at Rufus. He shouted, "Couldn't you have waited until nightfall to take those men off the ship? People were watching."

"Don't tell me what to do." Rufus spat toward Crawford's foot, missing his shoe by inches. "That strange sickness is spreading to more of my crew. I may not be able to pilot my way back to sea. And I doubt I'll find more crew in this rat-infested town. I don't care about your damn wool."

"You're not leaving those men in my warehouse."

"They're dead to me. You can figure out what to do with them. And Parr too. Since you failed to take the brother, I have no further use for this whole affair. Now, get off my ship or I'll throw you off."

Crawford left; it was pointless to argue. "You'll regret this, Rufus," he grumbled under his breath. He turned and looked back. Rufus coughed. "Serves him right." He pictured in his mind's eye Rufus's emaciated body floating face down in the sea.

At the warehouse, he checked on William and the two sick crewmen. They lay in a far corner of the dimly lit storage room now filled with twenty pipes of wine and twelve sacks of grain.

William sat slumped over. Vomit stained his beard and shirt. Sweat plastered his auburn hair. His chest heaved as he labored for breath. The other men continued to cough and spit up frothy blood, too weak to move.

Crawford kept his distance. He scratched his head. "Now, what to do with you three? I've got to be able to move this wine and I can't have anyone see you." A movement on the sacks of grain caught his attention. He jumped. "Damn rats. I hate those horrid creatures."

With two of the sheriff's men at his side and Searle behind him, Lord Parr pounded on the door of the warehouse. The sound of a bolt sliding past an iron latch preceded the creak of wood as the door flung open. "Who are you?" a man said.

"That man is Crawford," Searle said.

"I am Lord Geoffrey de Parr. We are here under the authority of the High Sheriff of Bristow. We are looking for my son, Sir William de Parr. You will step aside while we search this building."

"It appears that I have little choice in the matter."

"You are correct." Lord Parr motioned to one of the sheriff's men. "See that this man does not leave."

Moments later, Lord Parr found William and the crewmen of the *Lady of the Seas* at the back of the warehouse. He hurried to William's side. An unusually powerful and sickly odor hung in the air around the men. He shook William's shoulder and called his name. William remained unresponsive.

"Bring a litter. We must get him to St. Bartholomew's."

Lord Parr walked along beside the sweat drenched body of his son. It pained him to see William struggle for breath.

At St. Bartholomew's infirmary, a nun showed them to a bed in a guest house with a small chapel. "This should serve to restore his soul," she said.

"Thank you, sister," Lord Parr said. "Have you sent for a priest?"

"Yes, my lord," Searle said.

Lord Parr stood immobile, unsure what to do. He watched as the sheriff's men moved William from the litter to the bed. Moments later, the priest arrived; the tassels of his linen cincture flopped against his white robe as he hurried to William's bedside.

"How is he?" the priest asked.

When Lord Parr did not respond, Searle said, "He has not spoken, Father."

"What is that smell?" The priest rubbed his nose. "We must see if he can be awoken so he can confess and receive absolution." The priest put a hand on William's sweaty forehead. "He has a fever. Get some cool water. It might help to bring him around."

A nun brought a bowl of cool water and a rag. She wrinkled her nose as she wiped William's forehead and cleaned vomit out of his matted beard. She pulled back William's shirt to clean his neck. A hard lump appeared. The nun cringed. "Dear God!" she exclaimed. "Look at his neck—that large, blackened growth. What is it?"

Lord Parr ripped open William's shirt. A rush of putrid air forced everyone to step back, a look of shock on their faces at the state of William's body. Sadness deeper than anything he had known gripped him. His heart skipped a beat and his throat tightened. He stared at his son in disbelief. William's skin appeared pale and clammy with reddish purple blotches scattered about. A large black bubo the size of a hen's egg swelled under each arm and a smaller growth, just as horrific, grew at the base of his neck. Pus exuded from around the buboes. The memory of William as a helpless baby, full of hope, flashed in Lord Parr's mind. A promising future now destroyed by an unknown sickness. *What evil caused this ruined body?* "Lord have mercy."

Lord Parr placed a cool rag on William's forehead. William gasped and coughed a loud, hacking cough.

"Father, please hurry," Lord Parr begged. "William's soul is in danger. William, can you hear me? You must confess your sins."

The priest anointed William with oil.

"William. Please." Lord Parr knelt by his son and held his hand.

"Father?" William asked.

"Yes, William. I am here. Please listen to the priest."

"William, dost thou believe the principal articles of the faith and the Holy Scriptures and dost thou forsake heresy?"

William's response was no more than a whisper. "Yes."

"Dost thou know that thou hast often offended God?"

"Yes."

"Art thou sorry for thy sins?"

William coughed for a long moment. "Yes."

"Dost thou desirest to amend?"

"Yes."

"Dost thou forgive thy enemies?"

Silence.

The priest repeated, "Dost thou forgive thy enemies?"

"Yes."

"Art thou willing in all manner to make satisfaction?"

"Yes."

"Dost thou believe that Christ died for thee?"

"Yes."

"May the Almighty God have mercy on you, and forgiving your sins, bring you to life everlasting. Amen." The priest raised his right hand. "May the Almighty and Merciful God grant you pardon, absolution, and remission of your sins. May our Lord Jesus Christ absolve you, and I, by his authority absolve you from every bond of excommunication and interdict as far as I can and you may need. I absolve you from your sins in the name of the Father, and of the Son, and of the Holy Ghost. Amen." As he said the names of the Trinity, the priest made the sign of the cross over William. "May the Passion of our Lord Jesus Christ, the merits of the Blessed Virgin Mary and of all the Saints, what good you have done or what evil you have suffered be to you for the remission of your sins, growth in grace and the reward of everlasting life. Amen."

The priest placed a sliver of consecrated bread on William's lips and nudged it into his mouth. William's chest stopped moving. His hand went cold. Lord Parr lowered his head and wept.

The pestilence secured a foothold in Bristow and claimed its first life.

Chapter
FIFTEEN

Bristow, England, Tuesday, July 29, 1348

The distant bells of St. Augustine's tolled for vespers. Supper at the refectory had ended, but Thomas remained in his father's room at the Golden Fleece Inn. He paced while he waited for word of William's arrival.

His stomach, queasy all day, managed to keep down the bits of leftover bread and cheese his father left behind. But when he caught a whiff of cooked meat from the inn's kitchen, hunger returned. He stared out the window at the fading shadows.

Someone knocked.

"Thomas, it is Abbot Michael. Please open the door."

Thomas ran and unlocked the latch. "Where is my father?"

"Your father has been delayed. He was worried that you have not eaten all day so he asked that I come by and see to it that you got a meal. Come, let us go downstairs."

Thomas followed Abbot Michael along a narrow hallway that led to a stairs and the ground floor dining room. Geometric designs painted in gold covered the white plaster walls. A gold fleece hung from a branch mounted above the fireplace. Other guests, most of them well-dressed merchants in their colorful attire, sat around candle-lit tables.

The worn and scuffed floor planks squeaked as Thomas and Abbot Michael found their way to an open table. They sat next to a window that looked out on a darkening sky. The smell of smoke and cooked meat filled the dining room.

Thomas had a hearty serving of pork. The food found welcome in his stomach as he shoveled it down with little regard for spillage. Bread to soak up the meat juices and a bowl of cooked carrots rounded out his meal. A mug of ale washed down the lot. At his first sip of the ale, he shivered.

Abbot Michael appeared uneasy, and his face was drawn. "Are you not hungry, Father?" he asked over the din of conversations.

"No. I will just have some ale. You finish up. Then, we will go back to your room."

Once back in his room, Thomas couldn't help himself. "Is there something wrong, Father?"

"It is William. Searle and your father...they found the *Lady of the Seas*. Your brother was on board."

"William is here," Thomas interrupted. "May I go see him?"

"Thomas, please. Let me finish. Searle discovered that Crawford and the captain of the *Lady of the Seas* were going to take you and William hostage and then steal the wool. The sheriff now has them both in custody. It appears that William was kept in the ship's hold and he became sick." Abbot Michael's voice faltered. He looked away.

"Father, what are you saying? Has something happened to William?" Thomas paced desperate to release a surge of uncontrolled energy. "I prayed to God to keep him safe. Is he not safe?" Anger invaded the tone of his voice like a slow pain not yet realized.

"Thomas, please be calm. God hears your prayers. I know this is hard. William made his confession. His sins were forgiven. His soul was saved. He is now with our Lord and Savior." Abbot Michael reached out to embrace Thomas.

Thomas recoiled. "No! It must not be. God was supposed to keep him safe." His chin quivered. "Why is this happening?"

"Your father was by William's side when he died. Your father is now at the abbey church. He wants you to come to him."

"Why did God not listen to my prayer?" Thomas clenched his fists and tears streaked his face.

"Let us go back to the abbey." Abbot Michael tried again to embrace Thomas.

"No. Leave me alone. I hate God!" Thomas ran out of the room, down the stairs, and into the dark and colorless street. He ran down Broad Street and bumped into a man. He kept going; he didn't care. He had to run. His anger consumed every thought. He ran without regard to where or why. He ran through St. John's Gate and over the bridge that crossed the Frome. The steep road leading north toward St. Michael's Church finally sapped his inner rage. He collapsed by the side of the road a hundred yards past the church. His strength gone, he had nothing left to cry, or scream, or pound his fists on the ground. But he wanted to do all of that, and more.

North of Bristow, England, Wednesday, July 30, 1349

Noisy blackbirds stirred Thomas out of his sleep. The hard ground felt damp. Light broke through the darkness to the east. The dull gray of Bristow's stone walls looked sinister in the dim light. He sat up and tugged on some strands of grass as he stared off toward St. Michael's Church.

William was dead. Thomas pushed the thought deep inside where the pain could not hurt him. He cursed God. "Why did You ignore my prayers? I can't go back now. I can't serve You. I've lost everything."

The light of a torch farther up the road attracted his attention. He squinted to see who was coming, not sure if he should hide or sit still. When he heard a man humming a happy-sounding ditty, he relaxed.

The man's pace slowed as he neared. "God's blessings, young man."

"Excuse me, sir. Where does this road lead?"

"If you keep going north you'll come to the main road to Gloucester. It's a dangerous road. I wouldn't recommend it for someone traveling alone."

"How far is that?" Thomas asked.

The man paused. "How far is what?"

"Gloucester."

"I've no idea, young man. My brother went there once. I think it took him two days, maybe three. Whatever it was, it was a long way."

"Thank you, sir."

"You're welcome. God be with you." The man nodded and continued on his way, humming his tune.

In that instant, Thomas made up his mind. The chance for a life as a monk ended when he cursed God. God would never forgive him. Even more, he didn't want to forgive God. Thinking back served no purpose. His actions couldn't be undone. He stood, brushed the dirt from his breeches, and set off toward Gloucester.

As the man said, he came upon a well-traveled road. Wide, barren grooves, like trails of mud, marked the way. He looked south. Trees now blocked his view of Bristow. For all intents, Bristow no longer existed. He turned north and kept walking and tried to think of nothing but the road ahead. Yet, with every step, the gentle tug of Tintern Abbey called for him to fulfill his destiny—to be the monk everyone expected. The farther he went, the harder it became to keep going. He brooded over his dilemma. The ease at which he started walking confused him. After three miles, he found no comfort in the endless possibilities his mind conceived. He reasoned that he had no choice; his legs kept him moving forward.

The village of Filton lay ahead. A gentle breeze carried the sounds of cackling chickens, mooing cows, and squealing pigs. The land looked poor. Villagers worked in the meager wheat fields sodden with rain, some with sickles, others gathering and stacking stalks of grain. Thomas watched the villagers, curious if any of them thought of a life different from what they had. His approach drew stares.

The gray stone tower of the parish church rose above the trees, a lone sentry proclaiming God's presence. A collection of thatched cottages, most with lime-washed walls, lined either side of the wide dirt road and beyond. A few larger homes and the shops closest to the church had walls made of wood planks. Seeing the church reminded Thomas of the hateful words he said against God. He looked away, not yet ready to confront his anger and sadness.

More villagers went about their business. Some carried sacks or buckets. Others, holding tools for weeding or harvesting, plodded along the narrow paths between buildings.

In an instant, Thomas's mood changed. *Isabel!* Isabel lives in Filton. His desire to see her broke the lingering ties to Tintern Abbey. He had to find her.

An old woman with a dark cap covering her stringy white hair stood in front of a tidy cottage tending her chickens. He hesitated a moment. To offer God's blessings didn't feel right.

"Greetings," Thomas said to the old woman.

"Greetings, young man. God's blessings to you." She threw crumbs from a pile held in her napron as she talked. "What brings you to Filton?"

"My name is Thomas de Parr. I met Hugh Fiske and his daughter, Isabel, at the market in Bristow on Saturday. They invited me to visit. Is their cottage nearby?"

"You may call me Beatrice." She looked Thomas up and down, pausing to look into his blue eyes. Apparently satisfied with her assessment, she pointed with a crooked finger. "Their cottage is over there. The last cottage to the west. They will be tending their fields about now. If you wait, everyone takes a rest at mid-day."

"Can I help you with anything while I wait?"

Beatrice again studied Thomas. Her expression was blank, as if wondering what to do. Then, a jovial grin appeared. She motioned for Thomas to follow. Behind her cottage grew a little vegetable garden. She handed him a hoe. "Do you think you can manage to rid me of those weeds?"

To Thomas's delight the good plants grew tall next to the tiny weeds and lots of space separated the rows. He set about showing Beatrice that he knew how to hoe a garden. He concentrated so hard on his task that he didn't realize someone stood behind him until he felt a tap on his shoulder. He turned to find Isabel standing there.

"God's blessings, Thomas. I'm so happy to see you."

Isabel put her arms around Thomas and squeezed him. Her embrace trapped his arms as he held tight to the hoe. He teetered on the verge of falling.

"Greetings, Isabel," Thomas said once she released him. His memory of Isabel was matched with the perfection of the woman who now stood before him: beautiful, cheerful—her green eyes enchanting and mystical.

With the tone of her voice subdued, she asked, "Is there something wrong?"

"No. You startled me." Thomas lowered his gaze a moment. "I'm very happy to see you. I wanted to come for a visit." The ease of the words surprised him. He convinced himself that the answer to Isabel's question was not a lie; there wasn't anything wrong with him coming to Filton. Isabel's father invited him after all.

"You picked a cloudy day for a visit. Come. Father is getting our dinner ready. If I'm not there to see what he does, there's no telling what it might taste like." Isabel took Thomas's hand and led him out of the garden.

Thomas followed savoring every moment she held his hand. He returned the hoe to Beatrice who, with a chuckle, mouthed a "thank you." Walking along with Isabel brought a bounce to his steps. He longed to put his arms around her in a proper embrace and kiss her lips.

From a distance, Hugh Fiske's cottage looked like the smallest cottage in the village. Worn spots marred the lime wash on its walls and the thatch looked like the fur on a scared cat. A scythe and a hoe leaned at a precarious slant against one wall. Several different-sized buckets sat in a line as if waiting for someone to pick them up. A small window on the west side was open; its shutters lay on the ground below. Walking past the window, Thomas heard movement within.

"Isabel. Is that you?"

"Yes, Father. I brought someone along to join us."

"What is that, my dear?" Hugh opened and closed the frail door, careful not to strain further the one operating hinge. "God be praised. It is wonderful to see you, Thomas."

"Greetings, sir."

"Father, Thomas came for a visit. Is that not delightful?"

"Indeed. It is kind of you to come all this way. Please join us for our humble dinner. It is not much, but it keeps the hunger away. Let me get another bowl. Have a seat over there by the fire."

Outdoor eating presented a vast change from the quiet formality of the grand refectory at Tintern Abbey. An unsteady log standing on end served as Thomas's chair. Three other logs stood around a fire pit of hot coals. Above the coals, a pot hung from a hook on a tripod.

Isabel stirred a handful of needle-like leaves into the pot, let it simmer a while, and then scooped a serving of the contents into each bowl.

"This is vegetable pottage," she said. "I hope you like it."

Thomas took the bowl and nodded his thanks.

"Wait." Hugh said. "Isabel, what is the matter with you? We have not said grace. What would your mother say?"

Thomas froze. How could he say a prayer of thanks to the God who wouldn't save William? His muscles tensed. Hate burned his skin. He wanted to run.

"Forgive me, Father," Isabel said.

"For your carelessness, you will say grace for a week."

"Yes, Father."

"I am truly sorry, Thomas," Hugh said. "Isabel knows better. We are good Christians who believe in all the proper forms."

"Please. I'm not offended." Thomas took a deep breath and exhaled as quietly as he could. He set his bowl on the ground, bowed, and waited for Isabel to say grace. He heard the words, but he refused to let them enter his fractured soul.

After the prayer, he tasted the pottage, which looked like a thick, cream-colored soup made of grain and vegetables cooked down until it became a mash. It had a lumpy texture and an earthy aroma.

"We are out of bread, dear," Hugh said.

Thomas chewed with care, trying to identify what the pottage contained. The lumpy bits tasted of carrot and turnip. He didn't have a cook's sense of flavor to identify the rest. It made him think of a soup Brother Samuel once made that accidentally sat in a pot all day and got cooked down until it became one big mushy flavor.

"It's very good," Thomas said. He didn't want to offend Isabel if she was the cook. Brother Samuel's soup tasted horrible, and he said so. That honesty got him a slap on the head.

"Can you taste the sage?" Isabel asked.

"Sage? Like that sprig you showed me at the market?"

"Yes. Those little green leaves are sage. They give the pottage flavor."

When they finished their meal and rinsed their bowls, Thomas offered to help out in the wheat field. As if on cue, the cloud cover began to break and bolts of sunlight poked through. Everyone looked up.

"May the heavens be praised," Hugh said. "You must come more often, Thomas. We have little enough good wheat as it is. This sun is a Godsend."

Thomas didn't see the sun as a Godsend. To him, God only mocked his misery, which made him more determined to stay away from Bristow.

"Have you ever worked with a scythe before?" Hugh asked.

"No. But I watched the lay brothers at Trelleck Grange harvest grain."

Hugh stroked his snow-white beard and squinted. "Maybe Isabel can show you how to stack the stalks of grain. That would be a lot safer—for all of us."

"I'd be happy to show Thomas how to do that, Father."

Isabel's glee was immediately contagious. The cares of Bristow were buried under the pleasures of working alongside Isabel. But with the sun, so came the heat and humidity. Thomas's tunic stuck to his skin. He dripped sweat from his nose and chin and down his neck. He put the discomfort out of his mind and persevered. Isabel's patient teaching motivated him to work hard. Every time she spoke, the melody of her voice, a sound more beautiful than any birdsong, seemed to soothe the buried pain of William's death.

"You take a handful of stalks in each hand, like so," Isabel explained. "Twist them together like this. Then lay this bit on the ground and put an armful of stalks over the top. Grab the ends of the bit you twisted together and tie that around the stalk twisting the ends like so. Now you have a sheath of grain. We stand several sheaths together in a little bunch like this to ripen."

Thomas wiped his brow with a dry corner of his tunic.

"You'll feel much cooler if you take off your tunic," Isabel said.

He hesitated.

"There's no reason to be shy. I can tell the work is hard for you. You'll feel much better."

His muscles tensed. He had worked shirtless before, but never with a woman around. A vision of the naked woman in the woods flashed in his mind—her skin must have felt cool as she lay on the forest floor. He relented and took off his tunic.

The sudden breeze on his bare chest proved to be more stimulation than he could handle. He reached for a sheath of grain to cover the growing bulge in his breeches.

"You did that on purpose."

Isabel giggled.

He wanted to take off all his clothes and run through the field screaming for joy. *Isabel likes me.*

By the time Thomas thought vespers should be called, they finished a good amount of work. It seemed strange to hear only the rustle of Hugh's blade as it swooshed through the air cutting stalks of grain. No sound of bells calling the monks to service—no sound of bells telling him what to do. There was only the work at hand. And Isabel.

Lost in the rhythm of Hugh's sickle, Thomas recalled the day when he left Kendalwood Manor for Tintern Abbey. He sat in a cart next to Edgar, his father's head servant, feeling excited, but already missing his older brother William. When he turned for one last look at the home he might never again see, William stood waving, his sad face spotted with tears. William wanted so much to be a soldier in the king's army. Thomas thought if he had not been born, William would have received more attention from their father. There would have been more money available to send William away for proper training as a knight. Things would have been different. William may not have gone to France. Then, he might not have been on that ship. Somehow it had to be his fault William died. If only things had been different, William would be alive.

"Thomas," Isabel said. "What are you looking at?"

"I'm sorry." He turned and quickly put on a happy face. "As you said, the work is hard."

"Maybe we should finish up for the day. It's getting late."

"Isabel, you should have said something sooner. It is too late for Thomas to walk back to Bristow now. The roads are not safe."

"I didn't know," Thomas said.

"Father, can Thomas stay with us tonight?"

"That is up to Thomas."

The lack of foresight to think about where he might find lodgings suddenly struck him, a worry he hadn't considered when he dashed out of the Golden Fleece Inn. "If I may, I would like to stay."

"Good, then it is settled," Hugh said. "I believe we have enough fresh straw to make a place for you in the cottage. But mind yourself if you get up after first sleep. I wake easily."

"Father, please." Isabel giggled.

Chapter
SIXTEEN

Tintern Abbey, Wales, Wednesday, July 30, 1348

Three large canvas sacks, each the weight of a stout man and stuffed with coarse wool, sat in a cart outside Tintern Abbey's stables. The smell of hay and manure tainted the rain-washed air as Andrew guided one of the strong mares into place and secured the harness and bridle. Neighs and snorts broke the silence of the otherwise peaceful morning. He worked quickly with expert hands fitting every clasp in the proper order. At the clap of loose-fitted sandals he turned to greet a stern-faced Brother Samuel; whenever Abbot Michael left on a prolonged journey, Brother Samuel took to heart the rigors of running the monastery.

"God shines on your journey," Brother Samuel said. "The sun has found its way clear of the clouds."

"I hope it lasts."

His tone formal, Brother Samuel held a piece of parchment and pointed as he talked. "Be sure to ask for Gruffydd ap Maelor when you get to the warehouse. There should be men there to help unload the wool. Be sure to have Gruffydd put his mark here and then have him make a check here to confirm that all three sacks were delivered in good order."

"Yes, Brother Samuel."

"You may stay with the Benedictines if you need to wait."

"Brother Gilbert said I can stay at the castle so I can learn about sword fighting from Eudo. I think he'll be much more fun to be with than the Benedictines."

Brother Samuel shook his head. "If you must. But be careful. Let me know when you return."

"I will."

Andrew brought along an extra tunic. It was the same tan color as the one he had on, except this one lacked the fashionable holes that marked him as a poor laborer. He wanted to make a good impression with the merchant—and perhaps Eva.

Cart wheels sloshed in the muddy ruts along the quiet road. Soon, only the sounds of creaking wood, grinding wheels, and clomping horse hooves kept him company. He lost track of time staring at the road and thinking of his last encounter with Eva. Quicker than he expected, Chepstow's imposing town wall loomed ahead. Semi-circular towers periodically jutted out from the thick stone barrier. As a reminder of all the rain that had fallen over the past months, water collected in the ditch in front of the wall. In its current state, the ditch could almost pass as a moat.

Andrew recognized the guard and nodded as he passed through the gate. He thought it best to deliver the wool to the warehouse before checking to see if Eva was at home. The meandering streets led past the sandstone walls of the Benedictine priory. Andrew slowed the pace of his horse to accommodate the steep slope of the main road as it led down to the wharf. The impressive walls of Striguil Castle loomed to his left. He quickly changed into his good tunic.

Six piers jutted into the muddy river, the ebbing tide now halfway through its cycle. Several empty long boats tied to the piers banged against their moorings in the strong current. Andrew drove the cart up to a row of tall, single story, wooden warehouses. Four men stood in front of the largest building. Gusts of wind caused the warehouse door to sway and groan on its hinges.

"I'm looking for a merchant by the name of Gruffydd ap Maelor," Andrew called out. "I have a delivery of wool for him."

"You're in luck, boy," a man holding an oar said. "He's just inside. I'll get him for you."

"I'm Gruffydd ap Maelor," a man said as he walked out of the warehouse. His black hair and beard were unkempt, and his clothing looked no different from the other men: dusty breeches and cream-colored tunics spotted with sweat. The fabric clung to his body like loose sack cloth.

"I have your wool, sir," Andrew said. He got down from the cart and approached Gruffydd. He thought it odd that a merchant looked so common. But then, he never made a delivery before and was unsure what to expect. Maybe Gruffydd kept his finer clothes packed away. "Brother Samuel gave me this parchment for you to place your mark…just here."

"I'm sorry, lad. I don't have anything to write with. You just leave that with me and I'll have a messenger bring it to Brother Emanuel."

"Brother Samuel."

"Yes, sorry. Brother Samuel." Gruffydd winked at one of the other men.

In an instant, Andrew's suspicions were aroused.

Gruffydd shouted, "Grab him."

Andrew turned and bolted. He slapped his horse on its hind quarters and yelled sending horse and cart charging at the men. Without looking back, he ran for the castle gate. Memories of his days foraging the streets as an orphan flashed in his mind. The two men who chased him were no match for his speed. He climbed over and around obstacles, leaving the men to see only footprints in the mud.

He sprinted up the hill to the massive stone gatehouse of Striguil Castle, the two round towers like giant sentinels. Guards in their cuir bouilli armor and open-faced helms stood outside the barbican holding long glaives. Andrew yelled, "Is Eudo here? Some men attacked me by the wharf."

Bran spoke up, "What's that, Andrew?"

"They have my cart and horse!"

"Alert the watch," Bran told the other guard. "How many men?"

"Four, maybe five. I had no time to count. They tried to grab me."

A man dressed in the commander's uniform of the countess's livery hurried from the gate. "What betides?"

"Eudo! I was supposed to deliver wool to a man by the name of Gruffydd ap Maelor, but they took my cart and horse too."

"Steady, Andrew," Eudo said. "Not long ago a merchant by that name came to the castle. Said he was waiting on a delivery of wool. A little demanding if you ask me. As far as I know, he is still in the castle."

"In that case, they have his wool."

Eudo addressed Bran. "Bring the watch to the wharf as quick as you can. Leave your sword for Andrew."

Andrew didn't wait for Eudo. He grabbed Bran's short sword and raced back to the wharf.

The men who had chased him now worked to secure two sacks of wool in one of the long boats. Two other men held the bridle of his agitated horse while the imposter Gruffydd struggled to heave the last sack out of the cart.

"Stop!" Andrew shouted. He ran straight for the boat and jumped in, shoving one of the men into the river. The other man grabbed an oar and swung without purpose. Andrew ducked. The oar brushed his hair. The man again swung wildly. With all of his might, Andrew brought his sword down on the oar, splitting the handle in half. The man broke off the long end and used it like a staff. Andrew matched his steps to the sway of the boat. His strikes chipped away pieces of wood from the oar. Unable to keep his balance, the man fell into the river with a splash.

Andrew jumped out of the boat to confront the imposter Gruffydd who now wielded a long hunting knife.

They crossed blades for several parries. Out of the corner of his eye, Andrew saw Eudo standing by the pier watching the action. When the imposter went on the offense, Andrew lost his confidence. He dodged a thrust, but the blade tore through his tunic. He again looked at Eudo. Eudo hadn't moved. Andrew's heart pounded as he countered the parries and swung as hard as he could. After deflecting another thrust, he managed to strike the imposter's arm. The man dropped his blade, ran to the pier, and jumped into the river.

By this time, four men-at-arms ran down the hill from the castle. The last two men who still fussed with the cart stopped what they were doing and followed their mates, plodding through the muddy bank to jump into the river.

Andrew ran to his horse. "Steady, girl." He patted her neck and looked about for injuries. She appeared unharmed. He rubbed her nose and, with a calm voice, tried to ease her fear.

"Unless they are strong swimmers, I am afraid we have seen the last of those men," Eudo said. "The tide will pull them out to sea. A shame that is. We have not had a chance to use the stocks in a long while." Eudo watched the bobbing heads and splashing arms drift down river.

"Can you help me load those sacks of wool onto the cart?" Andrew asked.

"Sure, son." Eudo said. "That was some fine sword play."

"I see your sword is still sheathed."

"Brother Gilbert told me you wanted to learn about sword fighting. There is no better way to see what you can do than watch you in action. It was an opportunity I could not let pass. I would not have let him hurt you."

Andrew tried to think of an appropriate insult, but decided silence was better.

The real Gruffydd ap Maelor waited in the lower bailey of the castle near the great hall. The sight of the merchant's extravagant garb reminded Andrew of a fat rooster. Gruffydd wore a bright red linen tunic cinched at the waist by a belt partially hidden under a huge, overhanging stomach. A bit of red-green plaid trimmed the sleeves and neck. His gray hose was stretched around fat, stumpy legs. A dark blue surcoat draped over his left shoulder and a matching hat with a long, peacock feather completed the costume.

"Is that my wool?" Gruffydd demanded.

"This wool is for Gruffydd ap Maelor," Andrew replied. "Is that you?"

"Yes, yes. Who else would I be?"

"My apologies, my lord." Andrew found it hard to keep from laughing.

As if taking offense at the title, Gruffydd said, "I am no lord. At least you made a timely delivery. Brother Samuel assured me that I would not have to wait long."

"I'm sure you'll be satisfied with the quality of the wool."

"I expect nothing less than the highest quality." He stabbed at one of the sacks with a small dagger, its shiny blade unmarred, and pulled out a tuft of wool. After rubbing the fleece between his fingers, he shoved the wool back into the sack. "I take lodgings at the Three Monks Inn. You will deliver the wool to the wharf tomorrow, no?"

"The first high tide is after terce. Your wool will be well protected inside the castle."

"As it should." Gruffydd strutted out the gate.

Andrew took off his tunic. "Look at these holes," he said, holding up the ruined fabric to Eudo. "And all for the sake of that old rooster's wool."

"Toss it here," Eudo said. "One of the maid servants is good at fixing such things. I will ask her to take a look."

"How long will that take?"

"That depends on how well I charm her." Eudo winked.

"Brother Gilbert said I can stay for a few days. I hope you have the strength to keep up with me in the practice field."

"Remember that cockiness, son. You will be crying soon enough. Size and strength are not the only things you need when matching wits with another man's sword. You need subtle moves. You need to learn to see what is coming before it comes. Let us have a go, shall we?"

Andrew clashed swords with Eudo at the west end of the lower bailey. He lost his cocky attitude after Eudo swatted his backside several times. His reactions paled in comparison to Eudo's quick and free flowing movements. Once he got into the rhythm, his stance improved and the workout turned to glorious fun.

"Remember, the key in any fight is speed, agility, and dominance. Think where your feet are. Keep a wide stance.

"Like that....

"Good....

"Your stance will help with balance. Focus on your opponent's eyes. They will tell you what he plans to do. Then you can defend and counter.

"Again....

"Better....

"Time your attack to my movements and thrust forward when you see an opening. Watch for my ward and counter-ward."

After a break for dinner, the drill continued. During long parries, when the back and forth and clang of metal rang out, they drew a crowd from the guards who then cheered on one or the other. The constant ducks and turns taxed muscles Andrew didn't realize he had until the burn of exertion took its toll on his stamina.

"What is the matter, son? Are you out of breath?" Eudo asked, his hand resting casually on his hip.

"All this strange moving around—swinging, moving forward, back, and sideways." Andrew bent over with his hands on his knees. He labored to control his breathing. Sweat shined on his back. "I didn't expect it to be so difficult."

"Do you think your opponent will stand still like that training pole over there?" Eudo chided.

Andrew shook his head.

"The more you train, son, the better you will be. We will use the training pole tomorrow so you can concentrate on how to swing and thrust."

Andrew grimaced as he stood and stretched his back. "I can't wait."

"Your sorry state will not get you pity. If you want to stay alive, you need to know more than your opponent."

A fleeting thought of lying with Eva turned to dread as the pain in his muscles bit him with every move. He doubted he would be able to make love and enjoy it—Eva would have to wait. For now, he had to force a smile and hope to recover some feeling in his limbs by morning. "What's to eat?"

Chapter
SEVENTEEN

Bristow, England, Wednesday, July 30, 1348

andles burned low in the church at St. Augustine Abbey. Throughout the night, Lord Geoffrey de Parr prayed in the secluded Elder Lady Chapel for the repose of William's soul. Without provision for masses to be said, he feared William's soul might never reach paradise.

He knelt before the altar in the hundred-year-old chapel dedicated to the Blessed Virgin Mary. A life-size stone statue of the Virgin, faithfully painted to inspire devotion, focused his prayers. Graceful lines depicted the Virgin with hands folded at her breasts and head bowed at a slight angle as in prayer. A golden halo encircled her head. Her robe was colored a gentle blue and trimmed in gold with white undergarments; her hair was painted a soft brown; her face, hands, and feet radiated a warm, fleshy pink.

Large stained-glass windows portraying biblical scenes let in the morning light and brought warmth to the cool chapel. Free standing columns of blue lias stone accented the walls and primary columns. Whimsical carvings of animals and foliage decorated the arcading, details reserved for those observant few who spent many hours in prayer.

He felt a presence and turned; Abbot Michael stood at the bottom of the steps into the chapel. Lord Parr crossed himself and slowly rose to his feet. His knees ached from his prolonged vigil.

"My dear Abbot Michael, may God have mercy on us. These are indeed sad times. I never expected to be the one praying for the soul of my son. Yet here I am. How is Thomas?"

"My lord, it pains me to tell you that Thomas did not take well word of William's death. It upset him deeply. He ran off to find release for his anger. When he did not return after compline, I asked Searle to keep watch for him and I alerted the sheriff."

A burst of adrenalin awakened Lord Parr's tired spirits. "We must find him!"

"We will, my lord. There was nothing more we could do during the night. Abbot Ralph will say a special prayer at this morning's mass. You must take care to not tire yourself. You need your strength to return William to his home."

"How can I rest with my youngest son missing?"

"Searle assured me that he will begin a search this morning. We accomplish nothing by scattering ourselves in every direction. If Thomas returns, we must be here for him."

"But—"

"Please, my lord. There is nothing more to do. Come; let us go to the guest house. You must rest."

A knock sounded at Lord Parr's guestroom door. He sat up and rubbed his temples. His voice hoarse, he called out, "Enter."

"My lord, forgive my intrusion," Searle said. "I bring dire tidings." Searle opened the shutters to let in the late afternoon light. He took a cup and filled it with water from a pitcher on the small table near the window. "Here. Have a drink."

Lord Parr drank greedily as if he had been lost in a desert. "My head hurts. What is it Searle? Have you found Thomas?" He gestured for Searle to sit in the chair across the room from the bed.

"We have not found Master Thomas. What I discovered is much worse. Those men who were on the ship with Sir William...they died."

"They died? How?"

"As I walked along the Key earlier today, I met a captain arriving from Bordeaux. He talked about the deaths there caused by the pestilence. I described the way those two crewmen died, coughing and spitting up blood. He said he saw others die in the same manner and he knew them to have been stricken by the pestilence. And when I told him of Sir William's symptoms, he thought for sure Sir William died of the pestilence as well. Those large black growths we saw—the captain said that was a sure sign of the cruel plague. He said some people die quickly coughing and spitting up blood, others linger and develop those horrible buboes."

"How could this happen? William has never done anything to offend God. There must be some mistake."

"I believe not, my lord. We were all with him when he died. You saw the marks on his body. It is a blessing that Sir William was able to confess his sins and receive last rites. The captain said many victims are possessed by demons before death takes them and they are unable to confess. What is more, I fear for us. We all looked into Sir William's eyes. It is said the deadly humors can jump from one person to the next by an ill-timed look."

"Dear God, what evil have we done to deserve this?" Lord Parr stared out the window.

"If you are able, it would be wise to seek a priest and confess. I have done so already this morning."

Lord Parr stumbled over his words. "Confess? Yes, of course. That is wise advice." He looked at Searle. "What of Thomas? We must keep up the search for him."

"We are. The sheriff's men are out looking. No one has seen him. There is also the matter of the wool. I must see to other arrangements and advise the countess that our plan to deliver the wool to Calais has failed. I will then continue my search for Thomas farther out from the town walls."

"The wool." He gritted his teeth. "I had forgotten all about it. Of all the things to deal with, there is yet that damn wool. Please feel free to negotiate on my behalf for whatever terms you can find. Maybe there is a merchant from Flanders who is willing to take it."

"I believe the countess has existing contracts we may be able to supplement."

"Very well. I must speak to Abbot Ralph. For now, William will have to be interred in Bristow. I cannot leave here until I find Thomas."

After Searle left, Lord Parr washed his face. The cool water failed to relieve the dull throbbing in his head. Unsteady on his feet, he sat down to put on his shoes. His joints ached. He shook it off as tiredness from unusual sleep and left his room to search for Abbot Ralph.

Brother Ezekiel directed him to the abbey church. There, he found Abbot Ralph talking with Abbot Michael in the north transept near the Elder Lady Chapel. Their tone was hushed and secretive.

"God's blessings," Abbot Michael said.

"God's blessings to you both. I must speak to you Abbot Ralph about William. We must find a suitable place to bury him as I cannot leave Bristow without knowing what has become of Thomas."

"It would be an honor, my lord, to offer a resting place for your son here in the abbey cemetery, even if it be only temporary. I understand your distress. Allow me to have Brother Ezekiel make the arrangements. You have more pressing matters, I am sure."

"You are kind. Your generosity will be remembered." Lord Parr bowed. "I also wish to pay for thirty masses to be said in William's name. Will you do this for me?"

"We will be most pleased to provide the devotion."

"Have you any word of Thomas?" Abbot Michael asked.

"Searle was here not long ago. There has been no word. The search continues." He reached to steady himself against a pillar and fought against the fatigue that drained his ambition.

His tone suddenly quiet, Abbot Michael said, "There have been rumors that the pestilence has arrived in Bristow. Several of the crew of the *Lady of the Seas* have died of a strange sickness that some say is the evil pestilence."

"Word travels quickly, I see," Lord Parr said. "Searle mentioned this to me. He fears William died of the pestilence."

"We must encourage people to live good Christian lives and stay free of sin. Abbot Ralph and I decided that St. Augustine's canons must do their part to inspire the faithful. They will go out to churches in and around Bristow to help organize special masses to be said on Sunday. We must all pray for protection from this evil that approaches. If the pestilence has found its way to our shores, we must have faith that God's purpose will be revealed."

"I pray we will not be too late," Lord Parr said.

Chapter

EIGHTEEN

Filton, England, Thursday, July 31, 1348

Muffled voices woke Thomas. He looked around. It wasn't a dream; he had found Isabel and had slept the night in her cottage. A man's voice called his name, Isabel's father.

The voice again called, "Pottage is almost ready."

As he rose to his feet, his muscles ached from the prior day's labor. His bed of prickly straw laid under the only window. The morning light brought the oddest feeling; there was no lesson to recite and no mass to attend. His structured life ended when he ran from Bristow. He now had the freedom to choose what the day might bring. But choose what?

Against the longest wall of the sparsely furnished cottage, a mound of straw piled in a frame and covered with canvas served as a bed for Hugh and Isabel. Blankets lay folded at one end. Next to the bed, a clay lamp sat on an oak chest, its corners worn and its front panel scuffed. When he touched the latch to open the door, he heard Hugh's voice say, "Careful of the hinges, Thomas." The wobbly door jolted his sleepy senses.

Isabel's eyes shined. "Good morning, Thomas."

"Good morning, Isabel. Good morning, sir."

"I am sorry we did not have a tick for you to sleep on. You must certainly be used to much finer beds than our humble cottage has to offer."

"I slept fine." Thomas stretched to ease the stiffness. He sat on the stump next to Isabel with slow and deliberate movement. Hugh scooped a serving of pottage into a bowl and passed it to him.

As Isabel said grace, he let his mind wander, avoiding any thought of God. He tried to imagine how Isabel might feel lying next to him on a cool bed of grass. Only the sweet melody of her voice penetrated his vision.

"What more is there to do today?" he asked, when Isabel finished the prayer.

"Thank you for asking, Thomas," Hugh said. "There is a little more wheat to harvest. The yield is poor so we need to gather as much as we can. And the vegetable garden needs tending. But, what we need most is bread. Maybe you and Isabel could go to the bakery and trade herbs for a loaf or two."

"I'd be happy to go," Thomas said. He watched Isabel eat her pottage, mesmerized by the way the soft morning light illuminated her beauty. "I've two pence that I can contribute."

"That is not necessary, Thomas. It is kind of you to offer. Best eat your pottage before it cools." Hugh coughed.

Thomas felt his face flush. At least it was only Hugh who caught him staring.

After gathering sage, early blooming lavender, and mint, Thomas and Isabel set out for the bakery. Isabel wore the green gown she wore when he first saw her. He liked the way the fabric moved as she walked, giving slight hints to the form of her body beneath.

"My mother taught me a lot about herbs when I was younger," Isabel said. "I think God gave us herbs so we can take care of ourselves. I've seen it with animals. If a horse is sick, it seeks out certain plants like dandelion and nettle. If we pay attention, we can learn from them."

"What happened to your mother?"

Isabel appeared lost in thought for a moment and then smiled as if touched by a happy memory. "My mother was very beautiful. I loved her beyond all measure of words. Yet, God saw fit to call her to heaven. She died giving birth to a son."

"I'm sorry. I shouldn't have asked."

"There is nothing to be sorry for. That was five years ago. I was angry with God for a time. Father said God's need was greater than mine and I should be happy Mother was in heaven. I didn't want to believe that because I was sad and lonely. I wondered how God could do such a cruel thing. Father told me that even the wisest priest isn't able to explain God's will. What happens to us may seem to be good or evil. But, who are we to say which it is or why? It's God's will."

"Is it that simple? I mean, did God forgive you for being angry with Him?"

"It was hard to argue with God and not feel selfish. Once I figured that out, I confessed my sin and did my penance. I believe God has forgiven me."

Isabel's response sounded too simple to be true. His own mother died when he was two. He wasn't old enough to remember what it was like to have loved his mother and then lose her to God's will. Thomas wondered if God could forgive him as He must have forgiven Isabel. The thought encouraged him. He knew then that he had to find a priest, but not yet. His misery felt too comfortable. He changed the subject.

"How do you get your vegetables to the market? I saw no horse or cart by your cottage."

"The village cares for several horses. Everyone gets to use them. And Beatrice lets us use her cart. We usually get to Bristow every few weeks. Last week we went on Thursday and Saturday. I'm so glad we did because we had the chance to meet." Isabel took Thomas's hand in hers and squeezed it. She bit her lower lip.

The touch of her hand and the acceptance reflected in her eyes made him forget the effort he expended to maintain his despair. His gaze traveled to her irresistible lips. He wanted to kiss her. He leaned toward her.

Isabel pulled away, a giddy smile brightened her face. "The baker's shop is over there," she said as she ran ahead, tugging on Thomas's arm. "The baker likes sage so maybe we can make a good trade for the herbs."

The baker indeed appreciated the offer of herbs. Isabel convinced him to take all they had for three large loaves. Outside the bakery, they noticed a crowd of people congregated in front of the church. An Augustinian canon dressed in a white robe and mantle stood on the top step talking to the crowd. As they neared, Thomas recognized the canon as one of those in residence at St. Augustine's Abbey.

"We must gather this Sunday for a special mass," the canon said. "All the churches around Bristow are holding masses for protection from the evil pestilence that lays waste to sinners in foreign lands. God's vengeance is coming. We must prepare ourselves and be righteous in all things. Only with prayer and rejecting our sinful ways will God save us from the scourge that has afflicted so many. Repent and seek absolution of your sins. Spread the word. Everyone must come and hear the message of your priest."

Murmuring spread through the crowd. The sound grew louder as more people joined in.

Isabel pulled at Thomas's hand. "You must stay with us. There are too many sinners in Bristow. I've seen the way people ignore God's commandments. You'll not be safe there. You'll be overcome by the bad humors. We must get home and tell Father."

Thomas thought of his own father and Abbot Michael. He wondered if they were safe, if they prayed for absolution. He resisted Isabel's tug. Maybe he should seek forgiveness for his own sins.

Isabel tugged harder. "We must go. Father will know what to do."

Thomas wavered. He looked into Isabel's eyes and saw her fear. He wanted to comfort her, but he also wanted to make his confession. If he stayed to confess, Isabel would know the unspeakable thing he did. She might not understand. Yet, she also had been angry with God. He searched for the courage to say something.

"Please!" Isabel pleaded, her face contorted by the power of fear that filled the church yard.

He relented. "Yes. I'm sorry."

Striguil Castle, Chepstow, Wales

Andrew spent the night in the guard's lodgings at Striguil Castle. The men slept on thin straw-filled ticks, side-by-side, in the cramped space of their ground floor room. A chorus of loud snores offered little to help pass the night and ease the soreness of his workout. The stuffy air hung thick with the odor of sweat, old leather, and straw. His body ached all over, but he refused to wear his discomfort on his face. Determined to prove his stamina, he got up early to tend to the cart of wool.

When he returned from dealing with the colorful merchant, he charged into his training with the zeal of a heretic. He and Eudo spent the afternoon slashing away at the training pole.

"Your swing is too choppy," Eudo scolded. "Follow through. You need to learn to take the blows and recover. Your opponent is not going to wait for you to catch your balance."

Andrew sighed and moaned under his breath. A series of swings followed, all ineffective.

"Stop! Every swing has to mean something. You attack or you defend."

Andrew tried again.

"Good. With practice, you will learn the correct force. It is not necessary to use all your effort with every swing. Once your muscles learn to respond without thinking, then you can work on deception, forcing your opponent to make the ward or counter-ward you choose. The last move we will work on is the longpoint."

"The longpoint?" Andrew cocked his head.

"That is the thrust. You must know when to use it and you must know which ward is best against it. Master that and your chances of walking away alive are much improved. Now try again."

Andrew concentrated on sweeping blows and the impact of the metal blade on the hard, wooden pole. The rebound jolted his hand and arm up to his shoulder, through his chest, and all the way to the pit of his stomach. The sword became an extension of his body.

Before supper, Eudo played the part of the training pole. A moving target increased the challenge, but Andrew maintained his focus. His determination to defeat any threat drove his resolve.

"That is better," Eudo said. "Now, let us try a sequence of moves. The order is important. Pay attention to who dominates. When you dominate the fight, you perform the attack and then the counter-ward."

That evening, as the men sat outside their quarters chewing on salted pork, several of the guards encouraged Andrew to join their company. "I saw how you gave Eudo a good fight," Bran said. "None of us can hold up like that."

"Sword fighting is fun," Andrew said. "But I'm not sure if I want to join the guard."

At that moment, Eudo walked up to join his men. "You may think sword fighting is fun during practice, but you will get no satisfaction from killing a man."

St. Augustine's Abbey, Bristow, England

Lord Geoffrey de Parr slept little—first chills, then sweats. Dawn came too early to his room in the guest house of St. Augustine's Abbey. His headache lingered and several times during the night he had to run to the window to vomit. His coughing got worse. When the bouts went on for any length of time, his chest hurt like being pierced by an arrow.

He needed to get dressed to attend mass and then find something to eat. The thought of food made him run to the window again. This time, he saw blood in what little vomit he expelled.

He took a damp rag to wipe his face. The relief of the cool cloth led him to feel his forehead; it was hot to the touch. A bout of coughing ensued. He used the rag to cover his mouth and muffle the sound. When the coughing subsided, he spotted blood on the rag. A deep horror permeated his entire being. *I have it. The pestilence has taken me. Lord forgive me.*

He had to find a priest to confess and ask forgiveness for his sins. To lose his soul to the great deceiver frightened him to the core of his beliefs.

His knees buckled. Another coughing spell racked his body with excruciating pain. He crawled to the door, reached for the latch, but missed. He lay for a moment then raised himself to try again. The door opened. His mind slipped into a haze of muddled thought as he crawled into the hallway. "My dearest Katherine, I did my best to protect our boys, but I failed." He shouted for help. "Dear Lord, forgive my sins. I repent."

Abbot Michael stood outside the guest house. He waited for Searle to cross the inner courtyard. "There is nothing more we can do for him," Abbot Michael said as Searle approached. "Lord Parr has received the blessing of the sick and last rites, but he has been unable to confess. I pray demons have not possessed him. I believe he truly wants to confess."

"This came so suddenly," Searle said. "He seemed fine yesterday. The stories, then, are true. This great mortality of man has finally come to us. Is there nowhere safe from its evil intent? We pray for forgiveness and still it comes." Searle's shoulders slumped.

"Do not despair, Searle. God knows the righteous among us. Those who seek to confess their sins and repent will be secure in the protection of Jesus Christ, our Lord and Savior. 'As I live, saith the Lord God, I desire not the death of the wicked, but that the wicked may turn from this way and live.' God is truly merciful. We must believe."

"I want to believe that, Father Abbot. But is there hope?" Searle's face was drawn.

"There is always hope." Abbot Michael folded his hands. "It is faith that we must be careful not to lose, faith in the divine will of God. We do not always know or even understand his will. But without faith, we are lost. Our souls will fall prey to the evil one. Keep your faith, and God will always be with you."

"Your words are a comfort. I pray that Lord Parr has found peace."

"I am sure he has. He is an honorable man. Has there been word of Thomas?"

"I fear he is no longer in Bristow."

"Thomas is in God's hands now. We must pray that God will grant him the wisdom to know what he must do."

"It pains me to say that I must go back to Striguil Castle. The countess's business awaits. I cannot ignore my duties. This morning, I arranged for the sale of all of the wool stored in the cellars. The countess will see to it that you receive payment."

"Thank you, Searle. I am glad that business is finished." Abbot Michael reached out and patted Searle's shoulder.

"I have left word with the men at the warehouse to keep watch for Master Thomas. Should he return there, the men are to send word to me in Chepstow. I will pass on the information to you."

"When must you leave?"

"As soon as I can arrange a long boat. When I last spoke to the sheriff, he refused to believe the truth behind the rumors of the pestilence." Searle's voice grew louder and more agitated. "It will not be long before others are found to be afflicted. Then panic will spread throughout Bristow. The special masses planned for Sunday may come too late."

"Let us pray that such events do not play out as you say."

"I am sorry, Father Abbot. I should not let the sheriff's lack of action frustrate me. Do you have any messages that I may pass on to the abbey?"

"Yes. That would be most kind of you. Brother Samuel must be told what has happened. I will wait at least another week to see if Thomas returns. Abbot Ralph may need help with the sick if it comes to that. And I will need to send a message to Lord Parr's eldest son, Robert. If I go to Kendalwood myself, I will let you know. God be with you, Searle." Abbot Michael made the sign of the cross. "In nómine Pátris, et Fílii, et Spíritus Sáncti. Amen."

Confident in divine protection, Abbot Michael returned to Lord Parr's room to sit in vigil over the body and soul of his friend. He left the door and window open to allow the bad humors to blow away.

Lord Parr continued to moan and wheeze. Abbot Michael moved his chair closer to the bed. In the silence, he bowed and prayed.

The sky grew dark as night approached. He placed cool rags on Lord Parr's forehead, but they failed to rouse him. After a bout of coughing, Lord Parr made a soft groaning sound. Moments later, the wheezing ceased.

The pestilence took another life.

Chapter
NINETEEN

Filton, England, Friday, August 1, 1348

Thomas pretended to be asleep while Isabel and Hugh got up to pray between first and second sleep.

"Thomas," Isabel whispered. "Will you join us for prayers?"

He ignored her. His thoughts were stuck replaying the conversation with Hugh when he and Isabel returned from the village church the day before. Hugh became as fearful as Isabel when they told him of the special mass to be said on Sunday. He forbade Thomas from returning to Bristow. "The evil humors will seek out the innocent," he had said. Every time Thomas found the courage to speak up about his running off spiteful of God, Isabel or Hugh interrupted and fed him reasons to stay. The prospect of staying with Isabel won the day. Thomas pushed away his guilt and embraced the vision of one day lying next to Isabel—an experience he once believed might never be realized.

After Hugh and Isabel finished praying, they returned to their bed and the dark silence returned. Time passed slowly as Thomas wrestled with whether to ask God for forgiveness. He longed for the physical exhaustion that carried him away the night before. It came as no surprise, then, when a disturbing dream finally imposed itself on his restless sleep.

Thomas stood in front of the church in Filton, its stone tower rose above the surrounding landscape like a banner. A thunderous clang of bells called the parishioners to service. When the people arrived, they shoved him aside and filed into the church. They chanted, "William is dead. Where is his brother?"

"I'm here," he said. But no one paid him any mind. The crowd packed the church and continued their chant. Then, a single voice, an evil voice that brought shivers down his spine, spoke above the others, the words like shards of death. Quiet prevailed. In dark tones, the evil voice resumed the chant, "William is dead. Where is his brother?" The congregation echoed the words in unison like a practiced response to an invocation.

The cruel voice then cried out, "We must find him."

Thomas ran from the church as a black fog poured out of the doors and windows, the sinful essence of a thousand lost souls unworthy of heaven. From the fog, a new chant arose, "An innocent. An innocent." The fog chased him. He found refuge in a tattered cottage that looked exactly like Hugh's. Only, the inside of the cottage was as large as the nave at St. Augustine's Abbey. Sitting on a grand dais where the altar should be, an evil presence, cloaked in blackness and ancient death, held a gavel. With a loud bang, it proclaimed, "You have sinned. I claim your soul."

Thomas collapsed to his knees. Regret stabbed him in the chest. "Forgive me Lord," he cried out.

"It is too late for that. You are mine. I am the evil that covers this land in misery."

Thomas's body shrunk to the size of a pea in the presence of evil. He fell into a crack between the tiles of the floor. Above, he heard shouts. "I will find you. You cannot hide."

The glow of first light broke his sleep and ended the dream. He sat up with a start. Isabel and Hugh lay sleeping. He listened to their gentle breathing and his own respiration calmed, but the memory of the dream chant remained. He shivered as a cool breeze blew in through the window above him. The chill air urged him to get up and tend to nature's business.

Rather than returning to his bed, he sat cross-legged by the fire pit and tried to think on the meaning of his dream. What was it about these dreams that forced him to confront evil? What did it mean? Why did he lack the courage to fight back? It was natural to flee from evil, wasn't it? Perhaps Satan found a way to steal his soul from within his dreams. The slow creak of the door brought him to attention. Hugh came to start the morning fire.

"There you are. God's blessings, Thomas."

"Greetings, sir."

"Did the talk of the pestilence keep you awake? I hope you can see it is best to stay away from such evil."

"I was thinking of my father and Abbot Michael."

"Did you not tell them where you went? I am sure they will send for you when your brother arrives, no?"

Thomas swallowed hard. His sins mounted as he again thought to twist the truth. The way out came to him. "Yes. You are right. They will send for me." He repeated the words in his mind to remember the story he told. If his father knew where he was, word would come. It wasn't a lie. He didn't have to return to Bristow unless asked. He could stay with Isabel.

"It is settled then." Hugh looked at the clouds above. "Praise the Lord, Thomas. Your presence has turned our fortunes for the better. See. The sky is clearing once again."

Thomas smiled in acknowledgement, too ashamed to contradict Hugh's delight. How can a sinner bring good fortune?

All day Friday and Saturday Thomas helped Isabel tend the vegetable rows and collect herbs. He often thought of the garden at Tintern Abbey. The work at the monastery dragged on and frustrated him, while gardening with Isabel was much more productive and enjoyable. He also adored the soothing sound of Isabel's voice as she talked about the different plants.

The longer he remained with Isabel, his desire grew greater to stay. He saw no comparison to life at Tintern Abbey. The Holy Spirit required a belief in something intangible. Isabel's spirit manifested itself in physical form. Thomas ached with a longing to hold not a belief, but a beautiful woman.

"Are we going to the special mass tomorrow?" Thomas asked Hugh over a supper of newly made pottage cooked with fresh long beans and onions.

"It is what we have been called to do. We must do our part to help keep the pestilence away. We must pray for sinners and for our own salvation. God will forgive those who turn from evil and repent. Is that not what the canon said?"

"How do we know that will save us?" Thomas poked at his pottage with his spoon.

"It is God's will that such things happen, Thomas. You should know this. Those who are evil will perish in the flames of hell."

Thomas closed his eyes and thought of William. William was not evil. He must have died of something other than the pestilence, some other sickness that God saw fit to give him. *Why did William have to die? Was it truly God's will?*

In the silence of the moment, Isabel spoke up. "We must believe that God will save us. We are taught that all things are the will of God. Then it must be that the pestilence is God's will. There must be so much evil in the world that this is the only way for God to cleanse it for the pure of heart."

Thomas nodded. He dared not reveal his fear at attending the service without first making his confession. His stomach churned. There seemed to be no way to avoid going to church.

"Isabel is right," Hugh agreed. "We must believe. Our prayers will be answered. God will save us. After the service, Thomas, we will make a frame for your bed."

Striguil Castle, Chepstow, Wales, Saturday, August 2, 1348

Andrew sat with Eudo near the kitchen cellar on the landing that over-looked the River Wye. They took a break from training to have a mid-day meal of soup and bread. The view captured the serenity of the fast-flowing river and the forested landscape of Gloucester to the east.

All was quiet until Searle thundered down the stone stairs. Struggling for breath, he said, "I am glad I found you."

"Did everything go well with the wool?" Eudo asked.

"I am sad to say things did not go well. I need to get word to the abbey. Abbot Michael will be delayed."

"Delayed?" Andrew asked. "Is Thomas staying with him?"

"Master Thomas has run off, and we have been unable to find him."

"What do you mean, 'run off?'" Andrew stood up, spilling his soup.

"It has been unsettling. When Master Thomas learned that Sir William died—"

"Thomas's brother is dead?" Andrew interrupted.

"He became upset and ran off. It is possible that Thomas does not know that his father also died."

"Thomas's father too? How can this be?" Andrew sat down with a thud. He looked at Eudo and then back to Searle. "Is anyone looking for Thomas?"

"I am sorry, Andrew. In my rush I forgot Thomas is your friend."

Andrew jumped to his feet. "I want to help look for him."

Searle held up his hand. "Many are looking for him. The most important thing at the moment is to get word to the abbey." He finished relating the circumstances surrounding Crawford and the wool and the likelihood that the pestilence had come to England. "Brother Samuel needs to be informed. I dislike having to put this on you, Andrew. Someone must go. Given the light remaining, please take one of the horses. You may return tomorrow."

"But I want to go to Bristow."

Eudo put his hand on Andrew's shoulder. "Now is not the time. Searle is right. Someone must get word to Brother Samuel. We will talk tomorrow."

Andrew ran to the guard's lodgings to retrieve his satchel. Bran helped him saddle a horse for the short ride to Tintern Abbey. More than ever, he wished he could have gone with Thomas. He knew it was unrealistic to think so. All the same, he wished it.

Vespers had already started by the time Andrew arrived at the monastery. He paced under the arcade in the main cloister while he waited for the service to end. Occasionally, he sat on one of the stone benches, but his unbounded energy kept him from sitting still for any length of time.

The clang of the latch on the heavy oak door jarred his attention. The monks, dressed in their undyed woolen habits and black scapulars, filed out of the church in pairs. Near the end of the line, Brother Samuel ambled along, the flop of his sandals unmistakable among the patter of quieter feet. Andrew waved.

Brother Samuel put his finger to his lips and motioned toward the parlor.

"What is it you wish to say?" Brother Samuel asked, once he closed the door behind them.

"I have urgent tidings from Abbot Michael." Andrew's narration rushed through the high points of events like a stone skipping on the surface of a lake. Brother Samuel had to ask several times that he slow down and repeat his words.

"Thank you for speaking to me in private about this." Brother Samuel wiped a tear from his eyes and rested a hand on Andrew's shoulder. "We must have faith in God that Thomas will be safe. I know how much his friendship means to you. Be comforted to know he feels the same."

The excitement in Andrew's voice continued. "May I go to Trelleck Grange? I want to speak to Brother Gilbert about helping to search for Thomas."

"That is noble of you. But let us not run too quickly into danger ourselves. I am sure Abbot Michael is doing everything he can. We must give him a chance."

"Thomas doesn't know how to take care of himself."

"If the pestilence has truly come to England, you will not help Thomas if you fall under its evil influence. Have patience. After you return with the cart tomorrow, you may go to Trelleck Grange. Brother Gilbert will need you to salvage what we can from this poor harvest. God will hear our prayers. I will inform the rest of the brethren so that we may pray for God's forgiveness. At mass on Sunday, we will also pray for the repose of the souls of Sir William and Lord Geoffrey de Parr and ask God to help Thomas find his way."

"As you wish." Andrew gritted his teeth and slammed the door to the parlor as he left.

Chapter
TWENTY

Filton, England, Sunday, August 3, 1348

"Hurry with your pottage, Thomas," Hugh said, as he cocked his head to the clang of church bells. "We will be late."

Thomas took his time chewing his morning pottage. He had stalled as long as he could. There was nothing more he could do to avoid the special mass at Filton's parish church. He had to go. Hugh led the way from their primitive campfire as they joined other villagers along the path to the village square. Isabel held tight to Thomas's arm.

"Greetings Beatrice," Thomas said.

Beatrice waved. "Lovely morning," she said to Jane and Walter, her neighbors to the north.

"Yes, it is," Jane said. "But clouds are headed this way." She tugged Walter's arm making him walk faster.

Thomas held back as people assembled on the west side of the church. The hum of muted voices abounded; people exchanged quick nods. The crowd shuffled forward up the stone steps, bodies packed together like sheep in winter.

"The nave is not large enough for all these people," Hugh said.

Thomas tried to say he agreed, but his mouth was too dry.

Forward motion slowed as they approached the door. Thomas allowed others to pass. God would not forgive him unless he confessed his sins. He thought he may yet avoid entering the church. But, at the last moment, the way gave and the three of them slipped past the threshold.

"Please, my children. Remain quiet so all can hear," the priest began. "By now, I am sure you have heard of the strange illness, a great and evil pestilence, which has come upon foreign lands. Sinners there die in dreadful numbers. That same pestilence now threatens England. Do not despair. This is a sign from the most merciful and almighty God who seeks to turn you from your sinful ways. God is angry at your wickedness. Too long have you ignored confession. Too long have you strayed from the righteous path that is God's will. The pestilence is God's means to rid the world of sinners. As the Bible teaches us, God has sent many plagues upon the earth. You must believe that God does this to cleanse the world. He is trying to save you. By confessing your sins and doing penance, you prepare yourselves for eternal life. Just as the people of Nineveh were saved by performing penance, so too must you seek God's forgiveness in prayer and penitential processions."

A burst of murmurs interrupted the momentary silence. Parishioners glanced around, their heads bobbing as waves breaking a calm sea.

The priest continued, "You must pray every day to ask God for his forgiveness and for the salvation of all sinners. On every Wednesday and Friday, I will lead a procession around the village. We will start and end here at the church with readings from Psalms. As you walk along the procession, you will remain peaceful while reciting the Lord's Prayer and repeating the Hail Mary as often as you can. At various points, I will offer prayers and a message. Everyone who participates in the processions will be granted an indulgence of forty days. You must set aside your worldly duties. Come repentant with bare feet and bowed heads."

Whispers grew louder. Worried looks darted from person to person. Somewhere amid the crush of humanity, a small child cried. That cry sparked others on the verge of fear to let loose cries to God for forgiveness. Near the front of the church—where there was room—desperate souls went prostrate, begging God for mercy.

The priest called out, "Be still, my children. God hears your righteous pleas." He led the congregation in a recital of Psalms and, in time, a unified chant took hold.

After several more verses, the priest started his sermon. "To sin is to turn from God. To be free of sin is to embrace God. When you live a life free of sin, God's love will reward you with bountiful blessings. When you sin, God's wrath will destroy you. Your soul will be lost to Satan and you will burn in the fires of hell forever. If you repent and truly seek God's forgiveness, you will be saved. Our Lord, Jesus Christ, forged the way for all sinners. Confess your sins. By your confession, God's mercy will be granted to us all and the evil pestilence will pass. You must live righteous lives and honor God's commandments, or all will suffer the perils of Satan's influence."

Parishioners stood mesmerized by the drone of the priest's rhetoric. The sermon continued long after Thomas felt an ache in his legs and feet. If the priest intended to put fear into the hearts of his flock, it appeared he succeeded. But Thomas lacked faith in God's power to save anyone from the evils of the pestilence. If God failed to save William, why would God save anyone else?

After they left the church, Hugh struck up a conversation with Beatrice. While they talked, Thomas led Isabel to a nearby oak tree. He looked into her eyes. In that moment, he saw a reason to hope that God could save someone from the pestilence. If Isabel became afflicted, he would stay with her and do anything to save her. He put his arms around her and held her tight.

She relaxed in his arms.

Strange feelings puzzled him—feelings of care for someone other than himself. He felt a powerful urge to give himself to another, to Isabel. He tilted his head and kissed her. She did not resist. The sweetness of her supple lips took away the bitterness of William's death. Her warm body and tender heart soothed his soul.

"There is something I must do, Isabel," Thomas said.

"What is it?" Her face flushed.

"The priest was right. I have ignored confession for too long. I must make amends. Go home with your father. I'll be along as soon as I can."

Thomas returned to the church to find the priest. "Father, my name is Thomas de Parr. I'm a visitor to your parish, but I hope to make this my home. Your words today inspired me to ask, in the name of the Lord, that you hear my confession."

"That is wonderful to hear, my son," the priest said. "I am Father Lawrence Grey. Welcome to our parish. Come, let us sit."

"Forgive me, Father. I haven't made a confession in over three months. I, a sinful creature, acknowledge my guilt and sins, both deadly and venially, with all my heart and mouth to Almighty God, to the Blessed Saint Mary, to the holy saints of heaven, and to my Ghostly Father. I took the name of the Lord in vain and cursed Him in my selfishness, and I spoke lies when I knew the truth. I repent and ask for forgiveness and mercy." Thomas told Father Lawrence about his reaction to William's death and how he pushed away the thought of God as a source of comfort.

"Having a loved one move on from this world is never easy," Father Lawrence said. "But it is at such times that communion with the Lord is most important. You rejected Him and lost your way. Let that be a lesson to never turn from the Lord. Do you know the Lord's Prayer and the Hail Mary?"

"Yes, Father."

"Your sin against God was grievous. Yet, I see cause to consider the conditions that led to your sinful acts. You are young, and your heart is strong. You come willingly to seek God's mercy and I see in you a true desire to repent. For your penance you will walk around the village square and church yard for the rest of the afternoon barefoot, head bowed, and hands folded while repeating the Lord's Prayer. If you join the processions, you may reclaim your shoes on Friday. This is the public penance you must make to atone for your willful rejection of God and the lies you have spoken out of pride. Each morning until then, you will recite quietly to yourself both the Lord's Prayer and the Hail Mary ten times. This is the private penance offered between you and God so that He may see good cause to grant you forgiveness."

Thomas forgot the last time he walked as far barefoot. His soles were as soft as his honesty. Reciting the Lord's Prayer helped him concentrate on something other than the pain. He raised his head once he reached Hugh's cottage. The bed frame sat finished by the door.

Isabel pointed at his bare feet. "Thomas, your shoes, where are they?"

Thomas's face was expressionless as he disregarded the pain. His voice was strained, almost monotone. "They're at the church. It's part of my penance."

Isabel ran to Thomas and hugged him. "Your feet are swollen. We must wash and soak them in cool water. Father, bring one of those buckets."

Isabel helped Thomas to the nearest stump and then, with great care, washed his feet.

"Here, this should take the swelling down." Isabel put Thomas's feet in the bucket of cool water and added crushed lavender to remove the bad humors. "We finished your bed. Beatrice gave us enough canvas, so we can make a tick for you."

"I'm ashamed to tell you that I haven't been truthful about why I came to visit." Thomas swallowed hard and grabbed hold of his thighs to steady his hands. "Do you mind taking a rest while I tell you my story?"

"You need not to tell us anything, Thomas," Hugh said. "Whatever your reasons for coming, they are between you and God. We are just glad you found your way here to us. We love you as you are."

"Thank you, sir. I must be honest, or I'll never be able to love myself, let alone offer the love I feel for Isabel." Thomas looked at Isabel and managed a slight smile, the sincerest he could make.

Isabel blushed. She held Thomas's hand.

Thomas told Isabel and Hugh every detail that led up to his arrival to Filton. When the story ended, a relief beyond imagination cleared his mind and settled his spirit.

"I love you too," Isabel said. "I can see that the innocence I first saw in your beautiful blue eyes has returned."

"My father will have left Bristow to take William's body back to Kendalwood and Abbot Michael will have returned to Tintern Abbey," Thomas continued, his voice steadier as the cool water soothed his feet. "When we go to market, I'll ask Abbot Ralph or the men at the countess's warehouse if they might relay a message. Until then, there's no need for me to go to Bristow and risk the evil humors of the pestilence. I need to participate in the prayers and processions to complete my penance."

"I'm very happy that you want to stay with us." Isabel leaned over and kissed him on the cheek.

"You are welcome to stay as long as you wish, Thomas," Hugh said. "I think you will find Isabel a perceptive woman. Any man who wishes to marry her would be wise to listen to what she says."

"Father, please." Isabel giggled.

Chapter
TWENTY-ONE

Striguil Castle, Chepstow, Wales, Sunday, August 3, 1348

Andrew saddled his borrowed horse and left for Striguil Castle after morning mass. All through the service, his only thought was how to get to Bristow. Even if fear of the pestilence drove people to flee, there had to be a way to get there. When he arrived at the castle, he found Searle talking with Bran in the lower bailey. He heard the word "pestilence" and then Bran marched away with a scowl.

"Greetings, Andrew. Many thanks for delivering Abbot Michael's message."

"Are ships still sailing to Bristow?"

"I believe so," Searle said with a quizzical look. "But, that may change if the pestilence spreads and more people become ill. Why do you ask?"

"I want to help search for Thomas."

"Your offer is honorable, Andrew. But as I said yesterday, many people are already looking for him."

Andrew's jaw tightened. He didn't want to hear excuses. "Thomas might already be in trouble."

"I understand. But we must wait for further word from Abbot Michael. He may need your help if he goes to Kendalwood. Until we know his plans, the danger of the pestilence is too great."

"But—"

"I will let you know if word of Thomas comes to me. I may need to return to Bristow in a few weeks."

"May I go with you, then?"

"Patience. Going to Bristow is not a trip I favor."

Annoyed at Searle's lack of aid, Andrew stomped off to the stable. His thoughts too unsettled to train with Eudo, he retrieved the abbey's horse and cart and began the slow and bumpy ride home. On the way back to Tintern Abbey, he wondered what Thomas must be thinking, alone and unprotected. Why wouldn't anyone help him get to Bristow?

At the abbey's stable, he unhitched the cart and led his horse into a stall. As he removed the bridle, two lay brothers walked up and stood outside the open door. Apparently unaware of his presence, they spoke in hushed tones. Andrew froze to listen to the conversation.

"He said special masses are being called," Brother Elias said.

Brother Leofwin's voice noticeably louder and tinged with surprise said, "Where?"

"The merchant did not say. He was looking for grain. Poor harvests are everywhere. I told him we have nothing to sell."

"Where is the pestilence now?"

"He said there are rumors it has come to England."

"Already?"

"Not so loud."

Andrew crouched in the stall and remained quiet.

Brother Elias continued. "We must pray for God's forgiveness."

The brothers moved away, their conversation too distant for Andrew to understand. Searle must be correct; the pestilence has come to Bristow. Hopefully, Thomas ran from the city. Then, he'd be safe. But there was still danger, wasn't there? Andrew hated thinking so much. To clear his thoughts, he set out for Trelleck Grange at a quick pace.

Brother Gilbert sat at a small grinding stone near the manor house, sharpening the blade of a scythe. Sparks flew from the whirling wheel and the screech of metal oscillated with the speed of his foot pumping the pedal. He poured water on the stone and lifted his brown robe over his knees. "Welcome back, son. Did you learn anything from Eudo?"

Andrew sat on the ground beside Brother Gilbert and told him about his days in Chepstow and tidings from Bristow. Brother Gilbert's feet came to a halt when Andrew got to the part about Sir William's and Lord Parr's deaths.

"Dear Lord, have mercy on their souls." Brother Gilbert bowed and crossed himself. "Such a tragedy for Thomas. I'm sorry you had to be the one to relay the message."

"I need to go help look for Thomas."

Brother Gilbert put his hand on Andrew's shoulder. "I understand. It's what I'd want to do. But I sense there's something else that troubles you?"

"Brother Samuel wants me to wait until we hear from Abbot Michael. That might be another week or more. And Searle wants to wait at least a fortnight." Andrew plucked a handful grass and threw it.

"Yes. Caution is a difficult answer. But, I'd have to agree with them on this."

Andrew groaned.

Brother Gilbert held up his hand. "Hear me out. Sometimes we have to let our friends find their own way in the world. I can only guess at the reasons why Thomas ran off and what keeps him away. If you want to help him, then give him the time to figure out what it is that troubles him. Many things can change what's important. In time, he'll no doubt need you and that's when you must be there for him."

"But what if he needs me now? The pestilence—"

"Patience."

"How can I be patient when the pestilence may overtake Bristow at any time?"

"I know this is hard. The future is never predictable. I thought I'd die in battle serving a mortal master in war. But here I am, serving God and talking with you. Look to your feelings. If there's no word from Thomas, you'll know when it's time to leave. Then, I'll support your decision."

Andrew took a deep breath and exhaled slowly. He had never disobeyed Brother Gilbert before. How could he? Had it not been for Brother Gilbert, he likely would have died on the streets of Chepstow years ago. Against all his inner turmoil, he resolved to wait.

Brother Gilbert led them in a prayer: "Merciful God, we commit to Thy care the souls of Sir William and Lord Geoffrey de Parr. We ask Thee to let them pass through purgatory. Send Thy angels to guide them and usher them into paradise. We also ask Thee to protect the humble spirit of Thy servant, Thomas, as he seeks to find his way. Through Christ our Lord. Amen."

Andrew decided to let go and let God's will play out. After all, he accused Thomas of thinking too much. He needed to follow his own advice.

Bristow, England

The special Sunday masses in Bristow brought varying degrees of panic and resignation. For the most part, the panic manifested as wailing, zealous commitment to penance, and prostration before the altar. Only a few people ran into the streets intent on seeing the end of the world and looking for ways to hasten it. The sheriff's men put a quick stop to these displays.

After several days of sun, the rain clouds returned to cloak the city in a veil of gloom. Abbot Michael took care as he traveled from church to church looking to offer assistance to the overworked priests. He perceived a change in the mood of the town. People averted eye contact and passed each other at a distance, sometimes choosing to step in mud or manure rather than risk physical contact.

Back at St. Augustine's Abbey church, Abbot Michael knelt in the quiet of the Elder Lady Chapel. He prayed over the choice before him: to stay or to go see Robert de Parr, now the Lord of Kendalwood. Robert had to be told, but the people of Bristow needed spiritual guidance. Conflicted between his desire to help and the duty he owed the family of his friend of many years, he listened to the chants of the Augustinian monks as they recited the Psalms. When vespers ended, he sought out Abbot Ralph.

"I regret that I cannot stay to help you with all the people seeking comfort. I have prayed long about this and I feel the matter may no longer wait. I must be the one who relates the ill tidings to Robert."

Abbot Ralph clutched the gold cross that hung around his neck. "I understand. I am thankful for the time you have spent helping with the needy. Please advise Robert that there is no hurry for him to decide on Lord Parr's and Sir William's final resting places. And we will honor Lord Parr's request for masses to be said in their names."

"I am sure Robert will appreciate that. It troubles me that I must leave without knowing Thomas's fate. I would like to return to St. Augustine's as soon as I can."

"Do you think that wise now that the pestilence is seeking lost souls in Bristow?"

"I am concerned. But, the world cannot stop while the pestilence does its savage work. I owe it to Lord Parr to find his son. Maybe, if enough time passes, Thomas will let us know where he is. He will then need our help accepting his father's death. Our prayers must be unfeigned. We must trust in God to keep us safe, so we may go about His business. We cannot hide in fear. That will only feed the power of the evil one."

"We will continue to pray. God's blessings to you, my dear friend. May our Lord Jesus Christ watch over you and protect you on your journey." Abbot Ralph gestured a blessing. "I bid you peace."

Bristow, England, Monday, August 4, 1348

Abbot Michael walked along the Welsh Back, looking for anyone traveling to Chepstow. Most wouldn't acknowledge his presence as they quickly went about their business of loading or unloading cargo. He approached a man who appeared to be set to shove off from the pier. The man gave him a nervous glance.

"Might you be traveling to Chepstow?" Abbot Michael asked.

"I've a load of cloth to deliver to Striguil Castle."

"Then you must know Searle."

The merchant nodded. "You look familiar."

"I am the abbot of Tintern Abbey. I have important business and need transport up the River Wye to Ross. God would look kindly upon any man giving aid during these uncertain times."

"I'm more interested in surviving this pestilence, Father Abbot. But, if offering you the use of my long boat will aid my penance, you are welcome to it."

"Bless you." Abbot Michael made the sign of the cross and climbed into the boat.

By the time he reached Tintern Abbey, the monks had already gathered in the cloister for vespers. An excited Brother Samuel greeted him with an embrace. They ducked into the parlor to speak.

"Praise the Lord," Brother Samuel said. "We have been worried since Andrew came with word about Lord Parr and Sir William. We have said prayers for the repose of their souls at every service since. Is there anything new about Thomas?"

"I am sorry to say that I have learned nothing more about Thomas. It is my feeling he is not far from Bristow. At least, that is what I hope."

"Are you going to Kendalwood?"

"Yes. I will leave in the morning. I may be gone the rest of the week. Then I must return to Bristow."

"But—"

Abbot Michael waved his hand. "I will have no discussion on the matter."

Filton, England

Thomas eased himself onto his new bed. The unevenness of the straw stuffing mattered little as he laid his head on the rough canvas. After a second day of penance, his feet had toughened, and the swelling lessened. Isabel seemed to delight in the task of tending to his discomfort. Sleep and a strange dream soon seized him.

He reached out for Isabel; a look of terror distorted her kind face. He tried to come closer to comfort her, but she drifted away. Then, he stood next to her. He held her tight in his arms. He looked into her eyes as green as a vibrant forest. But she didn't see him; she stared with a blank look as if he wasn't there. His arms vanished, and she walked away. His legs disappeared; he couldn't follow. Only sight remained as he watched her fade into an approaching cloud of blackness. He forced his body forward. His legs returned. But when he ran to follow her, he remained in place. Suddenly, he found himself standing on a rock in the middle of empty space. A dark void hovered around him in all directions.

"There is no escape from me now," a voice said.

With one foot poised over the edge, the dream ended.

Jolted awake, Thomas shivered as he reached for his blanket tangled at his feet. He lay awake for a long while as he tried to make sense of the dream. Yet the more he thought about it, the less he wanted to understand the meaning.

Tintern Abbey, Wales, Tuesday, August 5, 1348

Andrew woke early to rouse the oarsmen tasked with taking Abbot Michael to Kendalwood. He hadn't been able to speak to Abbot Michael about Thomas and this seemed his best chance.

"Thank you, Andrew, for seeing to things this morning. I hope to be back on Friday."

"Do you think we'll hear from Thomas?"

"Brother Samuel told me of your concern. I am concerned as well. Do not be discouraged. I believe Thomas is stronger than we allow. When he is ready, he will come to us."

"That's what Brother Gilbert said."

"Brother Gilbert speaks wisely. Please take heed of his advice."

"I miss him."

"Your devotion is commendable. For now, your prayers will serve him best."

"As you wish, Father Abbot. God be with you."

Andrew helped Abbot Michael onto the pier and into the long boat. He stood and watched until the boat rounded the bend. While he still felt uneasy about staying, God seemed to be telling him to wait—for now. He could live with that decision.

Chapter
TWENTY-TWO

Filton, England, Wednesday, August 6, 1348

The village procession started at sunrise with Psalms recited in the nave of Filton's parish church. Some parishioners came dressed in sack cloth. Some of the men, stripped to the waist, covered themselves in ashes. Everyone was barefoot. Overnight rain left the ground cool and damp.

Father Lawrence led the parishioners around the perimeter of the village in a solemn line three abreast. Thomas walked between Isabel and Hugh. He allowed God's spirit to cloak him in divine armor against the evils of the pestilence. He resolved to fight the plague with all his soul and never again let Satan find a weakness and cause him to sin. Four times the group stopped to say prayers. Father Lawrence encouraged atonement. The penitents circled back to the church yard to recite more Psalms and sing the litanies.

When Thomas and his new family returned to the little cottage at the edge of the village, he helped Isabel with the midday pottage. As Isabel said grace, he gladly joined. Filled with earthly nourishment and God's blessings, Thomas felt safe from the pestilence and more at ease than he had ever felt. A fleeting image of Tintern Abbey flashed in his mind. It seemed odd that he had gone all day until now without a thought of the abbey or his soon-to-be life as a monk. Perhaps it was God's will that he stay with Isabel.

Friday, August 8, 1348

Friday saw a repeat performance of the zealous procession. At the end of the service, Thomas retrieved his shoes, confident that God had forgiven his sins. He was whole again.

After he left the church, he saw Isabel and Hugh gathered with a group of people near the Gloucester Road. The crowd surrounded a cart headed north. Thomas joined them. "What's all the ado?" he asked Isabel, who shrugged.

A villein shoved his way through the group to the front. "What talk of the pestilence?" he asked the carter.

"How many deaths?" another shouted from behind.

Interrupted with new questions as he tried to respond, the carter spoke in brief spurts over the din of voices: "There've been deaths—I've no idea how many—Folk are nervous, real cautious about looking at each other—The sheriff won't say if anyone's died of the pestilence—He's got extra guards walking the streets—The processions on Wednesday and earlier today got some folk afraid and wanting to leave—Fewer ships are docking and those that do, don't stay long—I had to wait several days for these goods I'm hauling to Thornbury—I'm glad to get out of there."

The clamor of questions continued. The carter waved them away saying he didn't know anything else. "Watch out!" he yelled. He snapped the reins. People continued to ask if he knew this person or that person. He ignored the questions and kept going.

"Do you think it safe to go to market tomorrow?" Hugh asked Thomas.

"Maybe I should go alone. I must get word to Abbot Michael and my father. You and Isabel stay here. We can all go another day. With all of us participating in the processions the pestilence can't last forever."

"Are you sure?" Isabel asked, she gripped Thomas's arm.

"I'll be fine. I must do this," Thomas said with a new-found confidence that surprised him. Filton was now his home and he wanted to stay.

"If you must," Hugh said. "Take care on the road and keep your gaze away from the eyes of strangers."

Saturday, August 9, 1348

At first light, Thomas rose and went out to the fire pit. He checked the contents of the pot. The pottage was cold, but a few spoonfuls took away the morning hunger. Out of habit, he sat on one of the stumps and said the Lord's Prayer. He wondered if his father recited the prayer at William's grave.

Clouds drew near from the west. It amazed him how Hugh could forecast the weather. Maybe he should pay closer attention now that he wanted to stay. He peered through the window of the cottage as he departed; all was still.

The walking and physical activity of the past week improved his stamina. He managed a steady, unfamiliar pace. The view along the way triggered uneasy memories from the first time he traveled the road.

He regretted the way he treated Abbot Michael. His anger blinded his reason. Isabel helped him see that. She taught him that William's death came as God ordained. God's will needed no explanation. Life itself was a pilgrimage, one step on the journey toward the ultimate goal of perfection and a seat in paradise—a path that everyone must follow.

The flutter of a flock of partridges caught his attention. He crouched low and looked for cover by a large oak tree. Men's voices sounded in the distance. Sturdy limbs within reach made for an easy climb as he scurried up the tree. He tried to remain still as he watched and waited, wedged in a crook of the tree to keep his balance.

Four men tramped along the road. They stopped beneath him. The smell of their sweat drifted into the branches. Thomas measured his breathing to keep as quiet as he could. Arrows rattled like thunder in the quiver slung over the back of the man who carried a bow. At their belts, each man carried a short sword. They wore tattered tunics and leather breeches. The largest man, the one who stood directly below him, swatted at a fly that buzzed his head. Thomas pressed himself into the rough bark and froze as the man looked up to see where the fly had gone.

"Damn fly," the man said.

"Stop fooling around, Jagger," the man with the bow said. "All we've seen today are well armed merchants or fleeing peasants."

"Those peasants should be easy, Dix." Jagger said. "We should stop some. They're bound to have something of value."

"They come in bunches," one of the other men said. "And they scatter. It's too much work to chase them down. Worse, they may have the pestilence."

"Listen," Dix said. He cocked his head. "Horses…and carts. Let's go. There's a better spot down the road where we can check to see if they have guards." He motioned for the men to follow.

Thomas let out a sigh. Carts could mean a merchant caravan, and that may translate to safer roads to the south—at least for a while. Soon, four carts passed by his tree. In each cart, next to the driver, a sword-carrying guard in crisp leather armor watched the road. After the grind of the wheels faded, he climbed down and continued his journey.

Near to Bristow, people who toiled in the fields or stood in front of their cottages kept to themselves. None looked up or acknowledged him as he passed.

He made his way to the bridge that crossed the Frome. The tide was out. Cogs along the Key stood motionless in the muddy riverbed. Crewmen worked on rigging without the usual loud chatter.

The foul stench of mud, urine and rotten food slapped him in the face as he entered the old town. Passersby looked at their feet. Hushed conversations replaced noisy arguments and rambunctious camaraderie. An eerie silence dominated the streets as if death watched from above waiting to snatch anyone who spoke out. Shops along Broad Street were open, but the merchants did not run out to greet customers.

Thomas turned onto Corn Street and paused in front of the Golden Fleece Inn. He remembered a boy full of anger running out the door to an uncertain future. Now he saw his future settled. He wanted a life apart from Tintern Abbey—a life entwined with the beautiful Isabel, the woman he loved.

At St. Nicholas Street, he turned toward the countess's warehouse. No one answered the locked door.

He retraced his steps through the uncrowded streets and headed for the abbey. At the gate, memories of his arrival with Abbot Michael brought a touch of doubt to his choice. Should he give up a life as a monk for Isabel? He shoved the thought aside. The same stableman who met him when he and Abbot Michael first arrived greeted him and led him to the inner gatehouse. "Please wait here," the stableman said. "I believe everyone is in the refectory. Abbot Ralph will be overjoyed to see you."

Moments later, a white-robed man appeared from the direction of the refectory. Abbot Ralph ran to the gatehouse; the gold cross around his neck swung to the beat of his stride. "Thomas, my son. God be praised. You have come back." Abbot Ralph embraced Thomas and kissed him on each cheek. "God's blessings to you."

"God's blessings to you, Father Abbot. I'm sorry that I ran off as I did. Please forgive me."

"We have been so worried. Do not feel shame. We are sorry for your loss."

"Is Abbot Michael here? I need to speak with him."

"Abbot Michael wanted to be here when you returned, but he went to Kendalwood to see your brother."

"Why would Abbot Michael go to Kendalwood? Did he go with my father?"

"I am sorry. I should have realized. Please, come with me. I have some things to tell you."

Abbot Ralph ushered Thomas to the Elder Lady Chapel and told him what happened to his father. Thomas stood still as he looked at the stained-glass window above the altar and the painted statue of the Virgin Mary. His eyes watered, and his throat tightened, but tears did not fall. His senses dulled but for the tranquil view before him.

"I wish I had known him better," he said at last.

"Your father loved you very much. He refused to leave until you were found."

"He wanted me to come to him." Thomas lowered his head. "How could I have been so foolish? I could have spent more time with him. We could have left Bristow together. Then he would still be alive."

"Do not regret your actions. God leads us to do many things we do not understand. Had you stayed, you may also have died of the evil pestilence. It took your father quickly. Be thankful for the time you had with him."

"Show me where they are buried."

Mounds of dirt marked the spots in the abbey cemetery where Sir William and Lord Geoffrey de Parr lay. A simple wooden cross marked each grave. Thomas started to say the Lord's Prayer, but the onslaught of grief soon choked his voice.

Abbot Ralph continued the prayer.

An intense sadness grew within Thomas. The reunion with his father was too short. He tried to recall the sound of his father's voice. He rubbed his cheek remembering the itch of his father's beard as his father held him after the ordeal at The Goat's Head Inn. He would never see William or his father again—only memories remained. The tears came at last, but they were not hateful tears.

Abbot Ralph continued with a prayer of absolution. When he finished, Thomas's tears subsided. A nagging pain remained, a pain of missed joy. Then, a glimmer of acceptance crept into his consciousness. He understood that death for William and his father came as God decreed. God's will needed no explanation. His father and William had begun their final ascent to heaven. They had broken all mortal bonds and were no longer tormented by infirmaries or tempted by sin. Paradise lay before them.

"Thank you, Father Abbot, for your kindness. I had doubts if a life as a monk was for me. But, now that my father is dead, I have no one to account to. I must go back to Filton. I have been staying with Hugh Fiske and his daughter, Isabel. I do not want to continue my studies at Tintern Abbey. I love Isabel. She helped me overcome my anger at William's death. I hope now she'll be there to comfort me over my father's death. I want to spend the rest of my life with her."

"I understand, Thomas. You have a confidence about you that I did not see when you first arrived. I pray you will come see us again. You are always welcome. Abbot Michael plans to return. May I tell him where you are?"

"Yes. I want to tell Abbot Michael myself that I plan to stay in Filton."

On his way back, Thomas followed several families fleeing the evil scourge laying waste to the people of Bristow. He paid little attention to their chatter. His thoughts focused on Isabel and all the things that needed attention around the cottage. Maybe Andrew would come to visit one day. In that instant, Thomas realized he had not thought of Andrew in a long time. He had shoved his dearest friend into the far corners of his mind. Uncertainty returned. He missed Andrew's guidance. *Am I doing the right thing staying with Isabel? How could I have forgotten you, Andrew?*

Tintern Abbey, Wales

With two people cutting and four stacking the wheat, the meager harvest progressed at a good pace with little grain lost to the field. Still, only half the grain ripened as the year before and the damp threatened the rest of the abbey's crop. After days working from dawn to dusk, Andrew returned to the abbey to help with chores there. He wanted to talk to Abbot Michael, but Abbot Michael was late returning from Kendalwood.

After dinner on Saturday, Andrew hurried to clean the tables in the lay brother's refectory. As he carried bowls to the kitchen, he overheard Abbot Michael and Brother Samuel talking. He paused just outside the door not wanting to interrupt their conversation.

"I told Robert that I made a promise to his father that I would try to find Thomas," Abbot Michael said. "I am aware of stories of violence in Bristow following the processions, but it is at times like these when the church must step forward and guide the people back to God. The righteous will be protected. Have faith, Brother Samuel."

"I do have faith, Father Abbot. It is the pestilence and the violence that I fear."

"Fear is a lack of trust in God. I must go to Bristow. I would be a fool to think it is not dangerous. The people of Bristow need help. I cannot turn my back on them as I cannot turn my back on my promise to Lord Parr."

"I am sorry I questioned you, Father Abbot."

"I am not angry, Brother Samuel. I would not be so forthright if I did not have faith in your judgment and your ability to carry on in my stead."

Andrew decided it best to not listen to any more of the conversation. He returned to the refectory, quietly set the bowls on the table, and went to see what help he could give at the stable.

Chapter
TWENTY-THREE

Bristow, England, Sunday, August 10, 1348

Abbot Michael surveyed the Welsh Back as the oarsmen rowed the long boat up to the pier. Fewer ships lined Bristow's wharf and fewer men loaded and unloaded goods. Even for a Sunday afternoon, the pace of activity was restrained. The oarsman at the front of the boat fidgeted. His gaze darted up and down the wharf as he secured the lines and helped Abbot Michael onto the pier.

Vacant stares and hard frowns marred the faces that greeted Abbot Michael amid an unnatural quiet along the wharf. He headed toward St. Nicholas's Gate fortified with compassion for these fear-laden souls. The rank smell of death and the muffled cries of pain and suffering gave him pause, but he pressed on.

Along High Street and Broad Street, he saw that many shopkeepers had closed their shutters and locked their doors. He fondly remembered the day he and Thomas walked the busy streets oblivious of the impending doom. With God's strength, his determination to help calm the fears of parishioners and bring awareness of God's divine protection filled him with purpose.

At St. John's Gate, a man with tears falling from sad eyes came up to him. "Father, please help me," he pleaded.

"I am not a priest, but how may I help you?"

"It's my friend. I went to his flat this morning. When no one answered the door, I went in. It was horrible. I think they're dead. Unsure what else to do, I came to find a priest. But, I haven't found the priest."

"Show me where your friend lives. Maybe I can see if anything may be done."

The man led Abbot Michael to a warehouse along the Key. Abbot Michael paused a moment to read a notice posted on the warehouse door. The notice read: "Property of Edward Crawford. Forfeited by Order of the Crown." The man continued up a flight of stairs to a first-floor landing where an open door invited entry.

"I was so afraid I didn't close the door behind me," the man said.

"Wait here."

A sickly-sweet odor lingered around the door. When he entered the dimly lit room, the dense smell snatched his breath. He held his stomach and forced down an urge to vomit. A man, woman, and two children lay on the bed. A perverted stillness fouled the peaceful scene. Abbot Michael covered his nose and mouth with his hand and took a step closer. A rat scampered across the bed and dashed out a hole in the wall. His doubts dispelled, he hurried out of the flat.

"We must notify the sheriff," Abbot Michael said to the man who now stood half-way down the flight of stairs.

"Is it the pestilence?" the man asked.

"I do not know. It is likely. The sheriff will know what to do."

The man ran down the rest of the stairs and vanished.

Unfazed by the man's actions, Abbot Michael searched for guards to whom he could report the deaths. He found several of the sheriff's men near the customs office. He led them to the miserable setting.

"You'll remain quiet about this, no?" the guard said. "Stand watch and let no one enter. We'll send for a cart to haul away the bodies."

Abbot Michael waited by the stairs. After half a summer's hour, a cart driven by two scruffy men rolled up the street, their noses and mouths covered with wide rags. To his horror, he saw that the cart already contained at least six corpses; entangled arms and legs made it difficult to be sure of the count. Several wore little clothing, their ashen skin shriveled, the tips of their fingers and toes as black as coal. One by one, the men hauled the bodies out of the flat, the father and mother wrapped in bed linen. They plopped the remains onto the cart like trash.

"Where are you taking them?" Abbot Michael asked.

"We dump the bodies in a pit for the poor outside of town," one of the masked men said.

"Do you not have a priest give last rights or offer prayers?"

"We are not paid to worry about that."

Abbot Michael made the men wait while he said a quick prayer over the bodies and then continued his trek to St. Augustine's Abbey where he found the gate closed. He pulled on the bell chord. Brother Ezekiel came to greet him.

"I am sorry, Father Abbot. We must be careful who enters the abbey. The pestilence has knocked on many doors these past few days."

"Where may I find Abbot Ralph?"

"He is in the Elder Lady Chapel," Brother Ezekiel said. "I will take you to him."

Brother Ezekiel opened the iron gate to the chapel; the loud creak of the hinges echoed throughout the church.

Stepping into the chapel brought back memories of Lord Parr kneeling before the altar after Sir William's death. The circumstances seemed no less somber. Abbot Ralph rose to his feet. Before he turned to greet Abbot Michael, he crossed himself with his long, narrow fingers and bowed to the painted statue of the Virgin Mary.

"My dear Abbot Michael. I bid you welcome. God's blessings to you." He reached out to embrace Abbot Michael and gave him the kiss of peace.

"God's blessing, Abbot Ralph. I returned as soon as I could. The mood in Bristow has changed since I was last here. People are frightened. I was just at a flat along the Key where an entire family lay dead, likely due to the terrible humors of the pestilence."

"The priests are having a difficult time tending to all of the needy."

"I assumed as much when no priests were available to look after that poor family."

"Rumors run wild and people over-react. The sheriff's men keep watch as best they can for anyone who may be sick. But, I have much better tidings that will raise your spirits." Abbot Ralph grinned from ear to ear. "Thomas came to the abbey yesterday. He is well."

"That is indeed wonderful to hear." Abbot Michael's sorrow vanished. "Did he say where he had been?"

"Yes. He is in Filton staying with Hugh Fiske and his daughter, Isabel."

Abbot Michael shook his head. "I should have known. Isabel must be the young woman he met at the market." He clutched Abbot Ralph by the shoulders. "Thank God he is safe."

"He was very sorry to have run off and wants to see you. He asked that you come to Filton."

"I doubt there is anything that will change his mind."

"Change his mind about what?"

"About becoming a monk, of course."

"How did you know?" Abbot Ralph asked.

Abbot Michael smiled. "I will leave in the morning."

Filton, England, Monday, August 11, 1348

After a morning spent picking herbs with Isabel, Thomas sorted the plants into piles. "What is lovage good for again?" he asked.

"In a broth, lovage helps to calm the stomach," Isabel said.

"How much for a sprig?" a man asked.

Thomas turned, his eyes wide. Abbot Michael stood by the corner of the cottage with a happy smile and outstretched arms. Thomas stuttered, not sure if what he saw was true. "Father Abbot!" He dropped the sprigs of lovage and ran to embrace Abbot Michael. "Father, I'm so glad you came. I was lost in grief. I was ashamed to come back. I'm sorry."

"I am sorry too."

In a serious tone, Thomas said, "I saw where William and my father are buried."

"Yes. Abbot Ralph told me. I wanted to be there to tell you myself, but that was not possible. Your brother sends his love and prays for your safety."

They hugged again for good measure.

"Father, let me introduce Hugh Fiske and his daughter, Isabel. You may remember Isabel from the market in Bristow."

"Yes, I remember. It is an honor to meet you," Abbot Michael said.

"Would you please join us for dinner?" Hugh asked.

Over pottage and bread, Abbot Michael told them about his trip to Kendalwood. Robert wanted to retrieve the bodies of William and their father, but Abbot Michael recommended against the plan. With the pestilence ravaging Bristow, it would be best to wait. Mention of the pestilence drew worried looks from Isabel and Hugh.

"We heard from a carter that fear has overtaken Bristow. Is that so?" Hugh asked.

"Many people are afraid that they will not be spared from God's vengeance even if they confess. Sinners and unbelievers take joy in causing mischief at the expense of those in need. Itinerant preachers have appeared selling to anyone who will pay the price pieces of wood claimed to be from the true cross or bits of bone claimed to be of a saint's body. I question these acts, but the people who buy them feel comforted by the chance that the divine power of these items will help keep them safe. Others buy herbs and potions that do little but make the person sicker. Prayer and penance in the name of our Lord Jesus Christ will cleanse one's soul of sin. That is the best protection from the evils of the pestilence."

"Is it safe for you to return?" Thomas asked.

Abbot Michael paused. "I will stay as long as Abbot Ralph feels there is a need. I am sure Brother Samuel can manage, but I would like to be back at Tintern Abbey in a few weeks. I must be at Citeaux by Holy Cross Day for the General Chapter meeting."

"Then I pray that God will bless your travels and keep you safe," Thomas said. He held Isabel's hand.

"You know your father wanted you to have a safe and secure future."

"So much has changed, Father. I no longer see myself as a monk. My place is with Isabel. There is much I can do here and at the parish church in Filton. My father's hopes for me died with him. My destiny found a new path. You prepared me well to be of service. Only, that service is not to be within the walls of a monastery."

"The Lord's work is accomplished in many ways, Thomas. You will always have a place at Tintern Abbey, if you desire."

"There is one other thing, Father. Would you please tell Andrew that I'm in good health and that I hope someday soon Isabel and I can come to visit?"

"Yes, of course. Andrew will be most pleased. He has worried about you."

"I'm sorry that I worried Andrew. I did not mean—" Pain gripped his chest and a lump in his throat stifled his voice. He remembered his last conversation with Andrew. The concerns they spoke of then now seemed so trivial. Thinking of Andrew brought back the doubt and confusion. He looked to Isabel for reassurance. She caressed his hand. His desire for her settled his mind and his heart.

"Do not regret your actions. I can see you have found peace. Take comfort that many people have been concerned about you and they will be glad to know you are safe. I am sure Andrew will be happy to see you again when that day comes. I am sorry I misjudged your friendship. There is a bond there that you should not let go. But for now, be mindful of the pestilence. Only God knows where it will strike next. Few who stand in its wake live to tell the tale."

After small talk about the constant rains, the bad crops, and the market in Bristow, Abbot Michael took his leave. He thanked Hugh for the meal and wished God's blessings on all. Thomas accompanied Abbot Michael to the edge of the village where they embraced and said farewell.

That evening, Thomas stayed outside after Isabel and Hugh went to bed. He gazed at the twinkle of stars shining through breaks in the clouds and thought of all that was beautiful in the world—and Isabel. His heart had settled on a love he could never have had as a monk. And with her love, he felt stronger in both body and soul.

Then, he remembered something Abbot Michael said as they parted: "You have grown up, Thomas. You are now responsible for finding the path God has set for you. No one can do for you what you must do for yourself. Listen to your heart and you will not go astray. If you make an ill choice, you have proved your manhood. None of us are perfect. It is what we learn from our choices that matters. God will be with you as long as you have faith."

The words settled into his memory. "Why do things have to change?" he asked over the raspy din of crickets.

When he opened the cottage door, the sliver of light from the new moon was not enough to break the darkness. He groped his way to his bed. As he sat down, he felt something next to him. A hand reached out to steady him.

"It is only me."

"Isabel?"

"I'm not Beatrice," she said.

Chapter
TWENTY-FOUR

Bristow, England, August 1348

Abbot Michael found one of the men at the countess's warehouse to relay a message back to Tintern Abbey. With Thomas's whereabouts no longer a mystery, his gratitude to God for allowing him to fulfill his promise to Lord Parr gave him added strength to continue the fight. He endured hours of prayer in the altar of the Elder Lady Chapel as he prepared his soul for battle against the evil one, confident in God's protective spirit.

Bristow needed him. He walked the streets and alleys looking to console anyone who appeared in need. Commerce suffered as people withdrew into themselves. Caution drove fear and fear drove isolation. Grass took root in the streets.

Along the Welsh Back, Abbot Michael stopped to watch the sheriff's men investigate a recently arrived ship.

"Line up on deck," the guard shouted, his short sword drawn. Two other guards stood behind him.

Seamen shuffled into place. The guard in charge examined each man closely. The process reminded Abbot Michael of the time he scrutinized a flock of sheep before agreeing to purchase them. After the guard finished his review, one of the seamen broke into a coughing spell.

"What's wrong with him?" the guard demanded.

"It's nothing," the seaman replied. "I swallowed wrong."

"I don't believe you."

"It's the truth," the seaman said. "I'm fine. Look. I have no marks on my skin." The man raised his tunic to reveal the boney chest of a man who spent too much time at sea.

"I don't care. No one is allowed off this ship. You'll leave with the next outgoing tide."

"But what of my goods?" the captain implored.

"Nothing is to be taken off this ship." He turned to the other guards. "Stand watch. Kill anyone who tries to leave the ship and throw the body into the river."

These precautions did little to slow the spread of the evil humors. People continued to become sick. Those living near the wharf and the warehouses seemed to be at greatest risk. The onslaught of the pestilence endured, in all its hideousness, with little regard for the futile countermeasures of a dejected population.

Abbot Michael visited many churches at the behest of priests who found it impossible to be available for all of their distraught parishioners. He had never seen so many people with such a great need for spiritual assurance.

The number of people afflicted with the cruel illness grew each day. The sound of carts rolling through the gloomy streets carrying the dead stacked like rotten logs brought tears to Abbot Michael's eyes. Death seemed to demand every second of misery possible before separating the soul from its mortal shell. Few recovered from the living nightmare.

The power of the pestilence swelled like a demon with an insatiable appetite, devouring the righteous and sinner alike. The faithful pleaded for priests; to die with unconfessed sins meant an eternity in hell. Gravediggers kept busy under the deafening clang of church bells until they also succumbed to the sickness and followed the stream of sad souls to their own graves.

People flocked to churches to seek absolution. Abbot Michael found his greatest service comforting the distraught and consoling the grief-stricken.

There was no lack of either. A careless foe, the pestilence targeted wealthy and poor, strong and weak, young and old.

"What have we done to cause Your wrath?" Abbot Michael asked as he prayed before the altar at St. Mary le Port church. He puzzled over the reason for God's indiscriminant punishment. He perceived no common thread but the air that people breathed. Everywhere there was speculation. Stories abounded as to the cause of their plight. Scholars looked to the heavens and blamed the stars or the planets. The clergy espoused the divine hand of God calling believers to repent.

The common folk of Bristow claimed the pestilence was simply the will of God. Their suffering was the result of God's anger toward the sinful lives of man, which fueled the fires of destruction.

In time, the responsibilities of the canons of St. Augustine's Abbey stretched to the limit. They asked Abbot Michael to visit the homes of their wealthy patrons and alert them when death approached so they could come and deliver the last rites. Servants often fled their masters taking as many valuables as they could carry. Such thievery did them little good when their own day of reckoning arrived. Abbot Michael went out unfettered by fear believing in the divine purpose of his mission, intent on seeing to the needs of desperate souls.

Tintern Abbey, Wales, End of August 1348

Andrew saw the messenger leave Tintern Abbey's main gate. He ran to the kitchen to find Brother Samuel. "What betides?" he asked as he panted.

"Have you come to help wash the bowls?"

"I can, if you wish. I saw the messenger. Is there word from Abbot Michael?"

Brother Samuel seemed lost in thought as he cleaned and chopped turnips. He pointed at the pile of dirty bowls.

Andrew waited by the door.

"Abbot Michael is staying in Bristow. He is helping the abbot of St. Augustine's Abbey comfort the afflicted. He is unsure when he may return."

"What of Thomas?" Andrew tapped his fingers on the door frame.

"Thomas is well. He is staying with a young woman and her father. He hopes to come for a visit as soon as he can."

"Is he not coming back?"

Brother Samuel turned to Andrew, deep worry drawn on his face. "I am sorry, but I do not know more than that. I am concerned that Abbot Michael wants to stay in Bristow. The messenger also related unpleasant tidings about the progress of the pestilence. More people die every day and other towns along the southwest coast of England are suffering its evil influence."

"Why did he not tell us where he was?" Andrew pouted. He recalled all the time he spent fretting about Thomas. His fist tightened into a ball.

"Andrew, you must be fair. Thomas lost his father and brother. No doubt he has been upset. We do not know what else has been on his mind."

"I can think of one thing—a woman."

With a stern look, Brother Samuel said, "Jealousy is unbecoming of you, Andrew."

"I'm sorry."

"Try to feel thankful that Thomas is well. I have never known you two to fight in anger. No one said what Thomas did was right in the eyes of God. He must seek his own penance. It is not for us to say. He is your friend, is he not?"

The direct question made Andrew pause. Of course Thomas was his friend, but he wasn't supposed to be—not anymore. Unsure how to answer, he nodded.

"Then you should know that a friend does not judge."

"But should a friend point out wrongs?"

"That depends." Brother Samuel scooped up the chopped turnips and dropped them into his cauldron.

"Depends on what?" Andrew pressed.

"It depends on your motive." The tone of Brother Samuel's words was tinged with a quiver of sadness. "If you feel you have been wronged, then you must tell Thomas your feelings. It is up to Thomas to make amends. To demand anything more is a reflection of your own selfish reaction to conduct that you do not fully understand. If Thomas has asked God for forgiveness, we can do nothing less than offer it ourselves, can we?"

Andrew had no response. His gaze fell to the floor.

"I think Brother Gilbert will need help finishing the harvest. After that, I am sure he will have other things that need to be done around Trelleck Grange. Our stores are in a desperate state. I will let you know if word comes from Bristow. Now, if you wish, there is fresh water in the barrel over there. We need clean bowls for supper."

Trelleck Grange, Wales

The rest of August turned cool and damp. Everyone at Trelleck Grange had to pitch in to make sure the grain remained dry so it could be threshed and winnowed. Andrew hated threshing; it was too easy.

When he had the chance, he snuck into the woods to chop down dead trees and saw them to length. The heavy exercise kept his thoughts from drifting to Bristow. He hated the confusion that stirred uneasy feelings—feelings he couldn't identify, feelings that made him anxious, edgy, and mad all at the same time. He reminded himself to let go of useless thoughts and stay focused on his task.

After the grain was processed and ready for the mill, Andrew decided to get back to practicing with his sword. His muscles played a well-orchestrated tune as he refined his skill. Brother Gilbert helped him build various contraptions on which to practice. The ones that hit back provided the best means to improve his reactions, but they also left bruises.

"Are you still angry at Thomas?" Brother Gilbert asked as Andrew hit the training pole with a force that made the hard oak mast wobble.

"No," Andrew replied. "I forgave him after I chopped down the tenth tree. I think I would have run off myself if a woman came into my life. I can't stay mad at him forever."

"That's a wise decision, son. Anger is one of those emotions everyone has but no one cares for. Like dung, it's best to get rid of it quickly."

Chapter
TWENTY-FIVE

Filton, England, August 1348

Thomas tried to make himself useful around the cottage without getting in the way. He had a lot to learn about living outside the protection of a monastic community. Not knowing where to start, he decided to fix the door. "Andrew would know what to do," he grumbled, as he fiddled with the rickety hinge.

In the time it would have taken him to walk five miles, he repositioned the iron straps to line up with new wood, secured the door with nails that Hugh had (fortunately) set aside, and remounted the door on its hinges—on the third try. The portal to his new home was now secure and functional.

When Isabel and Hugh returned for dinner after a long morning tending vegetables, Thomas had the pottage warmed and bowls set out. He watched Hugh out of the corner of his eye as Hugh reached for the cottage's door. His tone mimicking Hugh's, he said, "Careful of the hinges."

"I know how to open the door. It is me who reminds you to be careful," Hugh said. The door remained steady in Hugh's hand. "May God be praised. What have you done?" Hugh opened and closed the door several times, a happy grin brightened his face.

"I was tired of having to be careful. I decided to fix it." Thomas beamed, as he scooped pottage into a bowl.

"Isabel, come look. We have a working door."

"That's wonderful, Father. I told you Thomas was good for something." Isabel giggled.

In the days that followed, Thomas helped Isabel and Hugh with threshing and winnowing the wheat. By the end of August, the wheat was sacked and stored at one end of the cottage ready to be carted to the mill.

The never-ending list of chores kept them busy. Herbs needed to be collected and vegetables needed to be gathered. Thomas had an inexhaustible source of energy while he labored at Isabel's side. Work was fun. Best of all, Isabel never criticized him for doing something wrong. She took the time to show him the proper way to do things until he got it right. In those moments, Thomas knew for certain he had found his place in life.

After a morning of working in the garden, Thomas asked, "Have we gathered enough vegetables to sell at the market?"

Isabel looked over the baskets filled with carrots, turnips, onions, garlic, and peas. "I think so, but I'm worried about going to Bristow."

"We have no choice. Rent is due on Michaelmas, is it not?"

"Yes."

"Then we must go."

"But what of the pestilence?" she asked.

"We'll be fine. We've participated in the processions and we've prayed every day." Thomas took Isabel in his arms and held her close. He felt a need to protect her. He wanted to keep her safe. The gentle curves of her body pressed against him. "I'll check to see when others from the village plan to go. If we stay together, then the pestilence will pass us by. God will protect us for the penance we have done." Isabel relaxed in his arms. He glanced around; they were alone. "Come with me."

Thomas took Isabel's hand and led her to a small clearing at the center of a grove of trees near the garden. His heartbeat quickened. He looked into her eyes and lost all of his selfish desires. The words came out as if no force of nature could stop them. "I love you, Isabel."

"I love you too."

"I've never known such happiness. I want our love to last forever. Do you feel the same?" He wet his lips and forced a swallow as he tried to keep his mouth from becoming as dry as a desert.

"Yes." Her eyes sparkled.

"I know we're alone—there should be witnesses—but I can no longer contain the power you have given me. In this place, here and now, will you marry me?" The silence of the moment dragged on for what seemed an eternity. In a single word, yes or no, his life would change forever. Sweat streaked from under his arms and tickled his sides. He thought for sure Isabel could hear the beat of his heart.

Her beautiful lips formed a wondrous smile. "Yes."

The word echoed like a trumpet on a clear day. They embraced and kissed with a hunger forged from first love. The world beyond did not exist.

"But what of father and the church?" Isabel asked.

"In the eyes of God and the church, we only need our mutual consent. We can announce our espousal to your father as soon as we collect enough money to pay the rent. After that, we can have a grand ceremony in the parish church."

"You have truly made me happy, Thomas. I could not wish for anything more."

Holding Isabel's right hand, Thomas said, "I take you, Isabel, as my wife, to have and to hold, for better or worse, for the rest of my life."

Isabel held Thomas's right hand. "I take you, Thomas, as my husband, to have and to hold, for better or worse, for the rest of my life."

They kissed again and collapsed to the ground in a passionate embrace. Their unstoppable love, pure and unselfish, took control of their bodies. Their souls became one. Thomas held Isabel as he savored the innocence of desire and the wonder of God's blessing.

Filton, England, September 1348

The euphoria of Isabel's love drove Thomas to take on more work around the cottage. Tasks he once thought impossible now became opportunities to show Isabel how much he loved her. He repaired the worn thatch. The result was less than expert, but the tidied appearance kept out the rain. Buckets and tools that went untended found a place out from under feet. As the days passed, the cottage looked more and more like a place he was proud to call home.

When it came time to trade herbs for bread, Thomas asked Isabel, "May I do the bartering with the baker?"

Isabel kissed his cheek.

"What was that for?"

"For good luck. The baker doesn't give away his bread to just anyone."

"Are you saying he might think I'm not as pretty as you?"

"Save your flattery for the baker." She kissed him again and ran ahead through the trees.

He chased after her. When he caught her, he took her in his arms and kissed her moist lips. The embrace filled him with courage. He thought he could do anything as long as Isabel was by his side. He held Isabel's hand as they walked into the village. When they strolled up to the bakery, Walter and Jane stepped out of the chandlery next door.

Jane nodded. "God's blessings to you."

"Do you need vegetables?" Isabel asked. "We have extra."

"Thank you for the offer," Walter said. "Our crop was poor this year."

"That was charitable," Thomas said, as he held the bakery door for Isabel.

"Walter always shared his crops when he had plenty. They had a bad harvest this year so what else could I do?"

"I'm not disagreeing. I'm finding more reasons to confirm why I love you."

Isabel blushed. She glided into the bakery like an angel on wings.

The smell of fresh bread filled the air. The baker stood behind his waist-high counter stacking golden brown loaves on a shelf. "God's blessings, Simon," Thomas said.

"Isabel, Thomas. Welcome. Looks like you have some fresh herbs."

"Indeed," Thomas said. He stepped to the counter and laid out his offering. Isabel stood behind him and remained silent. "We gathered a dozen good sprigs of sage."

Simon looked to Isabel with raised eyebrows. When she didn't reply to his gesture, he said, "Nice plants. One loaf for the lot."

"That's not all. We also have some thyme and rosemary." Thomas set the other herbs on the counter. "These go well together. Let me show you an easy way to prepare them. For the thyme, take a stalk and slide your thumb and forefinger along the stem. All the leaves come off in a bunch." Thomas demonstrated the method. "For the rosemary, go the opposite direction along the stem. Then, nip off three leaves of sage. You only need a little. Lay the sage leaves out like so and pile the thyme and rosemary on top. Roll the lot into a tight ball and with your knife, chop the leaves into small bits. Now you have a nice mixture you can use whenever you want. If you make a large enough batch, all your loaves will come out the same and you don't waste anything. Use only as much as you need."

Simon's face lit up with a grand smile. "I never thought of that." He glanced at his basket on the counter that held three fresh loaves. With a nod, he reached for another from the stack on the shelf and said, "Here. Take these for the herbs—and the advice. You can return the basket tomorrow."

Thomas beamed. His many days helping Brother Samuel in the abbey's kitchen finally had its reward. He left the bakery with his chin high and his shoulders back. Isabel punched him in the arm when they got outside. "What was that for?"

"Four loaves!"

Thomas kissed her on the cheek. "It's all because of you."

On the way home, they passed Beatrice's cottage. The loud cackle of her chickens made him stop to take notice. "Have you seen Beatrice?"

"Maybe we should check to see if she's well."

Thomas waited while Isabel entered Beatrice's cottage. Moments later, she ran out. "Thomas, come quick. Beatrice needs help."

The unexpected smell of waste and vomit made Thomas cover his nose and mouth. Beatrice lay on her bed. "What ails her?"

"I don't know, but she needs food and water. Leave a loaf of bread and go see if we have any pottage. I'll get some water." Isabel shuddered. "I pray it's not the pestilence."

Thomas ran to fetch a bowl of pottage. By the time he returned, Isabel had Beatrice washed and the messes on the floor cleaned. She opened the windows to bring fresh air and light to the cheerless room.

"Bless you, child," Beatrice whispered. "I feel so weak."

"Don't worry. I'll take care of you." Isabel held a cup as Beatrice took sips of cool water. "Thomas brought some food. You must eat something."

After they saw to Beatrice's immediate needs, Thomas and Isabel returned home.

"Someone must tend her," Isabel told Thomas. "She has no family. We can't abandon her. With all she has done for the village and the church, God would never let her die of the pestilence. Would he?"

"We must keep her sickness quiet," Thomas cautioned. "If it's the pestilence and the village finds out, we'll be shunned. I saw how people ran in fear in Bristow."

"I'm afraid too, but she needs someone to care for her. You mustn't tell father. He'll worry. We must pray for God's blessings."

As careful as they were, suspicions grew. Villagers watched Isabel with curious looks as she came and went from Beatrice's cottage. Thomas ignored the stares as he took care of the chickens and harvested the ripe vegetables.

During the penitential processions that followed, villagers kept their distance from Thomas and Isabel. They refused to look them in the eye or to offer them the use of the horse and cart. Thomas overheard a couple claim that they once saw Beatrice consorting with evil spirits. "She is so old. She must have sold her soul to the devil," one of them said.

Fear escalated. Villagers avoided Beatrice's neighbors as the sense of panic spread. Friendships built over generations vanished overnight.

The next evening, Isabel asked Thomas to join her when she went to check on Beatrice.

"Is there nothing more we can do for her?" Thomas asked. "Are there other herbs you can give her or potions you can make?"

"I only know what's good for common ailments. If she has the pestilence, it's much too powerful. I've thought of sage to check the bad humors or wild thyme to heal those blackened growths on her skin. But she's not been able to eat. I don't think anything will stop the sickness now."

"I bought this candle from Father Lawrence. He said to light it and put it in the window when death is near." Thomas looked at Beatrice; sweat soaked her robe and matted her thin, white hair. She moaned and uttered unintelligible words. "Do you think it's time?"

"Light the candle."

Isabel sat on the bed and held Beatrice's hand while Thomas paced. The candle neared the end of the wick by the time Father Lawrence arrived.

From his belt, Father Lawrence detached the cross-shaped vessel he used to carry consecrated hosts and oil. He administered the last rites. Beatrice died a pitiful death unable to confess as delirium stole her last breaths. "I am sure it was the sickness that prevented her from making a confession," Father Lawrence said.

"Do you think it was the pestilence?" Thomas asked. He thought of William and his father suffering as Beatrice did. The images upset him.

"I do not know for sure," Father Lawrence said. "I have heard that some die quickly. Others linger. At least her torment, whatever the cause, has ended."

Beatrice's death received little response from the village. Her passing went as if she had been a lost beggar. Everyone seemed to fear acknowledging the unspoken truth—the pestilence had arrived in Filton.

Thomas and Isabel stood alone with Father Lawrence and the gravedigger as the earth reclaimed its dust.

The pestilence claimed another victory.

Chapter
TWENTY-SIX

Filton, England, September 1348

In the days that followed Beatrice's death, Thomas tried to understand the indifference of Filton's villagers. He had witnessed families coming together for penitential processions and long hours of prayer. But, when evil arrived, selfishness and fear replaced the common bonds of fellowship. The pestilence was evil and only evil people died of God's plague.

As more candles appeared in windows, the curious kept watch from a distance and no one reached out to offer help. People looked over their shoulders as if Satan peered around every corner, trepidation and apprehension their only companions. Hell was real, and no one wanted to go there.

Thick menacing clouds filled the sky on the morning Thomas rose to find Isabel restless and sweating.

"What ails you?" he asked.

"I feel sick," Isabel said. "I thought I'd be better once I had a good night's sleep. Now, I have this headache and it seems to be getting worse. And I feel stiff all over."

A sense of inevitable doom overwhelmed Thomas. "You should have said something. We must find help."

Isabel held her head as she sat on the edge of the bed and cried. "Thomas, what have I done? I only wanted to help Beatrice. The pestilence has taken me too."

"You mustn't say that." Thomas put his arms around her. He tried to sound hopeful. "There may be other reasons why you feel unwell."

"If you think I'm with child, I think it's too early to tell." Isabel managed a quick smile as tears rolled down her cheeks.

Every muscle in his body tensed. "There must be someone in the village who can tell us something."

"The way they treated us when we tended Beatrice? No one will come near if they suspect I'm not well. They'll abandon us as they abandoned Beatrice and her neighbors, Walter and Jane."

"We must go to Bristow. Abbot Ralph can help. St. Bartholomew's Infirmary is not far from the abbey."

"That's too far and too dangerous. You mustn't tell father. He'll be overcome with grief."

"We should tell him we're married."

"No. Please. The joy of marriage will only be a cruel joke for the pain to come."

Thomas sat with Isabel until they heard Hugh call out that the pottage was ready.

"What is with the sad faces?" Hugh asked when they sat down.

"I was just thinking about Beatrice," Isabel said. "I'll miss her."

"Yes, we will all miss her, I think," Hugh said.

Thomas let out a sigh at Isabel's quick response.

Throughout the day, Thomas stayed close to Isabel as they picked ripe vegetables and packed them for storage. She rested often. He fretted over her and encouraged her to save her strength. Work in the garden no longer provided enjoyment. His thoughts paid little attention to what he did. Instead, he strained to think of what to do to help her. The penitential processions failed to prevent the pestilence from taking hold in Filton. No prayer, no penance, no absolution seemed to appease God. Would God take Isabel as He had taken William and his father?

A fierce battle played out in Thomas's mind. He tried to rationalize God's will. The unending possibilities made his head hurt. *What must I do? Will you save her? You must save her. I love her more than my own life. I have confessed my sins. What other penance is there that I can do? Why must You take her? I need her. I love her.*

"Thomas, you have reached the end of the row," Isabel said.

The sound of Isabel's voice brought him out of his mental melee. As if awakened from a terrible dream, he looked at his hands; he dug for carrots a foot past the end of the row. The spirit in his voice left him. "Sorry. I wasn't paying attention."

That evening, the pottage didn't sit well with Isabel. She ran to vomit in the bushes. Thomas's face involuntarily saddened in reaction to Isabel's sudden departure. He shielded his eyes with his hand.

"It cannot be!" Hugh's face turned white. "Tell me it is not so. Not Isabel, my dear child." Hugh dropped his bowl and covered his face with his hands. "God has forsaken us."

The fields and gardens went untended as Thomas and Hugh took care of Isabel. For the first few days, she managed to move about the cottage and take short walks outside. But, as her appetite waned, she showed no desire to get out of bed. "The pain is like being stabbed by a thousand needles," she said. Fever drove out what little fluid she took in.

Thomas pleaded with God to let Isabel live and to take him instead. He didn't care about the pilgrimage to paradise. How could he look forward to such a journey without Isabel at his side, here and now, sharing this life one day at a time? Death may be God's will, but when that death might be Isabel's, he struggled for acceptance. Death was fickle.

He had given in to love and let his soul merge with Isabel's essence. Now, the force of that mortal bond hung by a tenuous strand. A way of life he once considered impossible, a way of life founded on a miracle, was under attack by a force he did not understand.

The third day brought desperate pleas to God as Isabel's breathing became labored. The buboes under her arms grew black, and foul-smelling puss exuded from the edges of the sores. Hugh was inconsolable. His mood swung from extreme rage to deep depression. Thomas kept Isabel comfortable as best he could. He honored his vow to stay with her for better or worse, but he didn't know what to do to help her.

"Is this the way it's to be?" he said to Isabel. He watched her lips for any sign of movement. He expected silence. "Are we to watch each other die at the hands of this terrible menace until no one is left?"

Isabel opened her eyes and looked up at Thomas. Her voice lucid and clear, she said, "Do not be sad, my husband. I go to the world of bliss and joy to once again be with my mother. Remember our love. We'll meet again in paradise."

"Isabel!" Despite her ashen skin and parched lips frozen in a grimace of pain, Thomas saw beauty in her tender, green eyes.

"Do not give up on God. I asked God to bring into my life someone who would truly love me. And he did. My prayers were answered. And He has forgiven my sins. I'll be with our Lord Jesus Christ in Heaven. I'll always love you, Thomas." Her eyelids fluttered.

"Isabel, stay with me." Thomas shook her as gently as he dared.

"Isabel, I love you." She remained silent and motionless.

Her weakened and dehydrated body stood little chance against the raging pestilence that devoured her existence, like a fragile flower under a dark cloud. In a way, her infirmity saved her from the worst of the pain and delirium. Death came quickly. There was no time to call the priest.

Thomas kissed Isabel's lips; they were still warm. He repeated her last words so as to etch them in his mind. She said his name as her last word. Thomas's emotions froze. He wanted to cry, but time seemed to stop.

He had to wash her body and find a shroud in which to wrap her. It pained him from the depths of his soul to see the state of her once-beautiful body. He tried to remember her as she looked the first time he held her close to his skin. Her warmth and giving nature radiated the purity of God's love.

After he washed her, he found a white linen sheet in the chest. He wrapped her body, careful to straighten her long, chestnut brown hair. He then went out to the fire pit and found a stick that was burned at one end. The blackened end he used to draw a cross on the shroud.

He then knelt beside the bed on which the love of his life laid. The hole in his heart that had been filled was now torn open. A new scar, deeper than before, tested his faith. He tried to think why God gave him such a perfect gift as Isabel and then took her away. Where did his destiny lead now?

The floodgates of his emotions broke. *What more can You take from me?* Then, Isabel's words came back to him: "Do not give up on God."

Isabel's plea saved him from renouncing anything good in the world. He was alive. He had memories and experiences to share. Most of all, he had the joyful memories of Isabel. God's will needed no explanation.

"I'll never forget our love. I promise you, I'll listen for God's will and do as He commands."

Thomas greeted Father Lawrence outside the cottage. Father Lawrence apologized for not being available sooner. He appeared nervous on entering the cottage. Hugh refused to greet him.

Father Lawrence anointed Isabel and then prayed: "O God, Whose attribute it is always to have mercy and to spare, we humbly present our prayers to Thee for the soul of Thy servant Isabel, which Thou has this day called out of this world, beseeching Thee not to deliver it into the hands of the enemy, nor to forget it forever, but to command Thy holy angels to receive it, and to bear it into paradise; that as it has believed and hoped in Thee it may be delivered from the pains of hell and inherit eternal life through Christ our Lord. Amen."

After the prayer of absolution, Thomas said, "I'll carry her to the cemetery."

"The gravedigger is waiting," Father Lawrence said. "Do you wish to have a service?"

"Yes. But we have nothing for payment. If you wish, you may choose from these baskets of vegetables. We have more than enough for ourselves now." Thomas looked at Hugh waiting for him to acknowledge the offer. When Hugh didn't respond, Thomas asked, "Is that acceptable?"

"Yes." Father Lawrence bowed.

Thomas picked up Isabel, her frail body lighter than he remembered. He led the way to the cemetery. Hugh followed, head bowed, his gaze fixed on the shuffle of his feet.

As they walked, Father Lawrence prayed, "May the angels escort thee to paradise, may the martyrs receive thee at thy coming and bring thee into the holy city Jerusalem. May the choir of angels receive thee, and with Lazarus, who once was poor, mayst thou have eternal rest."

At the gravesite, the gravedigger helped Thomas lay Isabel's body into the earthen tomb dug next to her mother. Hugh stared at his daughter's remains, his face as white as her shroud.

Father Lawrence cleared his throat. "O God, whose mercies cannot be numbered, accept our prayers on behalf of Thy servant Isabel. Grant her entrance into paradise, in the fellowship of Thy saints; through Jesus Christ Thy Son our Lord, who liveth and reigneth with Thee and the Holy Spirit, one God, now and forever. Amen."

The simplicity and brevity of the service epitomized Isabel's short life. She did not need a grand procession or multitudes of mourners. Thomas and Hugh provided the prayers to convey her soul to heaven.

The experience of the burial left Thomas unable to think of anything beyond grief. The vision of Isabel lying at the bottom of the grave shattered his will to live. He tried to accept Isabel's death as God's will, but he refused to let go of despair. He again reflected on Isabel's words: "Do not give up on God."

Isabel's plea became his salvation. He repeated the phrase all the way back to the cottage. Unsure how to accept God's will, he tried to find solace in the idea that God needed her. But, all he wanted to do was to crawl into the grave with Isabel and die. *"Do not give up on God." "Do not give up on God."* Maybe God let him live for some other purpose. Maybe there was more he needed to do to prove his worth to God.

"You must leave," Hugh said when they arrived at the cottage. "There is no reason for you to stay."

Hugh's request—no, his command—took Thomas a moment to process. And the force of Hugh's voice seemed odd from the despair exhibited since Isabel's death. "I can't leave you now," Thomas said. "What of all the work that needs to be done and the goods that need to be sold at market?"

"If the pestilence does not take me, grief will. I have nothing to live for. It is best that you take away happy memories of this place. There is only sadness now." Hugh took a stick and scattered the embers in the fire pit.

"Let me at least help you through Michaelmas."

"No. I will not have you see me wither like a dying weed."

Hugh refused to listen to reason.

"I'll leave in the morning," Thomas conceded.

"I am tired now. Please leave me alone." Hugh went into the cottage and closed the door.

Thomas sat by the fire pit and finished the little bit of pottage that remained in the pot. The momentary distraction of Hugh's obstinacy gave him a chance to think of something other than his own grief. He went to the vegetable garden and did his best to put his mind and body to the task of hoeing. When the light became too dim to see, he returned to the cottage and went to bed.

The pestilence did not sleep.

Chapter
TWENTY-SEVEN

Filton, England, September 1348

Thomas heard Hugh's voice outside the cottage. It sounded like Hugh chatted with someone. The occasional laughter seemed out of place for the morning after Isabel's funeral. He opened the cottage door unsure what to expect.

"Careful of the hinges, Thomas," Hugh said.

Hugh smiled an unnaturally happy smile as he scooped pottage into bowls. He placed two bowls next to empty stumps and handed another to Thomas before he took one for himself.

"You are late as usual, Thomas. You best hurry before Alice and Isabel start without us. Isabel added lots of sage. She knows how much you and her mother like sage. Is that not right, my dear?" Hugh talked to the empty stumps, rambling on about the beautiful weather despite gray clouds drifting overhead.

"Isabel will now say grace," Hugh said. After a moment of silence, Hugh raised his head. "That was lovely, my dear."

Thomas ate his pottage and watched. Maybe demons or some madness had found an easy host in Hugh's hopelessness. He agonized over whether to leave. The Christian thing to do would be to stay, but Hugh rejected his offers of help. If he could not remain with Hugh, no one else in Filton would take him in for fear of the pestilence. For his own sake, he had to leave.

He gave Hugh a hug and, without saying farewell, left the cottage he once called home.

He set out for Bristow. He knew of nowhere else to go. Maybe the Augustinians needed someone to help with the sick. If God willed, death would end his sorrow. Along the Gloucester Road, he met scores of travelers heading north with nothing more than a bundle slung over their shoulders. Some implored him to turn around and flee the evil humors infesting Bristow. Others refused to speak or even look at him as he made his way along the now familiar route. The smell of fear, as bitter as dried sweat, followed in the wake of the slow exodus. Even the bandits had fled.

In Bristow, fewer people walked the streets. Women held bouquets of flowers in front of their noses. Charms and amulets hung from around necks in plain view. He went directly to St. Augustine's Abbey. When he pulled on the bell cord, a man came and opened the little window set in gate. Thomas didn't recognize him.

"What's your business?" the man asked as if the question had been asked a thousand times.

"I need to see Abbot Ralph. I'm Thomas de Parr."

"Abbot Ralph is not here."

"This is important. Do you know when he'll be back?"

"We expect him any day. He went to Tintern Abbey."

"Why did he go there?" Thomas's heart skipped a beat. He swallowed hard.

"The abbot from Tintern Abbey died last week. He was helping the canons with the wretches who suffered from the vile pestilence and came down with it himself, poor soul."

The suddenness of the statement took Thomas's breath away. He stood for a moment, silent, glaring at the man.

"Did you know him?"

Thomas managed a weak "Yes."

"Seems like everyone knows somebody who has died of this dreadful sickness. I'm just glad the tolling of the bells stopped. I heard that one of the bells at St. Nicholas parish broke because it was ringing so much. If you want a good paying job, they need people to pick up bodies and haul them to the new graveyard. The field was consecrated this past Sunday. They have this long trench and they pile them in. No one knows who they are. They are just dead people."

Thomas scowled at the man. He wanted to scream, but the dull expression that stared back told him that it would be pointless. "I must go now," he mumbled.

"As you please. Come back in a few days. Abbot Ralph may be back by then. Do you want to see anyone else?"

Thomas left without responding. He repeated the man's words as he staggered back to St. John's Gate, "The abbot from Tintern Abbey died last week." With his heart still raw from Isabel's death, the death of Abbot Michael was too fantastic to believe. He refused to let the reality of the statement sink in. "Have I not suffered enough?"

The world deserted him. He had only one place left to go, Tintern Abbey. Maybe they would take him in. Abbot Michael said he would always be welcome. But how could he return to the life of a monk? He rejected the monastery and married the woman he loved.

He made his way to St. Nicholas Street. Some men stood in front of the countess's warehouse.

"I need to get to Tintern Abbey," Thomas said. "Is Searle here?"

"I think he's waiting on the tide right now. He's leaving from the Welsh Back. If you hurry, you may catch him."

Thomas ran down St. Nicholas Street to High Street. He dodged the few people who braved the open air. Moored to a pier, he saw two empty long boats. A little farther, he saw a third that appeared to have just shoved off. He ran to the end of the pier and spied Searle on board.

"Searle!" he shouted, waving and jumping up and down.

The oarsman continued to row the boat away from shore. "Master Thomas?" Searle called out. He looked surprised and pleased. "God's blessings. Have you heard about Abbot Michael?"

"Yes, I have."

Searle spoke louder as the boat moved away. "Terrible tidings. I am so sorry. What are you doing here?"

"I need to get back to Tintern Abbey. Isabel, the woman I was staying with, was taken by the pestilence. I must get back."

A man who stood nearby perked up and recoiled at the word 'pestilence.' "You have the pestilence?" he asked.

Searle stood and shouted, "What did you say, Thomas?"

"That boy has the pestilence! Run!" The man took off running.

A look of panic came across Searle's face. He sat down and motioned for the oarsmen to row faster.

"Searle. Wait!"

Two men approached Thomas with looks of evil in their eyes. The larger of the two pointed and yelled, "That boy has the pestilence. Kill him before he spreads it."

Thomas froze as fear seized him. He looked at Searle. Searle's boat continued down river. His choices gone, he forced himself to move. He ran back into the old town and up Worship Street. The men chased close at his heels.

He darted into the shoe shop, which he knew had a back door. The surprised shopkeeper got up to protest. Thomas dashed into the alley before the shopkeeper yelled, "Stop!" The two men chasing Thomas collided with the shopkeeper. All three went tumbling into shelves filled with wooden shoe forms. The noise of all the forms crashing to the floor sounded like thunder.

Thomas made his way through the alley and onto Maryport Street. When he got to High Street, he stopped and looked behind him. No one followed.

Trying to appear calm, he ambled up High Street. He passed The Goat's Head Inn and then turned down Corn Street toward the Key. He figured he might hide for a while in one of the warehouses.

An open door to a warehouse not far from the customs office looked inviting. A torn notice was posted to the right of the door. The legible portion said: "Forfeited by Order of the Crown." Thomas looked around to see if anyone watched and then snuck in. Sacks of grain filled the large space. The dusty, stale smell of the room made him sneeze. He found a spot in the shadows toward the back and hid.

His heartbeat pounded. Frustration drained his strength. *How could Searle leave me like that?* In the quiet, visions of Abbot Michael filled his mind—gray tonsure and beard, commanding looks, a soothing voice that never spoke a selfish word. He buried his head between his knees. Grief forced its way to the surface.

"Why did I ever leave Tintern Abbey? What am I to do now?" Doubt haunted his thoughts. He no longer trusted his choices. Yet, he sensed that his life depended on getting to Tintern Abbey. He had no idea how to find his way back. The chaos of Bristow surrounded him. People ran from the sight of anyone in need. His future was as black as the horrible growths under Isabel's arms.

His faith depleted and hope all but lost, he wanted to give up. Then, Isabel's last words came back to him, "Do not give up on God." Fatigue overpowered him. He leaned against the sacks of grain and fell asleep.

Bristow, England, September 1348

The sound of men talking jolted Thomas awake. He kept still and listened to the voices. One of the men had an Irish accent, the other sounded local.

The man with an Irish accent said, "If we do not get this grain moved soon, we will have to pay more to the crown for storage."

The other man said, "I'll raise the offer for shipping. That might entice a captain. But, I doubt there's a profitable market for grain to the south. With all the deaths from the pestilence, even if we found a ship willing to go to Guyenne, there's no demand. We'll have to go to Ireland or Flanders."

"Have you thought of Newnham?" the Irish man asked.

"Why?"

"I heard Newnham is still free of the pestilence. It may be twenty miles by road, but we may have a better chance of finding a ship willing to take cargo."

"I hadn't thought of that. If we hire wagons and take the Gloucester Road north, then west, there is a ferry that crosses the Severn at Newnham."

The two men grumbled about falling grain prices before their footsteps faded and the warehouse door slammed shut.

Thomas caught on to the idea and took it as a sign from God. Crossing the Severn at Newnham might be his only way to get back to Tintern Abbey. He crept to the door and peeked out. When all was clear, he slipped out and sneaked back into the old town. Walking along the back allies along the town walls, he caught a sickly, sweet scent. Through the open doorway of a narrow cottage, wedged between two larger timber-framed buildings, he saw feet sticking out from under a blanket. A rat nibbled at the toes. He covered his nose and mouth and hurried past.

Daylight fled as he put Bristow behind him. Once again, he found himself on the Gloucester Road. High clouds filtered what little light the waning moon provided. The dim light soon made it impossible to find his way. With the dark, came the cold night air. His linen tunic offered little protection. He shivered as he huddled by a large bush. To stay warm, he covered himself with leaves and drifted off to sleep.

North of Bristow, England, September 1348

At the break of dawn, his joints stiff and achy, Thomas struggled to his feet. He brushed off the leaves, hopeful that he would make good progress in the light of day. When he got to Filton, he stopped to check on Hugh. The open door of the cottage looked ominous; something was amiss. He looked inside—no one. Four empty bowls sat stacked next to the fire pit. A little pottage hugged the inside surface of the pot. He searched the garden and the field but found no sign of Hugh. Back at the fire pit, he stirred the cold pottage. It smelled unspoiled, so he gobbled what remained.

He waited until mid-day, hoping that Hugh might come back. The aches in his joints nagged him, as did a bothersome headache. A swig of water soothed his dry throat but did little else to settle his discomfort. He had an uncomfortable feeling that his body was fighting something. He rubbed his temples. Maybe some rest in a bed might help.

The moment he stepped inside the cottage, he smelled Isabel—not the sick smell of the pestilence but the sweet lavender smell of her hair. He looked at the bed on which she last laid. The rumpled canvas and the bunched-up blanket looked to be unchanged from when he carried her to her grave. He smoothed out the canvas and folded the blanket. When the light faded, he lay down and thought of Isabel and the future they could have had.

In a dream, Thomas stood in an open wheat field. A cold wind chilled his face. Unable to move, he watched a mysterious, black form approach, stalks of wheat shriveled before it. Evil radiated from the entity as heat radiates from a fire. He raised his hand to shield his face. As it gained strength, the edges of the form became defined like the outline of a shadow after a cloud slowly passes on a sunny day. Only, in his dream, the sky was covered by thick gray clouds. The shape became elongated, an oval standing on end. A sigh emanated from the darkness. "At last," a voice said. "Your soul will be mine." The form moved closer.

"Stay away," Thomas shouted.

"I am patient. It is only a matter of time now."

A group of people appeared behind him. He couldn't discern who they were, but he felt safe with them there. Their presence helped him to hold back the power of evil.

The blackness mocked him with laughter. "You cannot win. I have you," it said. "You will beg me to take your soul. There is no escape."

Chapter
TWENTY-EIGHT

Tintern Abbey, Wales, September 1348

"Why did he have to go back to Bristow?" Andrew clenched his fists. "You should have stopped him." The echo of his harsh words bounced off the kitchen walls.

"Andrew. Please be calm." Brother Samuel bent to one knee to kindle a fire. "We are all distraught by these ill tidings. You should know that once Abbot Michael made up his mind to do something—especially when he felt he was doing God's work—then no one could change his mind."

The truth hurt. Andrew knew that Abbot Michael would not shy away from helping those in need, just as he had done nine years ago when Brother Gilbert brought him, injured and unconscious, to the abbey. But knowing that didn't relieve the anger and sadness coursing through him. The only way he knew to silence the internal screams was to run to the forest with his axe. The first dead tree he came upon he swung at it as hard as he could. He chopped and chopped until nothing remained but scraps of wood.

In the days that followed word of Abbot Michael's death, he tried to make sense of his feelings. While the monks sought comfort in prayers said for the repose of Abbot Michael's soul, his own comfort remained elusive. He struggled to resolve his feelings and then admonished himself for wasting time thinking on such useless thoughts. Thomas was the one who thought too much.

Restlessness became a constant annoyance. Instead of the axe, he took up his sword as an outlet for his excess energy. He perfected his stance and the sequence of moves Eudo taught him. His focus was undeterred, as if he prepared for battle.

One morning, after rising from a worthless night of sleep, he was struck by a sudden desire to go to Bristow. While everyone expressed dread at the happenings in Bristow, he couldn't get out of his mind the need to be there. Something within, a powerful feeling he couldn't suppress or ignore, told him to go.

When he arrived at Trelleck Grange for his morning chores, he told Brother Gilbert, "I think we're well along in our work. If I may, I want to go to Chepstow."

"Who says we're ahead on our work?" Brother Gilbert asked, his hands on his hips in his military pose.

"The threshing and winnowing are finished. You said when I felt the time was right I'd know. Then, you'd support my decision."

"I remember. But tell me, son, where is it you want to go?" Brother Gilbert crossed his arms.

Andrew knew better than to tell a half-truth. "I have to get to Bristow. I'm worried about Thomas. I can't explain it, but I feel like he's in trouble. Last night, I slept little. I couldn't stop thinking about him. I thought I'd go see Searle and ask if he's going to Bristow anytime soon."

"You know stories from Bristow are bad. The pestilence is everywhere. Are you certain that's what you want to do?"

Andrew spoke with conviction. "I'm certain."

"This is not something to be done lightly."

"I feel like every part of me is running and I can't stop. I keep thinking something is wrong, but I don't know what it is."

Brother Gilbert stroked his beard. "Now you sound like Thomas."

Andrew rolled his eyes. "The thoughts just pop into my head."

"I've an idea. I'll tell Brother Samuel I sent you to complete a very important task. He doesn't need to know the true purpose, not yet anyway. I want you to find out what you can about Thomas. And I expect the task to be well done and the result to be good tidings."

A surge of energy brightened Andrew's mood allowing a grin to force its way through his melancholy expression. "As you wish. I'll be back as soon as I can." He embraced Brother Gilbert.

"Wait a moment." Brother Gilbert disappeared into the manor house. When he returned, he carried a shiny sword with a leather grip and a brass pommel. "This is no ordinary sword. It was a gift from the countess for twenty years of service. This sword will keep the troublemakers away. I think I have a hooded cape around here too. The nights are getting colder and the hood will keep the rain off your head. God be with you, son."

Andrew now had a purpose. He donned the heavy, ivy-green cape and pulled the hood up to cover his head; the flowing fabric hid the fancy sword. A cold mist began as he set out for Chepstow. He reached the town gate by late-morning. His pace brisk, he didn't stop until he reached Striguil Castle. When he saw the barbican, the thought struck him that Searle might not be at the castle. He discounted the idea—it was too late to turn back. He approached and shook the rain from his hood.

"Come for more sword play, Andrew?" Bran asked.

"I came to see Searle. Is he here?"

"He's worried about the pestilence and doesn't want anyone coming into the castle without his permission. Wait here while I get him."

Andrew paced the confines of the uncovered barbican. The other guard stood under the portcullis to hide from the rain. Searle soon appeared. Andrew asked, "Might you be going to Bristow?"

Searle looked around with cautious glances. "It pains me to relay this to you, Andrew. I was in Bristow several days ago. I saw Thomas as I was leaving."

Andrew tensed as a rush of foreboding filled him with uncertainty. "Why didn't you send a message? How is he? What did he say?"

"This is the unpleasant part; he may be unwell."

"What do you mean, 'unwell?'"

"What I mean to say is that Thomas may have—" Searle leaned close and whispered, "the pestilence."

"What?" A gut-wrenching pain struck Andrew in the stomach like someone stabbed him. "Are you sure?"

"I was in a long boat and Thomas was on the pier. I could not hear him well. A man nearby shouted out that Thomas had—" again in a whisper, he said, "the pestilence." Returning to a normal volume, he continued. "Then, two men started to chase him. There was nothing I could do. The oarsmen were rowing down river with the tide. I had no choice but to leave."

"You left him?" Andrew swallowed a scream before it left his lungs.

"As I said, there was nothing I could do."

"We must go back. Why did you not say something before?"

"I did not know for sure. Thomas may be well. Either way, it is too dangerous to go back. People are dying by the hundreds each day. Bodies lie in the streets. If a house is suspected of giving refuge to this sickness, the sheriff's men board it up whether or not those inside are living or dead. After a person dies all who have seen him, or even carried him to the grave, quickly follow him. God has forsaken us."

"But we have to go."

"I am sorry, Andrew. I will not return to Bristow. It is certain death. And I doubt you will find a boat and crew that will take you. All are frightened of the evil that lies in wait."

"Is there no other way?" Andrew pleaded.

"There is the ferry at Newnham," Searle said. "That is the closest crossing of the Severn."

"Then I'll go to Newnham."

"Andrew, wait. You will never make it before dark. It is almost twenty miles."

"I can't wait any longer. I must go."

"Traveling through the forest at night is dangerous."

"I can take care of myself." Andrew charged off. He ran across the bridge over the muddy River Wye and into the rugged land of Gloucestershire. He knew the way as far as Aluredeston Grange, having been there with Brother Gilbert. But after that, he would need to be alert.

He kept to the main road as its gentle slopes allowed him to maintain his pace. For much of the way, thick green forest populated either side of the road. He met a group of merchants hauling goods and coming from the direction of Newnham. Two men, swords in plain sight, sat on either side of the merchant in each cart. The men looked at him with obvious distrust as they passed.

From time to time, his thoughts wandered toward Bristow and how to find Thomas in a strange and fear-ridden town. If Thomas was ill, as Searle implied, time worked against him. He had to put aside his doubts and keep going. There was no other choice.

Preoccupied by the distraction of thinking too hard, he failed to notice a group of men walking out from behind a clump of trees until their footsteps startled nesting blackbirds. With his hood up, his face was hidden in shadow.

"Look here, Owen. We have someone who wants to give us a nice warm cape," one of the men said. He had long, dark brown hair as shaggy as a sheep dog.

The large, heavyset man with rust-colored breeches grinned. "I think you're right, Fane. That cape looks real nice. And it has a hood too."

A short, hideous looking man with a long nose and stringy black hair grunted.

Andrew stood at attention as the men drew closer. He saw immediately that the shortest man had a bow. The fat one in the middle held a short sword while the one called Fane carried a long hunting knife tucked in his belt. It occurred to Andrew that these were the same three men he and Thomas encountered at Trelleck Grange earlier in the spring.

With a bold confidence, Owen said, "Hand over that cape. I don't want to put a hole in it before I try in on."

Andrew calmed himself and concentrated on the way the men carried themselves. He readied his mind and body. These men were not going to hinder his journey. He waited, forcing Owen to make the first move.

"Didn't you hear me, serf." Owen strutted ahead a few paces swinging his arms and looking cocky. When Andrew didn't back down, Owen stopped. "Adwar, string that bow of yours."

Andrew lacked the skill to defend against an arrow. He had to disarm Adwar if he wanted to walk away unharmed. He raised the pitch of his voice, hoping to sound intimidated. "You can have the cape. Just let me be."

Adwar held the string with one hand while his other hand held the bow, ready to set the string. He stood still, his face empty of expression, as if waiting for orders.

Andrew took off the cape, taking care to keep his sword covered. In one swift motion, he tossed the cape aside and threw his knife at Adwar. The shock of Andrew's quick movements stunned the three misfits and gave the knife time to find its mark. Adwar had no chance. He crumpled to the ground like a limp fish with Andrew's knife sticking out of his chest.

Owen shouted, "It's that boy we ran into by them monks at Easter. Because of you, boy, we had to work for two weeks under that bastard of a monk called Gilbert."

"Brother Gilbert tried to help you," Andrew said.

"Kill him, Fane," Owen ordered.

Fane reached for his long, hunting knife and charged Andrew. Andrew drew his sword, widened his stance, and prepared to ward the attack.

Fane looked at the sword and hesitated.

Owen bellowed, "He's just a boy. Kill him."

Fane charged on. They struck blades several times. Andrew defended as he waited for the right opportunity to strike. Fane overextended himself and lost his balance. Andrew took the advantage and swung at Fane's arm cutting through flesh and bone. The knife and part of Fane's forearm fell to the ground. Fane dropped to his knees and held the stump of what remained. Andrew recovered and thrust his sword into Fane's chest.

Owen's expression changed from cocky to shock as he watched Fane die. "You bastard. You'll pay for that."

The rage on Owen's face shined like a beacon telling Andrew that Owen's attack would be wild and undisciplined. He held tight to the hilt of Brother Gilbert's polished sword; Fane's blood dripped from the tip. He taunted Owen.

True to expectation, Owen charged without purpose. Andrew crossed blades and stepped out of the way. Owen again charged swinging hard, his face red. Andrew held to defensive parries. He waited for Owen to tire. The clang of swords rang out shattering the silence of the forest.

Andrew replayed his lessons with Eudo in perfect form. At the first sign of fatigue in Owen, he went on the offense. His attack was relentless. The rage in Owen's face turned to fear, then terror. Owen's strikes became unbalanced and his body defenseless. Andrew seized the moment and thrust his sword into Owen's stomach.

Owen grimaced and shouted in pain as the blade cut deep; his arms stretched out flaying at the wind. Andrew withdrew the blade. He raised his arms over his head to build momentum. Before he let loose the final blow, Owen's expression froze, and his lifeless body fell to the ground.

Andrew stood over the carnage he wrought. Silence returned but for the intense throbbing of his heart. Three dead bodies littered the road.

Eudo's words came to him: "You will get no satisfaction from killing a man." The words were true, but there was no time for emotion and nothing to regret. He had to do whatever it took if he wanted to reach Bristow and find Thomas.

He searched the bodies and found a few silver pennies. After gathering the weapons, he dragged the bodies off the road into a brushy area and covered them with leaves and broken branches.

The lands of Aluredeston Grange lay a few miles ahead. He pushed on as fast as he could. He refused to rest. Each step brought him closer to his goal. His legs went numb as he reached into his soul for the strength to keep going.

In the dim light after sunset, he arrived at Newnham. Owen's short sword and Fane's hunting knife allowed him to barter for lodging for the night, a hearty meal, and passage on the ferry in the morning. He kept Adwar's bow and arrows.

Chapter
TWENTY-NINE

North of Filton, England, September 1348

When morning came, Hugh had yet to return. As Thomas sat on the edge of the bed, he rubbed his eyes. His head ached, and he felt nauseous like he had too much to drink. While it pained him to leave without knowing what had happened to Hugh, he needed to keep moving. Before he left the cottage, he looked in the chest for something heavier to wear. He found an old cape made of rough, undyed wool. The cape was frayed at the bottom and smelled of mildew, but it offered warmth.

The gentle hills north of Filton made travel less strenuous. When he could, he walked along with merchant caravans headed north. No one said much as suspicions ran high. But the pace of the carts was too much for him, and he soon fell behind. Alone again, he trudged along.

After a full day of walking, exhaustion slowed his pace to a crawl. The aches in his joints turned to prickly pains and his headache pounded with every step.

As he reached the top of a rise, he spotted a group of people in the distance. He lacked the energy to confront them, so he left the road to work his way around through the forest to the east.

Thick undergrowth made the going difficult. From time to time, spider webs plastered his face, and low branches scratched or scraped as he hurried along. Dead branches seemed to jump out of the ground intent on tripping him.

The trek through the forest reminded him of the times he and Andrew played in the woods near Tintern Abbey. Life was fun then. Now, desperation compelled him onward.

Without warning, crippling pain surged through every part of him. He collapsed to the ground and curled into a ball. The pain reached an unbearable crescendo. He cried out as if relief could be had by yelling. He gritted his teeth while he let the pain wash over him. The intensity was beyond anything he thought possible to endure. Blackness engulfed the world as he escaped into unconsciousness.

In a dream state, Thomas found himself lying naked on hot, barren dirt. The sun beat down on him with the force of an overheated forge. As if horses pulled on each limb, his arms and legs pulsed in agony. Piercing pain racked his body. He struggled to his feet and confronted a black form taking shape before him. Helpless, all he could do was watch as the form coalesced into the shape of a man, a dark and sinister man. Pure evil. The man came closer—his walk a swagger, his stare a lance of death.

"Are you frightened, Thomas?" he said with a malicious sneer.

Thomas cowered before the creature. Filth and decay oozed from its skin. The smell, a hundred times worse than the sickly, sweet odor he experienced in Bristow, choked his lungs. He tried to speak, but his voice was trapped by the pain.

"Your fear feeds me. Your flesh nourishes my existence. I will have every part of you. I am the Pestilence. I am the Great Mortality."

After an unknown passage of time, consciousness returned. Pain still burned within him. Thomas struggled to breathe between deep, gut wrenching bouts of coughing that seemed to tear at his lungs. His stomach joined the chorus by vomiting what little fluid remained in its domain. The extreme agony slowly subsided. He tried to get up. Weakness forced him to rise no farther than his hands and knees. A fever sapped his strength. Sweat streamed out every pore trying to keep his body cool. He sat cross-legged and held his head to keep it from exploding.

The darkness around him grew deeper. The forest floor got little light on a bright day, but nothing helped him judge the time of day. He willed himself to stand.

Without the sun to guide him, he lost his sense of direction. He looked for a tree with a big trunk. Andrew once told him: "If you're lost in the forest, look for moss on a tree. It only grows on the north side."

An old oak dominated an area about twenty yards away. He held his stomach and shuffled his feet through the damp leaves. His hand caressed the rough bark. A smile brought momentary relief as he felt the cool softness of a patch of moss. "Thank you, Andrew. I remembered."

He set out to the northwest where he hoped to return to the Gloucester Road. He stumbled along for maybe three or four hundred yards when he spied a round hut in the middle of a small clearing; smoke whiffed out a hole in its conical peak, sending the scent of burnt oak into the air.

Long pieces of rough bark served as shingles. Dried leaves and sticks covered the wattle and daub walls like camouflage. Small enclosures, butted up against the hut, secured chickens, ducks, and pigs. He watched for a while, uncertain if he should move closer. He was unafraid.

A coughing spell took hold forcing him to his knees. He held his sides desperate to keep the pain in his chest from bursting. The animals came to life cackling, quacking, and squealing. He wanted to run, but his body refused to listen. Then, the creak of door hinges quieted the animals. His coughing continued unabated. Gasping, he fell to the ground. Time seemed to stop as pain, unbearable pain, coursed through his body. He wanted to die.

Someone lifted his head and put a cup of cool water to his mouth.

"Gently," a soft, female voice said.

The water soothed his throat. The coughing stopped.

"Not too much or it will not stay down."

Thomas obeyed. The hand that held the cup looked old and wrinkled. When he turned to look, he saw long white hair and the hood of a dark gray cape encircling a warm face, creased with age. She reminded him of Beatrice.

"Come, let me help you inside."

Thomas struggled to his feet. The old woman guided him toward her hut, past a large, black pot that sat next to a fire pit encircled with blackened stones, and through an unsteady wooden door. Inside, an open fire burned in the center of the room. A piece of deer hide covered part of a small window. She led him behind a woolen drape to a bed of straw covered with canvas and helped him to lie down.

He quickly fell asleep.

Newnham, England, September 1348

With his strength restored and his stomach full, Andrew boarded the first ferry that crossed the Severn. The woman at the inn suggested he stay near Berkeley Castle or Thornbury as traveling after dark invited mischief.

Thieves presented the least of Andrew's concerns. Once he got to Bristow, he needed to meet with Abbot Ralph at St. Augustine's Abbey. To think beyond that goal served no purpose.

Nearing Berkeley Castle, he came upon a crowd of people gathered around a middle-aged man who stood on a large stump. The man's passionate tone drew the on-lookers close and his deliberate stare engaged each person in his rhetoric. His arms waved to the beat of his cadence.

Andrew stood at the edge of the crowd of twenty or so people who gathered to listen to the rants. All looked to be serfs by the condition of their shabby and drab mantles, tunics, and breeches. It was a sea of dirty browns and grimy tans. The faces were rough and the hands rougher. Some were barefoot.

"She's the one who has brought this evil on us," the man declared. His deep-set eyes gave him a crazed look. A receding hairline exposed a sweaty forehead.

"She's never hurt anyone," someone in the crowd said.

"How do you know?" the man replied. "She's out there in the forest conjuring the devil while we hide in fear at the coming pestilence. How long has she been out there? No one knows. What evil powers has she gained while we toil for our masters? Our priest tells us to repent and do penance for our sins. Have any of you seen her at church? She hides behind her demons. Her sins must be beyond count. God will punish us for the evil she does. The pestilence will come and destroy us all. I say we find her and put an end to her evil. If she'll not repent, she must be burned as a heretic."

Calls of "Find her" and "Kill her" came in response.

Someone asked, "How do you know she's out there?"

"Yes, how do you know?" another asked. "If no one has seen her, why should we believe you?"

"Because I've seen her." The man clenched his fist and pointed toward the forest to the east. His face red, he said, "She's out there and she's the cause of our fear. We must make her repent, so God will protect us."

Andrew remained quiet as the people argued over whether the old woman existed. Many complained how little light remained to finish the work they yet had to do. Some rejected the whole story. In less time than it would take to milk a cow, the crowd dwindled. Only four young men remained. Andrew guessed they were around his own age.

"And what speaks you, stranger?" the man on the stump asked.

The attention took Andrew unaware. He studied the men who now came toward him. They each carried a long dagger at their belt. The older man, the one who was on the stump, led the way. The other four men bore ill intent on their dirty faces.

"Have you no tongue?" the older man said.

"I'm on my way to Bristow."

"You seem well armed. Do you know how to use those weapons?"

In a confident tone, Andrew said, "It's not wise to boast."

The man looked Andrew up and down. He laughed. "My dear young man. You're modest, I'm sure. Have no fear. You're among friends. Let me introduce myself. I'm Richard."

Andrew nodded. "My name is Andrew."

"Well, Andrew. It appears we're the only ones who take seriously the evil that lurks in our forest to the east. I'd be grateful if you'd join us on our little quest. A man of your talents would be most helpful."

"I must be on my way."

"Suit yourself." Richard said. "Come along boys. The sun's still above the trees."

The men headed northeast into the forest. Andrew continued on his way south to Bristow. Not far down the road a young woman in a black cape came out from behind a tree and approached him. Tears flowed from her eyes.

"Please, sir. You must help," she pleaded. "Those men are looking for my grandmother. She's a kind and generous old woman. She wouldn't hurt anyone. She likes to live alone, that's all. When my grandfather died, she was forced out of her cottage and fled to the forest to get away from our steward. She's lived there ever since. You must help her. She's not evil. Please."

"I don't know what I can do. I'm trying to get to Bristow."

"Please. I beg you. All Richard wants is her animals. He cares nothing for the salvation of the village."

"It'll be dark soon and—"

The woman's tears became sobs.

"I suppose I won't make it to Thornbury before nightfall."

The woman took Andrew's hand and kissed it. "Thank you, sir. God bless you. My grandmother's name is Sarah. Tell her Gwen sent you. She'll be able to put you up for the night and then you can be on your way."

"But what if Richard comes back again?"

"He's a coward. Those four boys who went with him are useless. They'll tire of Richard and then he'll have no one to follow him."

"As you wish. I'll do what I can."

"God be praised. Your kindness will be rewarded."

Andrew followed the men as they stomped their way through the underbrush. They cut at small branches with their knives making lots of noise. They sounded cheerful and confident, boasting how they would defeat the evil powers of the old woman.

Richard led them through a small gully and up to a high spot. They stopped while Richard surveyed the area. Andrew crept closer.

"We should be able to see the old woman's hut at the top of that next rise," Richard said.

"Seems like you've been here before," the young man called Harry said.

"I know the area, if that's what you mean." Richard said. "Now keep quiet."

Andrew kept close and circled to their right. When it appeared that they located the old woman, Andrew hid behind a wide oak tree. From his vantage, he saw the clearing where a little hut sat surrounded by animal enclosures. Puffs of smoke drifted out the roof. Richard and his friends waited among a thicket at the edge of the clearing.

The door to the hut creaked and an old woman, wrapped in a dark gray cape, came out and fetched the large black pot that sat next to the fire pit. After she went back inside, Richard and the others stood up and walked toward the hut. The animals sounded the alarm.

Richard shouted above the noise, "Come out here, you old hag. We've come to end your evil and stop the pestilence from coming to our village." Richard smiled at the others. He held his dagger in the air like a call to arms.

"Did you hear me, hag."

"Go away," a voice from within said.

"You best come out or we'll burn you out."

When the door creaked, the animals settled down. The old woman came out carrying a crooked, wooden staff. "Leave me be," she said.

The men laughed.

"Is that your magic wand for summoning the devil?" Richard asked.

The men moved closer. The old woman stood her ground.

An arrow struck an old stump with a loud thud a foot in front of Richard. The men stopped and looked around.

"I would do as the lady asks," Andrew said. He had another arrow ready, and it was pointed at Richard.

"Now see here, stranger…Andrew, I mean. We must protect our village and this old hag is the evil that poisons the forest. Her sins draw the pestilence to us."

"Are you sure about that? Or, are you here to take her animals?"

Richard's face turned red. "I don't think you'll let that arrow fly. Surround him boys."

The four young men drew their daggers and raced toward Andrew.

Andrew aimed for the closest man and let loose his arrow. The arrow hit the man in the thigh; he tumbled to the ground. With one arrow left, he shot for the next closest and struck a shoulder.

He drew his sword just as the third man came within reach. Andrew's blade sliced into the man's arm. He screamed in pain and fell to his knees.

Harry, the last of the useless men, froze mid-step, terror in his eyes. He looked at Andrew's sword—blood dripping from the tip—wet himself, and took off running.

Richard's brows furrowed. He gritted his teeth and rushed at Andrew like an experienced fighter. They crossed blades in a clash that brought the animals back to life. Noise filled the forest. After several parries, Richard stepped back and threw his dagger. Andrew dodged, but the blade sliced into his sword arm.

As Andrew's attention was drawn to the pain in his arm, Richard charged, knocking the sword out of Andrew's hand. Andrew cried out as they hit the ground. They wrestled and punched. Andrew's wounded arm lacked the strength to counter his opponent. Richard gained a choke hold.

The glimmer of Richard's dagger caught Andrew's gaze; it lay a few inches beyond his reach. He squirmed to get closer. Ignoring the pain, Andrew stretched his bleeding arm as far as he could. His fingers tickled the handle. He struggled to breathe. With the strength that remained, he pulled himself toward the dagger, grabbed it, and cut at Richard's arm. Richard cried out and let go of the choke hold. Andrew turned and drove the dagger into Richard's chest. One last gasp and Richard was dead. Andrew looked for the others, but they had slipped away during the melee. The old woman who stood guard by her hut hurried to him.

"My dear young man. God be praised. I owe you my life."

"Are you Sarah?"

"Yes. But, how did you know?"

"My name is Andrew. Your granddaughter, Gwen, sends her love."

"Thank the Lord. Please, let me look at your arm."

Sarah washed and then dressed the cut with warm yarrow leaves wrapped between layers of bandages. "That cut went deep. You must be careful of those stiches. If the wound is not tended correctly, it will turn bad and fever will set in."

"I must get to Bristow. My friend is in danger. I have to find him."

"It is late. You will not get far before dark. The road is unsafe at this hour and that wound needs proper care."

"I feel fine." Andrew wiggled his arm, but the pain made his wince.

"Your face says different. You will not help your friend if you are dead."

Sarah's comforting voice and caring touch were too much to refuse. "I'll stay the night in case anyone comes looking for Richard."

"God will protect your friend as you protected me and the sick traveler who rests in my hut."

"Sick traveler?"

"A young man came to me out of the forest earlier today. He has a fever and pain tortures his body. I have never seen anyone so sick. When he is not sleeping, he moans like the devil had taken him. He thrashes about something terrible. Whatever illness he has, he seems to be fighting it with all his might."

"Is it the pestilence?"

"I do not know. I prayed that God might find it in His mercy to save him. He is young, and I feel his thirst for life."

Chapter
THIRTY

East of Berkeley Castle, England, September 1348

Andrew opened his eyes to the sight of a furry mouse sitting on the cool stone of Sarah's fire pit. The mouse twitched its whiskers and scampered off into the trees. Andrew rubbed his arms to get warm. A sudden shot of pain in his right arm reminded him of the dagger wound and the events of last evening. He looked toward the scene of the fight. Richard's body laid untouched, cold and rigid. Leaves, stained dark red, painted a picture of the struggle. He dragged the body farther into the woods. Burying proved more difficult than he anticipated. He managed only a shallow grave. His arm throbbed. By the time he returned to the hut, Sarah had pottage prepared. His stomach growled at the rich smell of leek and mushrooms.

"How is your arm?" Sarah asked as she handed him a bowl.

"It hurts if I move it around too much."

"Let me see." Sarah removed the top bandage. "I will have to change the dressing. You are bleeding again. I wish you would wait another day, so your arm can heal properly."

"I need to move on if I'm to make Bristow before dark."

"I know you are concerned about your friend, but that is your sword arm. How will you defend yourself along the road?"

"I can manage." Andrew held on to the thought that the wound was not serious.

Sarah removed the rest of the dressing. Andrew cringed as she pulled the last bit away from the cut. Crusty blood covered a three-inch gash held together by five stitches. Cracks in the scab oozed fresh blood. Sarah placed warm yarrow leaves directly on the wound and wrapped his arm with a clean bandage to help keep the cut closed.

Andrew's shoulders drooped. "That looks better than last night."

"It is better, but it could easily tear open. If you do not make it to Bristow before nightfall, where will you stay? How will you tend the wound? It is too dangerous."

"I have to go. You should be safe now."

Sarah scooped a ladleful of potage into another bowl. "Maybe God sent you to help the sick traveler in my hut. Did you think of that?"

"What can I do for him? I don't know him. My friend needs me." Andrew looked at the door of the hut.

"You risked your life for me and yet you did not know who I was. How is that different from the young man in there whose life may depend on the help you might offer? If he is to have a chance, I need more herbs. But I am unable to leave him long enough to collect what I need."

Sarah's compassion shamed him. He looked into her motherly eyes and saw a determined spirit. How could anyone turn away from her plea? "I suppose you're right. I've had my share of fights already these past few days. If it came to that, another fight might be more than I could handle. If God truly led me here to help you and your traveler, then I must have faith that God knows what's best." Andrew sighed. A strange sense of calm eased his anxious feelings. "I'll do what I can. What's in that other pot?" He pointed to a cauldron of bubbling liquid.

"A potion. I am making a broth of lovage, sage, and fennel to quiet his cough and settle his stomach."

"He must be really sick."

"I have called on everything I know to help him, but I do not have all that I need. He has a fever and I need pennyroyal to get it under control. And I could use lavender to help with his headaches."

"Is there somewhere I can get these things for you?"

"My granddaughter will know. Or, she may have some to spare."

"Where can I find your granddaughter?"

"Follow the road to Berkeley Castle. It is not far. Her cottage will be to your right when you reach the village. The parish church of St. Mary's will be on your left."

Andrew finished his pottage and set out to collect the plants. When he reached the Gloucester Road, he paused to look south toward Bristow. "Hold on Thomas. You best not die on me. What will I do without you?"

He stood a while and pondered his commitment to help the old woman and her traveler. If he continued on, no one would know. He might yet reach Bristow by nightfall. The sick traveler would likely die. What more could he do for him?

He hated wondering over choices. Things should be simple; follow your heart and don't look back. Why did God send him on this journey anyway? Why this place and at this time? He cursed his inexperience that led to his wound. "I should have been more prepared." He sat on the ground and held his head. "I'm becoming like Thomas. God help me."

Inside the hut, the heat of the fire kept the chill air at bay. Sarah removed Thomas's clothes, so she could wash him and apply cool rags to counter the fever. The carbuncles under his arms and in his groin were dark and oozed foul fluid. She applied a paste of crushed garlic, onion, and leek to draw out the bad humors and then covered him with a heavy wool blanket.

"My dear boy, I have some broth for you. Please wake up." Sarah shook him gently. "You must drink. Please wake up."

Thomas's eyelids fluttered. He moaned and then coughed. Sarah took a cool, damp cloth and wiped his face and neck. The sick odor of the pestilence mingled with the garlic and onion of the healing paste. She held the cup to Thomas's mouth. He took a few sips.

"That is good. Just a little. Let it settle a bit."

"Where am I? Who are you?" Thomas asked.

"I am Sarah. You wandered into my clearing yesterday. What is your name?"

"My head hurts. I feel sick."

"I know, my dear. Sarah will make you better. Just be patient. A kind young man has gone to fetch herbs for me. They will help with your headache and the fever."

"Where's Isabel?"

"I do not know Isabel, my dear." Sarah straightened Thomas's hair as best she could. It was matted and damp from all his sweating. "Come, my dear. Have a few more sips and then I will wash you down again with cool rags."

Sarah tended Thomas throughout day as he went in and out of consciousness. On occasion, she managed to get him to take bits of the healing paste and let it dissolve in his mouth. She hurried to the door anytime her animal guardians made a sound—but no Andrew.

As twilight descended, she went outside and stood a while at the fire pit as she ticked off all the remedies she thought might help her sick traveler. The crunch of leaves signaled someone's approach. She hushed her night watch and listened. Her keen ears discerned the rhythm of four feet. Soon enough, she spied Andrew and Gwen.

Draped in her black cape, Gwen waved. "Andrew needed help finding you. Is there anything I can do?"

"Thank you, my dear child. But it is best if I tend him. I do not want you to come down with whatever he may have."

"I'll check with you tomorrow then."

"Thank you for being my guide," Andrew said. He embraced Gwen. "I'm glad you came along when you did."

"I'm certain you made the right choice. God be with you."

After Gwen left, Andrew filled a pot with water from the cistern and positioned it over the fire.

"Our traveler has a strong will," Sarah said as she tore the herbs into smaller bits and dropped them into the pot to steep. "But, I fear the worst is yet to come. The fever has not broken. Tonight will be the test. If he makes it through the night, he has a chance."

"I hope my friend has someone like you to tend him. If he has the pestilence, I can't imagine the pain he must be in. The stories I've heard are frightening."

"This friend means a lot to you?"

"We grew up together at Tintern Abbey. We're like brothers. But he's the youngest son of a nobleman. He'll soon join the Cistercians. I'm just an orphaned peasant who was taken in by the monks."

"You are much more than that, my dear. You risk your life to find your friend. That takes great courage and love."

Andrew's eyes watered. He wiped away the show of emotion with his sleeve. "Long ago, when the monks found me, I'd been beaten up by a beggar over a loaf of bread. Hate took control of me. I was angry at everyone until one of the lay brothers taught me how to defend myself. All I want to do is be there to protect my friend. But, how do I protect him from the evils of the pestilence?"

"You must have faith in your friend and faith in yourself, my dear. Let me have a look at that wound again." Sarah changed the bandages and put fresh yarrow leaves on the cut. "It is healing fine. You mend quickly. I think it will be well enough by morning. Then you can be on your way."

In his sleep, Thomas fell into a dream world. The emptiness frightened him. He stood alone in the middle of an open field. Beautiful shades of green suddenly turned to noxious shades of brown. The familiar smell of death approached. Only the soft grass under his feet remained alive.

A hoe appeared in his hand. He used the hoe to hack away at the foul weeds covered in sharp thorns that overtook the barren landscape. He hacked and hacked, but the weeds grew faster and faster. Then, an evil laughter filled his mind with dread. He looked for the source, but the land was void. Blackness reigned everywhere.

"Where are you?" he shouted.

Silence.

He found himself sitting on a hard stone bench like the ones in the cloister at Tintern Abbey. Except, this bench sat alone on the edge of a cliff. Over the cliff blackness fell to infinity. To Thomas's horror, the blackness coalesced into the evil man that claimed to be the Great Mortality.

"Greetings, Thomas. I would say 'God's blessings,' but I do not believe you would find that statement genuine."

"What do you want?" Thomas commanded.

"I want you, of course, but you resist. It angers me when they resist." His cold, black eyes stared deep into Thomas's soul.

"They? What do you mean?"

"All those people who think they can overcome me. They come to me in the end. I laugh at their feeble efforts." He laughed a vile, menacing laugh. "You, on the other hand, have proved difficult. All the trouble I have gone through to get here. You would be amazed."

Thomas scoffed.

"I have been around for centuries. I have waited patiently for the perfect host. You would not understand my plight. Needless to say, I found my way into people again. Such a large and bountiful source of energy. Everything needs to grow, Thomas. I am no exception. Millions of people gave their lives, so I could live. Is that not wonderful?"

"No. You are evil."

"That is a matter of opinion, Thomas. It delights me to think of all the pain and suffering I caused. You may not know this, but pain to you is pleasure to me."

"That is sick and cruel."

"Maybe it is—from your point of view. As I was saying, they all come to me in the end. Like your dear father and brother and that wench you thought you loved."

"Shut up! I'll not go with you."

"I am not finished with you yet, Thomas. You will beg to let me take you. Your time is up. What do you have to live for? Your beautiful Isabel and that overconfident abbot left you behind to wallow in your miserable life."

"You cannot take my memories."

"I do not want your memories. I want you. Just give in and be done with it."

"No. Never."

Thomas shut his dream eyes as tight as he could. A soft voice brought him out of the dream.

"My dear boy. Please wake up. You need to drink. The fever is draining you."

Thomas opened his eyes. A kind old woman sat next to him holding a cup. He took it and drank. The liquid brought relief as it moistened his tongue and throat.

"Try to drink it all," she said. "It will work on the fever."

Thomas finished the cup. His stomach did not reject it.

She washed him and reapplied a healing paste to the bulging sores. The cool rags soothed his burning skin. In the momentary comfort, he drifted off to sleep.

Sarah went outside to rinse the rags. Andrew sat by the fire pit poking at the embers in the darkness. He threw a log on the hot coals and watched the explosion of red ashes shoot into the air as the fire came to life.

"How is he?" Andrew asked.

"Not well. He is so weak. And the fever burns the fluid out of him. We must pray to God that He will have mercy on his poor soul."

"Should I get the priest?"

"You will never find your way in the dark, my dear. There is no time. People die every day without a priest, my poor dear husband, rest his soul, among them. Our prayers are no less valid. God will hear them."

"I'll pray for him, then."

Sarah continued to watch over Thomas throughout the night. His breathing grew shallow, only a hint of movement to the rise and fall of his chest. She changed the rags on his forehead often. When he moaned and thrashed about, she tried to calm him with encouraging words. At times, she was able to get little bits of the healing paste into his mouth.

By dawn, Thomas looked like death waited at the door, eager to slip in with the slightest crack. Sarah strained to think of anything else she might do, but her mind was blank. She gathered up the rags and cups and went outside.

The cold air smelled fresh and invigorated her tired soul. Ravens called to each other welcoming a new day. Andrew sat by the fire pit minding the pot of water.

"We will need to change the bandage before you leave," Sarah said. "Thank you for getting the herbs, but I think our traveler has come to the end of his journey in this world. He is on the edge of death."

"Are you sure?" Andrew asked.

"I fear he is beyond all hope."

"Then we must have faith." Andrew threw another log on the fire.

Dreams again took hold of Thomas's restless sleep. He found himself in the nave of the church at Tintern Abbey, its grand arches rising to the very heights of heaven. The beautiful pulpitum conveyed the reverence of the carvers who toiled many long days to glorify God. Suddenly, out of the pulpitum, four figures approached. A brilliant light bathed them with a soothing glow as pure as God's love.

"God's blessings, son." The form of Lord Geoffrey de Parr came forward. Beside him walked Abbot Michael, Isabel, and William, young as Thomas last remembered him.

"Father Abbot, how is this possible?" Thomas asked.

"We are here to guide you, if that is your wish," Abbot Michael said, his expression radiated peace and serenity.

Isabel reached out and took hold of Thomas's hand. Her hand felt as smooth as silk. Her face shined with a beauty beyond compare. Her green eyes sparkled like brilliant emeralds. Her lips moved with the grace of God. "We will live together in the house of the Lord forever, Thomas."

"Must I go now?"

"It is your choice," William said. "The Great Mortality waits. He may take your body, but we are here to save your soul. Do not fear him, Thomas. We will stand by you and guide you to paradise."

Tintern Abbey vanished and Thomas found himself before an altar. It was dark and cold—so cold he shivered. Behind him stood his father, William, Abbot Michael, and Isabel. Their presence comforted his fear.

The black form of the Great Mortality came forward out of the altar. The stench of sickness and death surrounded him. The vileness of the black form's hideous laughter made the hair on the back of Thomas's neck stand on end. The Great Mortality wrung his hands and came closer. Nothing reflected off his black eyes but the emptiness and desolation of Satan's domain.

"It is time, Thomas. I have all of you. Your mortal existence has ended. Your soul is mine to command. There is no one to speak your name. Surrender your body. I will be ever so grateful." A wicked smile formed on the blackness of his evil face, the confident smile of a victor. "There is no hope. Your faith has deserted you. The moment you laid down with that ugly strumpet, you turned from your God. Let us end this before the real pain begins."

Thomas turned and looked at those beside him. His face was drawn. He felt the beat of his heart slow, the sound no greater than the fall of snow.

"God has forgiven you, Thomas," Abbot Michael said. "Do not be discouraged by your choices. They have made you who you are. Life is a preparation for death. Death is nothing to fear. Paradise awaits."

"What is your choice, son?"

Thomas looked at the Great Mortality. His shoulders slouched, and the innocence in his blue eyes retreated in defeat. He prepared to walk into the arms of death.

A thunderous boom reverberated from every direction. Thomas stopped and looked about as he tried to identify the source. Then, another boom shook the world, like the hammer of God crashing down on the Gates of Hell smashing Satan's minions. The Great Mortality retreated to his altar. He put his cruel hands over his despicable ears.

Another boom came and then another. A pattern emerged. Thomas cocked his head to listen. He smiled. His faith returned. A rush of energy more powerful than a thousand waves poured over him cleansing every corner of his body.

The Great Mortality cried out with all his cruelty and malice, "What have you done?"

"I'm not going with you," Thomas shouted. "Your power over me has ended. I want to live." Thomas turned to those beside him. "I know what I must do. You all have taught me so much. I'll never forget your love."

"I'll always love you, Thomas," Isabel said, as she stroked his cheek. "We'll be with you in your memories."

Thomas turned back to the Great Mortality, his clear blue eyes piercing with intensity. The loathsome creature writhed in agony at the force of Thomas's will to live.

"Be gone! You are not the victor here."

The Great Mortality sank into his altar, echoes of his melancholy wail dying into obscurity.

The booms continued. Thomas found himself back in his room at Tintern Abbey. His window was open. The musty smell of fresh plaster and whitewash mingled with the crisp air. A goldfinch sang its sweet song. Yet, something different nagged at his soul. The room seemed that of a boy full of wonder and innocence. But Thomas didn't feel that way anymore. Life in all its joys and cruelties changed that. The dream faded.

Thomas opened his eyes. The boom of his dream morphed into a softer *whack*. It was a beautiful sound, a sound that filled his broken heart with joy. He got out of bed. Pain and fatigue forced him to move with slow deliberate steps. He found his breeches and tunic and slid them on, careful to not cause pain to his sores. He edged his way to the door and looked out.

Tears welled up as he stepped outside into the cold morning air, his hair disheveled. "Andrew," he said. He spoke the name not as a question, but as a statement of faith, hope, and love. He voice was a glorious confirmation of death defeated.

Andrew turned. He dropped the maul. His mouth opened, but words failed him. He stared as if he didn't believe his eyes.

"Do you have to make all that noise so early in the morning?" Thomas slumped against the door frame.

Andrew rushed to catch him. "Thomas! It was you who Sarah tended. It's truly a miracle. I prayed to God that I'd find you. I was about to leave for Bristow, but I decided to split some wood to see how well my arm healed. I might have been gone by now."

"I don't understand?"

"We are together now. That's all that matters." Andrew put his hand on Thomas's forehead. "Your fever broke. You must get back to bed and rest."

Andrew whisked Thomas off his feet with his strong arms. He carried him back into the hut, laid him on the bed, and covered him with the blanket. He straightened Thomas's hair and kissed him on the forehead.

"I'm sorry, Andrew." Tears streaked from the corners of Thomas's eyes as he looked up at Andrew. "Will you forgive me?"

"There's nothing to forgive. Sleep well, my friend."

Chapter
THIRTY-ONE

East of Berkeley Castle, England, October 1348

After his fever broke, Thomas continued to battle the pestilence. He slept often, rising only to eat or relieve himself. Sarah lanced the buboes and placed crushed yarrow leaves directly on the sores. She alternated with applications of her healing paste and insisted that Thomas let some of the paste dissolve in his mouth. Under her watchful eye, his health improved.

Three weeks passed before he gained enough strength to wander farther than the fire pit in front of the hut. His appetite returned, and he no longer looked as pale as a ghost. While the mark of the pestilence remained as scars to remind him of his ordeal, he had defeated the Great Mortality—a feat not often boasted by those who survived.

While Thomas recovered, Andrew set about fixing everything that needed fixing around Sarah's hut. He made a proper thatched roof and repaired the walls. He added a room that Sarah could use for storage. The extra space allowed Andrew to have a place to sleep safe from the cold and wet October nights. He strengthened the animal enclosures, mended the gates, and split enough dead wood to last through winter. Thomas never again complained about the loud *whacks* of Andrew's maul.

As the nights grew longer, the pull of Tintern Abbey again tugged at Thomas's soul. He continued to wrestle with acceptance over the deaths of his father, his brother, Abbot Michael and Isabel. But, he found comfort in Isabel's plea: "Do not give up on God."

Whatever the reason, he was alive. He had hope for a future and a renewed faith in God. It saddened him to think that Abbot Michael's guiding hand no longer played a part in his life. When his strength returned, he could no longer ignore the choice he had promised the spirits of his dream.

"Are you ready to go back to the abbey?" he asked Andrew.

"Are you sure you can make it?"

"I've had too much time to think. I know what I must do, but it frightens me."

"Brother Gilbert told me to follow my heart. That's what led me to seek you out. I was frightened of the pestilence more than I wanted to admit. And there was much I failed to think about before I left—like fighting thieves and misfits. And I had doubts about whether I could really find you, but I never stopped believing in the journey I had to make. When you stepped out of Sarah's hut, I knew God set me on this path."

"I'm afraid to think what may have happened if you hadn't come."

"Then don't think of it."

"Is it really that easy?"

"No. But I can tell you've gotten much better at fending for yourself."

"We should tell Sarah it's time for us to be on our way."

The evening fire crackled as Sarah passed around bowls of pottage. Thomas said grace. The memory of Isabel saying the prayer at Hugh's cottage caused him to stumble on the words, but he persisted. When he finished, he said, "I owe you my life, Sarah, but I have nothing to give to repay your kindness."

"Nonsense, my dear. I did God's bidding. You are the one to thank. I have not felt this needed in a long time. You gave me purpose. This evil will not last forever. You will see."

"It's time for us to go."

"We must leave in the morning," Andrew said. "It'll take several days for us to reach Tintern Abbey, maybe longer if we have to stay off the roads."

"Do not fret. I knew you would have to leave some day. God is patient. But in the end, it is His will, not ours, that leads the way."

Gloucestershire, England

When morning came, Sarah prepared flat bread for Thomas and Andrew to take along on their journey home. Tears were shed as well as laughter and wishes for God's blessings at the parting. Thomas's pace was slow. He rested often. When they reached the ferry at Newnham, Andrew bartered Adwar's bow for the crossing. They used the few remaining pennies to pay for lodging and a meal at Newnham's inn.

"Are you boys heading to Gloucester?" the innkeeper asked.

"We journey to Chepstow." Andrew said.

"I heard the pestilence found a way past Gloucester's walls. Serves them right for shutting the town gates and turning away people in need. They say the deaths in Gloucester are now as bad as Bristow."

"What about the countryside?" Thomas asked.

"The humors seem to flow easily along the main roads. A merchant who passed through last week told me that villages along the king's road from Gloucester to London have been attacked. Some call it the Great Mortality. I suspect London will be next. At the first sign of sickness, I'm heading north."

The next night, they found refuge at Woolaston Grange, one of Tintern Abbey's granges east of the River Wye. The lay brothers treated them to a hot meal and more talk of the pestilence.

"It's well that you didn't go near Gloucester," one of the lay brothers said after the table was cleared.

"We heard about Gloucester while we were in Newnham," Andrew said.

An elderly, blind lay brother banged his cane on the table and said, "The end of the world is upon us. Our sins have provoked God's wrath."

"It's not as simple as blaming God's wrath," Thomas said. "Fear plays into Satan's hands. It's right to seek forgiveness for our sins, but God's wrath, if that's the cause of the pestilence, hasn't been deterred by any amount of penance or penitential processions. The pestilence doesn't distinguish between the righteous or the sinner. We must be content with the forgiveness of our own sins. The rest is up to God's will. His need is greater than our own. I—"

Andrew put his hand on Thomas's shoulder blocking Thomas from revealing the scar at the base of his neck. "I think what Thomas means is that God's wrath applies to each of us and it's our own truths that must be made right with God if we're to survive the evils of the pestilence."

Thomas nodded and lowered his hand. He suddenly felt shame for surviving the pestilence when so many have died.

"We thank you for your kindness in letting us stay the night. If Thomas and I are to get an early start in the morning, we should get some sleep."

"Of course," the lay brother in charge said. "Please be sure to let Brother Samuel know of our deep sorrow at the passing of Abbot Michael. We will say prayers for the repose of his soul. If you will follow me, I will show you to the guest chamber."

Climbing stairs took more effort than Thomas expected. He was glad visitors had the use of a private room rather than joining the rest of the lay brothers under the rafters in the second-floor dormitory.

"The straw is fresh," the lay brother said. "I hope you find the room comfortable."

Andrew poked at the mattress. "We'll be fine."

When they were alone, Thomas asked, "Why did you stop me from showing my scar?"

"Did you not see their faces? They're frightened of the pestilence. If you showed them you were infected, they might have chased us away."

"I'm sorry."

"I'm not mad. We just need to be careful. When people are afraid, they do things they might otherwise not do. We've a long day tomorrow. Best get some sleep."

From Chepstow to Tintern Abbey, Wales

On the afternoon of the third day of their journey, Thomas and Andrew reached Chepstow. They stopped at Striguil Castle to see Eudo. Andrew told Eudo of his encounters with the three misfits and the men at Sarah's hut. He was quick to add that he understood what Eudo meant by not getting satisfaction from killing a man.

"I am proud of you, Andrew," Eudo said. "You have proved to be a noble friend in deed."

"I want to keep up with my training. I still have lots to learn."

"Tell Brother Gilbert you are welcome any time."

After a tasty meal of steaming pottage laced with a healthy portion of rabbit and a loaf of fresh dark bread, Thomas and Andrew left for the final stretch of their journey. Even as Thomas lumbered along, the five-mile walk from Chepstow seemed to take less time than they remembered. When they turned the last bend in the road and descended to the banks of the River Wye, the sight of the magnificent abbey church liberated their tired faces.

Thomas stopped to take in the view. He sat on the ground, exhausted. "We made it."

Andrew sat beside him and quietly shared the familiar panorama.

Thomas sighed. "I never realized how unpredictable the future can be. Choices really matter. I'm sorry I ran from Bristow."

"I was mad about that for a while."

"Only a while?"

"It was hard to be angry and not feel selfish."

Thomas's eyes went wide. "Isabel said the same thing. She was mad at God after her mother died. Why do I never get thoughts like that? I have to do everything the hard way."

"You're not as smart as some of us."

He punched Andrew.

"Ouch, that's my sore arm."

"I'm sorry."

"I suppose I deserved that. Remember the day you crawled into my old hole in the wall?"

Thomas nodded.

"When I took Eva home that day, I stayed with her longer than I should have. It was not my first time with her. It's bothered me ever since that I didn't tell you."

"I was jealous of her."

"There's no need. She's horrible with a bow."

After a moment of silence, Thomas said, "What do you think it'll be like?"

"How do you mean?"

"I mean walking through the gate. Nothing will be the same."

"Why is that bad? Are you still confused about the future?"

"No."

"Neither am I."

"I'll miss Abbot Michael."

"I'll miss him too."

They sat a while in silence admiring the red and gold foliage of the hillsides. A cool breeze portended an early frost.

"Are you ready?" Andrew asked. He helped Thomas to his feet.

As soon as they passed through the abbey's outer gate, they were spied by Brother Elias and Brother Leofwin who were on their way from the stable to attend vespers. A great commotion ensued as word went out that they returned. Tears of joy abounded.

Brother Samuel, now Abbot Samuel, greeted them with open arms. "God's blessings, Andrew." He hugged Andrew, almost squeezing the life out of him.

Andrew gasped. "God's blessings, Father Abbot."

"Brother Gilbert will be so glad to see you. He will be here for vespers."

"It's wonderful to be home. I'm anxious to see Brother Gilbert too."

"Praise the Lord." Tears streaked Abbot Samuel's plump cheeks. He embraced Thomas. "Words are insufficient to express my grief for your loss. It has been a trying time for us all."

"Thank you, Father Abbot."

"Please do not think you have to make any decisions now about your future. Take your time. Your room awaits. When you are ready, then we can talk."

Thomas straightened his posture. With a clear voice, he said, "My mind is made up. I learned a lot about life and love—more than I ever dreamed when I left the abbey with Abbot Michael. I thought my destiny was set and that there was no other choice. What I found was that I do have a choice. God allows us to make choices. Sometimes they are good and sometimes they are bad. But, they are our choices. I turned away from God when I needed Him most and I paid the price. Had it not been for Andrew, I may have given up. Now, I have another chance. That's why I want to continue my studies to become a monk here at Tintern Abbey. It's what I want to do, not what I have to do. Abbot Michael prepared me well. This is my home. This is my family."

"Your words are commendable, Thomas. I can hear Abbot Michael's influence. He was a great man and will be missed by us all. I want you to pray on your decision, and if you feel the same in a week, then we will set a date for you to take your vows and begin your novitiate."

During vespers, prayers of thanksgiving were offered as well as prayers for a quick journey to paradise for the souls of Abbot Michael, William and Lord Geoffrey de Parr, and Isabel.

After the service, fatigue took its toll on Thomas. He took a moment to sit on a bench in the cloister. A passing cloud covered the stars and the moon and brought the gentle patter of rain on the tiled roof of the arcade. Andrew sat beside him.

"Do you really want to become a lay brother?" Thomas asked. "I mean, lay brothers and monks are not supposed to be friends—except maybe someone like Brother Gilbert—and that's only because someone has to take charge."

"If I take over for Brother Gilbert and you become the abbot, then I guess we'll be allowed to remain friends."

"You know what I mean."

"The way I see it, an orphan and the son of a lord are not supposed to be friends either. But here we are. I don't think the Cistercians have any greater power over us. Only God does, and I think He's the one who brought us together."

"Can we sit a while? I'm too tired to take another step."

"Shall I carry you?"

"You're always doing something for me, Andrew. Is there nothing I can do for you?"

"You can be my friend."

"I'm already that."

"I know."

Chapter
THIRTY-TWO

Sleaford Castle, Lincolnshire, England, October 1348

Each of the last three merchants that passed through Sleaford told Hastings the same story: Bristow, Gloucester, and villages to the east and south toward Weymouth were unsafe.

"I'm not going back," Rowan said.

Hastings stroked his beard. He cursed himself for being too kind to Lord Geoffrey de Parr. The man was clearly willing and able to raise the money. Maybe he should have asked for two thousand marks and pressed harder for at least a portion of the amount. No matter. What was done, was done. Cold winds blew dried leaves in a whirlwind in a corner of Sleaford Castle's courtyard. "By Christ's blood. There must be a way to find out if they're alive."

"I thought you said you had until the end of winter to satisfy Sleaford's desire for revenge?"

"I did."

"Then what's the hurry?"

"It's not Sleaford I'm concerned about. The chancellor wants answers too."

"With the pestilence moving toward London, the chancellor will be too busy to care about us. As long as the day comes when we can deliver what he wants, why the trouble?"

Hastings glared at Rowan. He hated it when someone else came up with an obvious explanation. "For once you surprise me."

"I'm here to please, my lord." Rowan gave an exaggerated bow.

"Careful. You may hurt yourself. We still have work to do." Hastings plotted his contingencies. The prospects were grim, but he had no choice. As each twist of his plan unraveled, doubt over his expected reward rose, as did the danger to his own life. There must be an alternative if the worst came to pass. He refused to consider defeat. Thinking on the worst brought the worst. Resolved to think positively, he said, "I'll humor Sleaford with the idea that Parr and his ambitious son are suffering from this dreadful plague. That should make him happy. Until it's safe to go to Bristow, we'll bide our time and enjoy the old sot's bountiful larder. Then, we'll decide how best to get to Bristow and, if necessary, how to find the younger son."

About the Author

Thomas Schultz grew up in Wisconsin where the winters are cold and the summers are short. After a career in financial regulation, he decided to pursue his passions for travel and history. An interest in medieval England led to a desire to create a novel set during the 14th century but containing themes modern readers can appreciate. The result was his first novel, *Plagues and Princes: The Great Mortality*, the first book in a trilogy of books that take place as the Black Death attacks England with a vengeance unseen since the Norman Conquest.